E. ARNOT ROBERTSON

(1903–1961) was born Eileen Arbuthnot Robertson, in Surrey, the daughter of a doctor. Her family moved to Notting Hill, London, when she was fourteen. She was educated at Sherborne, and in Paris and Switzerland. In 1927 she married H.E. Turner, general secretary of the Empire and Commonwealth Press Unions, later to become Sir Henry Turner, C.B.E. Her first novel *Cullum* was published in 1928, followed by *Three Came Unarmed* (1929), *Four Frightened People* (1931) and *Ordinary Families* (1933); the latter two are both published by Virago. Her other novels are *Summer's Lease* (1940), *The Signpost* (1943), *Devices and Desires* (1954), *Justice of the Heart* (1958) and *The Strangers on My Roof*, published posthumously in 1964. She also wrote *Thames Portrait* (1937) and *The Spanish Town Papers* (1959), both with photographs by Henry Turner, and a children's book, *Mr Cobbett and the Indians* (1942).

E. Arnot Robertson was a broadcaster, lecturer and film critic; she was at the centre of a famous lawsuit when she sued MGM who had tried to stop her attending screenings as a result of her 'hostile' reviews. She lived with her husband and son in Heath Street, Hampstead: ardent sailors, they would frequently cruise to France, Belgium and Holland on their yacht. After 34 years of marriage, Henry Turner was killed in a boating accident on the river, a loss from which E. Arnot Robertson never recovered. She committed suicide the following year.

VIRAGO
MODERN
CLASSIC

NUMBER
322

CULLUM

E. ARNOT ROBERTSON

WITH A NEW INTRODUCTION BY

RACHEL BILLINGTON

Published by VIRAGO PRESS Limited 1989,
20–23 Mandela Street, Camden Town, London NW1 0HQ.

First published in Great Britain by Jonathan Cape 1928
Copyright E. Arnot Robertson 1928
Introduction Copyright © Rachel Billington 1989

British Library Cataloguing in Publication Data
Robertson, E. Arnot (Eileen Arnot), *1903–1961*
Cullum.
I. Title
823'.912 [F]

ISBN 0-86068-598-5

Printed in Finland by Werner Söderström Oy

TO

JAMES McBEY

in affectionate recognition of his long,
fruitless efforts to make me a credit to
the Scottish race

Introduction

Cullum was E. Arnot Robertson's first book, published in 1928 when she was twenty-four. It was an immediate success, although the *Times Literary Supplement*'s critic was obviously surprised to find himself enjoying what appeared to be the subject for a woman's novel. 'The caddish behaviour of a young novelist, with a red head and inextinguishable charm, is the theme of *Cullum* by E. Arnot Robertson (J.Cape 7/6d) an old theme, indeed, but played this time with variations.' The variations, although the critic could not quite put his finger on them, were a cool wit and a complete lack of sentimentality. 'Mr Robertson,' the TLS reviewer ended, under a telling misapprehension, 'has a refreshing way of writing and a mere sketch of his plot does not do justice to his pleasant humour and clear thinking.'

'Mr Robertson' was, in fact, a young married woman, destined to be named Arbuthnot by her parents who wanted a boy and, in the event, given Eileen. *Cullum*, like many first novels, was based on the author's own experience, in this case of early unhappy love. It was published at a time when the novel, written by women for women, commanded a wide, although middle-class, and devoted readership, serviced mainly by excellent library systems. Ironically, it was the very popularity of these novels which caused male critics to attempt to put them in their place, that is, second place.

For many years even excellent writers like Rosamond Lehmann and Mary Webb were tarred by the indiscriminate brush of 'romance' which meant only that, like Jane Austen and Charlotte Brontë, they had dealt with the subject of love. It has taken many more years (and Virago's reprints) to uncover neglected writers of the period such as M.J. Farrell, now writing under her own defiantly female name, Molly Keane, and E.M. Delafield. Both

i

these writers have a satirical and abrasive approach to love and loving which could not be surpassed by any male writer. In fact, it is women who, if they are serious writers at all, turn the least sentimental eye on love. It is tempting, sometimes, to believe that it is not the romantic aspects of the novels which cause men to be over-critical but the very unromantic attitude to romance that threatens the male's image of himself.

It is a subject that preoccupied Arnot Robertson both in her work and in her life. In a way, *Cullum* is its blueprint, the story of a strongly independent young woman who allows herself to be bowled over by an obvious liar and cad. The question of what makes a woman need a man is as old as Adam and Eve. In married life Robertson was Mrs Turner, wife of Henry Turner (later Sir Henry) who among other public activities, founded the Empire Press Union. Robertson, herself an outspoken woman, who from the thirties onwards, spent as much time giving her opinions on the radio as she did writing novels, could not operate without her husband. According to one of her friends, he even tied her shoe-laces – because her fingers were too small. Certainly, she relied on him to read and approve all her work. When he was drowned at the age of seventy, she couldn't manage to live without him and committed suicide the following year. She was still only fifty-eight. With sad irony, she had forecast her dangerous dependence in a recorded debate entitled 'That women and children should be saved first'. She argued against the motion because she believed women could not live without men either emotionally or financially. She drew a picture of herself as an 'unappreciative widow', wishing she had not been saved. In another debate with fellow novelist Rose Macaulay, she went further and argued that women's emancipation had created 'mental stress' because women had a 'spiritual need of dependence and a much smaller range of intellectual interests than men'. She continued firmly, 'People, not things, are the centre of their thoughts. I think that will always be so. I don't think you can ever change that.'

This classic statement of the reason why women are drawn to the role of novelist appears to place her in a very unfeminist camp. Yet her heroines, such as Esther in *Cullum* or Judy in *Four Frightened People*, are exceptionally determined people. Esther has a

ii

clear sense of her own talents, both imaginatively as a writer and physically as a rider of unridable horses. She is no weakling, just as Arnot Robertson (shoe-laces notwithstanding), was no weakling. Indeed the picture of her that emerges from the non-fictional writing and radio talks of this period could be called aggressive. In 1934 she contributed to a collection of essays edited by Graham Greene and entitled *Old School*. Her comments on Sherborne, headed 'Potting shed of the English rose', are acerbic. 'It is nice to feel that no misfortunes that happen to me – neither illness nor poverty, the most probable – can possibly make me quite as unhappy as I was at Sherborne.' Her rage mounts as she describes Sherborne as an inappropriate second-rate copy of a boys' public school, centred on the idea of team spirit which she thought completely unnatural for girls. The religious regime caused an early loss of faith and she vowed never to enter a church again except for a wedding or as a tourist. Moreover, sex was considered 'something so beastly lying in wait for us that we were not to think about it'. She took obvious pleasure in recalling that the headmistress once told her that she prayed about her more than any girl under her care.

Later in life, Robertson's anti-conformist, anti-authoritarian stance led her to take on a battle with the vast film corporation MGM, who objected to her critical reviews on BBC radio and wanted her taken off the accredited reviewers' list. She sued for libel, partly with £7000 donated money, partly with £8000 of her own, and although she lost the last round in the House of Lords where, according to a friend, her left-wing lawyer antagonized their lordships, she was generally thought to have achieved a moral victory. The lawsuit took place in 1946 but the BBC had fair warning of her attitudes in 1935 when she defended herself against a producer's criticism of a piece as 'too sophisticated' with the fighting words:

I warned you I was an intellectual prig! My feeling about reviewing is that it is not nearly fierce enough – neither praise nor criticism are given with anything like freedom; books are treated as though they varied very little within the limits of competence. Writers should be damned far more often. This general tolerance is extremely bad for the few good ones there are.

Since the talk she was defending included a definition of the Hemingway school of writing, then enjoying much admiration, as 'tough whimsy' one can understand the producer's nervousness. Arnot Robertson enjoyed causing a stir and breaking restrictive shibboleths. Typically, it was she who, in *Four Frightened People*, first made reference in print to the unmentionable woman's 'curse'. Gradually an E. Arnot Robertson emerges who is anything but a romantic woman's writer – except that her prime consideration always remained the relationship between people rather than ideas – which makes it, perhaps, slightly less surprising that at one point this self-styled intellectual prig became 'agony aunt' for *Tit-bits*. In a talk about the differences between writers and journalists she said,

To me the end of a book is the end of a close partnership with people in whom I am passionately interested – far more interested than in people of the outside world; and I don't want to let go of them, because once the *book* is out they are dead as far as I am concerned.

However, unlike some novelists whose pleasure in characterization diminishes their interest in the plot, Robertson worked hard on an invigorating story. Even *Cullum*, the classic first novel in that it is based on reality and stays close to well-known backgrounds, includes a dramatic hunting accident and an even more dramatic suicide. Arnot Robertson was always keen on bold effects. *Four Frightened People* is mainly set in a Malayan jungle and the fact that the author had done her research from the comfort of the British Museum did not diminish the tremendous success of the book. Nor did the kill-joy reviewer at the *Times Literary Supplement* who commented that the frequent appearance of tree-swinging baboons was somewhat surprising since the nearest of the species would be found in Africa. He had completely missed the point of the book, which is about people and emotions, not documentary accuracy. Perhaps his irritation came from a deeper objection indicated in an earlier paragraph: 'they appear to have been so over-sexed that physical strain, illness and malnutrition did not prevent the two men from desiring Judy or Judy from becoming Ainger's mistress'.

Sex, in the twenties and thirties was not generally dealt with in as open a manner as in Arnot Robertson's novels. Whereas to the modern reader, the description of unmarried sex between Esther and Cullum may seem actually restrained, to a reader of the late twenties it would have seemed shockingly lacking in the proper romantic gauzes. Worse is to follow. Cullum confesses that he was thinking of another woman when he made love to Esther. Their love affair, since it is told by Esther with the power of hindsight, carries with it a strong aura of cynical bitterness. It is not comfortable reading. Once again Arnot Robertson proves herself a very unromantic novelist. Nicola Beauman, in her study of the woman's novel from 1914 to 1939, *A Very Great Profession*, points out that the average middle-class reader 'preferred their fiction not to threaten the status quo as they knew it, and still associated anything vaguely "indecent" with rubber shops'. On the other hand she quotes a *Good Housekeeping* of 1938 as deploring 'the obsession with sex which has prevailed now for some years'. It was not easy to reconcile the prudery of the older generation with the uninhibited outlook of a minority of the new.

Arnot Robertson went on after *Cullum* to write seven more novels. In the words of her *Times* obituary, the four published after the war did little 'to add to her reputation as a writer of fiction'. It seems that her determinedly broad canvas outweighed her control of her characters. *Devices and Desires* (1954) tells the story of a thirteen-year-old child leading a group of political refugees from Bulgaria into Macedonia and then visiting Aden and Trinidad as companion to a rich youth dying from spinal paralysis. *Justice of the Heart* has a journalist travelling from Cambridge to Zanzibar and Norway and *The Strangers on the Roof* (published posthumously in 1964) takes place in Hong Kong and Macao where the protagonist is a speech therapist working among the poor.

During all this later period Arnot Robertson was busy with non-fiction and her radio work, appearing regularly on such programmes as 'Woman's Hour' and 'My Word'. In 1955 she was asked about her reasons for becoming a writer. In her usual forthright way, she blamed it on her family, among whom she felt inferior. She described how at the age of about seven or eight, 'I got away by myself to the shrubbery and said: "There must be something I can do that they can't do. They're braver than I am – they're better-looking than I am. They've got no brains at all. All right, I shall write.'"

In *Cullum* and indeed most of her work, the theme of bravery is amply illustrated. Esther's physical prowess is an important part of her character but in the end shown to be pointless and self-destructive. Nevertheless the hunting scenes are an essential part of the book, just as the sailing scenes are integral to *Ordinary Families*. Boats and boating was the subject of her first radio piece which included the memorable line, 'there is no reason why any normally hefty girl, or a pair of them, should not run a boat up to about six tons'. Even after she decided she hated sailing, she and her husband spent much time on the River Thames – where he eventually met his death while untangling weeds round a propeller. Together they produced a book called *Thames Portrait*. Robertson's love of nature was a happier inheritance from her childhood which shows itself in *Cullum* with her individual and evocative descriptions of the countryside.

Ordinary Families includes the theme of sibling rivalry. Here the beautiful sister takes any man she wants, although not to her ultimate advantage. In fact E. Arnot Robertson herself was very good-looking, tall and slim with red hair, a striking image immortalized in a painting by her friend, James McBey. Yet her early family unhappiness (she never properly forgave her mother) doubtless reinforced the recurring theme of jealousy in her books and also encouraged the bouts of severe, almost neurotic, depression. She herself had one child, an adopted son, Gordon Turner. With Cullum, Robertson created a hero whose deficiencies gave ample reason for analysing the demon of jealousy. After her betrayal, Esther finds some consolation with a comment which could apply to so many passionate but unsuccessful love affairs, 'What I miss most isn't Cullum, but what he stood for in my imagination.'

This is the central reality behind all stories of romantic love but is very seldom expressed. In the year of *Cullum*'s publication, Arnot Robertson gave a talk in which she strongly argued the case for a realistic approach in fiction. However, her self-knowledge was not total, for she also described her reaction to a reader who nearly died of laughing at her novels. 'I take myself with sepulchral seriousness,' she responded, 'I like my characters all soggy and sapped with sorrow because then it's easier to push them into their proper places in the plot.' Happily this is not at all the impression created by her work. One of the most obvious features of *Cullum* and her best later work is the immense energy coming from the characters. The dialogue is always sharp, often witty and not immune to one-liners. Of course, her purpose was serious but she could never, in the end, resist being readable too.

E. Arnot Robertson often said she liked writing. Her real idea of pleasure was to spend a quiet afternoon changing 'which' back to 'that'. On the other hand she likened choosing a subject for a novel to falling in love, when you lose all free will. *Cullum*, even with its faults which mainly consist of a not unattractive clumsiness of style, reflects just that feeling of a first love affair. It survives the sixty years since its first publication not so much by careful construction or great use of language, but by the unromantic directness of its passion and as a hard-headed portrait of the kind of man who is on an eternal quest for the next woman.

Rachel Billington, London, 1988

vii

Contents

Chapter 1: *The Coles*

ONCE the glamour has faded it is hard to give a clear impression of a man whom one has loved, as he appeared while the magic endured. Feeling loses so much of its life in the translation into words that one has to be still a little bound by the spell, still partly convinced at least, of the reality of the broken enchantment, in order to be convincing, and in restrospect it is difficult to see the figure in its old perspective, unaltered by the light of after-knowledge, and to realize where the charm lay. Yet, in a way, I am still conscious of Cullum's charm.

It is not easy to express, but if I only succeed in making a comparatively colourless sketch of that laughing, vital young figure it will not be from lack of material, but because I must leave out much that is essential to the completeness of the picture. Though the artist as an impersonal instrument should come before the individual, there are some things which, even now, would hurt too much in the writing. The little group of people whose lives are the real records of his will understand and clothe the bare outlines of this account with the living stuff of memory. It would need his own style and brain to do justice to his own story.

Cullum Hayes and I, Esther Sieveking, were brought together by a common interest; we both wrote, or we were both trying to write, he with a certain amount of success already, while I was still making, in an amateurish way, tremendously ambitious experiments, which I scribbled in secret for fear of the scornful interest of my family.

Living in the country, among people who looked on books as a last resource for killing time when all other means had failed, I had never met anyone who cared at all for the things that I loved passionately. It was my sole grievance against fortune, for my lot had fallen in a fair ground, in Holmwood, set among the green and gracious Surrey hills; but I was desperately eager to find a companion who could enter into the intangible world of books and ideas, where I spent half my time, when I was not helping Father in the stables, grooming or exercising the unbroken hunter colts and confirmed rogue horses which it was his paying hobby to buy, break in and re-sell as soon as they became manageable.

Having no son, he had expected me, since I left school in France, to share the kicks, and make some of the ha'pence, on which we depended a good deal, for besides the money from the sale of horses, Father had nothing but his retired major's half-pay, which had to provide for my two small sisters as well. I enjoyed the work, but it left me more and more unsatisfied. Mental loneliness is hard to bear at all times, but hardest when one is young.

I was intensely excited when I heard, through village gossip, that a Mrs. Cole, who had taken a friend's house in the neighbourhood, was a well-known writer with several volumes of poetry to her credit. Knowing Holmwood's capacity for magnifying the few exciting things that came in reach of it, I discounted most of the story ; I had never heard of her; but I felt there might be something in it and I spent hours devising means of getting to know her. I lacked the courage to speak to her casually when we met in the post-office, though the post-mistress drew us both into conversation with her, while she served us simultaneously with stamps and sweets. It was towards the end of Mrs. Cole's three weeks' stay when I saw her one morning, from a distance, strolling along one of the open grass rides on the Holmwood common. Our bull terrier bitch, Justice, was with me, and we were hidden from Mrs. Cole by the thick, high gorse and holly bushes. Bent double in my efforts to drag the fat, indignant old dog with me, I set off at a run for a place where I could intercept her. Justice, mildest of creatures, had an alarming manner of sniffing at all strangers' heels, following them a little way with her head and tail stretched out and carried low, and her pink-rimmed eyes half closed, from indolence, but it looked like ferocity.

I cut into the ride just ahead of Mrs. Cole and sauntered in the same direction. Justice lumbered back to her and behaved in her habitual, well-meaning way, and Mrs. Cole was duly nervous. Peremptorily I called off the dog, who cocked a surprised, meek eye at me, but Mrs. Cole was grateful, and as we seemed to be going the same way she started talking to me. She was a small, fat, middle-aged woman with a chubby little pursed-up mouth and bird-like bright eyes. She was bird-like both in face and in her quick, jerky movements; she was never still for a moment, and conversation poured out of her in a flood. I marvelled at the rapidity with which she got out her words. I learnt in ten minutes that she was a vegetarian, a teetotaller, a non-smoker and an anti-vivisectionist, and that she had innumerable other fads. She was of the type that should have had many children, instead of only one son and many affectations. She had come down to Holmwood to

11

recuperate from recent nerve-trouble, having known the place many years ago; and she asked me to come to tea the next day.

I went full of great expectations; she had already confirmed the report that she wrote poetry, and, anxious for advice, I treated her with immense deference, prepared to accept everything that she said about writing as the word of an oracle, but I had no chance of asking her the many questions on points of style, the way to approach editors, and similar matters, that I knew no other means of getting answered, for in the short time that I spent with her she talked almost entirely of her own literary produce, which she some-times sold to magazines: she had not published any books. I was shown a collection of worn cuttings that had become illegible at the folds through constant handling. They contained sad little pieces of verse which always referred vaguely to 'you' in the last line. 'You' had either jilted her or passed away; it was impossible to tell which, but they were all melancholy and had the most comprehensive titles; 'Life,' dealt with in eight or ten lines; 'Love,' inaptly, being a little longer.

They seemed to me so inexpressibly bad that I spent as much time in reading them as I could, to put off the moment when she might ask me for my opinion of them, but she helped me out of the difficulty herself, talking so much and so fast of her ideals and enthusiasms that I had only to thank her without com-ment when I handed back the cuttings.

She spoke with dreadful verbal ease of matters which I could not discuss with anyone on first acquaintance, because they played too great a part in my life. I wanted a friend who could understand intellectual emotion, which seemed to me something so innately private that I should have been a little ashamed to admit feeling it; I did not want one who babbled of such things in banal phrases, but Mrs. Cole was one of those good women whose sense of reserve is entirely occupied with physical reticences; she was ready and eager to reveal the recesses of her mind to a new-comer; there was not much in it, but I was soon made welcome to all there was. Unaccustomed to people who paraded their inmost feelings, I found her explicit soulfulness extraordinarily embarrassing. It made me hot and uncomfortable to hear her gushing in ill-chosen expressions over poetry that, to me, was sacred. In their fierce mental privacy the young resent having their idols made ridiculous by the loud worship of fools. In time, shy minds grow a sheath of callousness for protection, but in the early years, speech on the sub-jects that lie closest the heart is either a supreme tribute or a desecration. Had I been older, or less in love with the love of words for their own sake, she would have amused me, but as it was she made me feel that my delight in books and my attempts at writing were rather silly. As a reaction from her super-sensibility towards all things artistic, I felt myself growing more and more of a Philistine. She kept impressing on me how easily trifles affected her; she was often moved, she said, out of all proportion to the cause of the emotion. From her keenness to explore her soul in my presence I guessed that her family, to whom she was returning in three days' time, took insufficient interest in it and that she suffered from lack of sympathy.

'Do you know,' she said seriously, leaning forward to tap my knee in emphasis, 'I'm a perfect pagan at heart! really; a perfect pagan.' She was such a typical little town woman that I nearly laughed, but she went on: 'When I get among those mysterious, wonderful pine trees, here in the Redlands Woods, I want to kneel down and worship! I'm sure you do, too.'

'No, I don't,' I said shortly, thinking involuntarily of a pond in those woods, up Coldharbour way, where I had sat one night in summer, watching the slim moon shadows of the pines stirring, with little silver gleams, on the surface of the water, as the wind touched it. People like Mrs. Cole have no right to litter such places with their silly thoughts.

She must have found me unsympathetic; she made no protest when I rose to go soon after tea. At the door she asked me if, as I was interested in writing, I had ever had anything in print.

'One thing,' I said.

'Oh, what in?'

I gave her the name of the periodical which had unaccountably accepted the first contribution which I sent them, with beginners' optimism, when I was seventeen. It was crude and slightly nasty verse, written just after I left school, in the inevitable realism phase, when I was consciously revolting against prettiness, and deliberately found inspiration in train lights disappearing into a tunnel or the mingled red and white of a crushed frog's entrails on a muddy road. (Less surprisingly, the Editor refused everything else with which I bombarded him for several years.)

The expression on Mrs. Cole's face changed into instant respect.

'*The Small Review!* But my dear! How marvellous. *The Small Review!* Oh, surely you needn't go yet! It's quite early, and this is so interesting.'

A literary lion-hunter, convinced that she had discovered a promising whelp, she said that I must come to dinner with her when I was next in London. I told her that I should be spending a day in Town the next week.

'Excellent, my dear. And I'll get Cullum Hayes to meet you! You know Cullum Hayes, the young author; son of Arthur Hayes, the ex-M.P. Quite a wonderful first book it was, his, you know; and such a great friend of my son's, of course.'

This was much better. I had only seen one recognized author before, and had never spoken to him. He had stayed in Dorking the previous winter and had hired from Father a hunter on which he sat precariously and intermittently, while the horse, of its own accord, followed the pack of hounds with which Father and I hunted. I had a strong tendency towards hero-worship; repeated proof of his incompetence in the field, which I had been brought up to consider disgraceful, could not lessen the anxious awe with which I watched the novelist fall. To meet an author in his own sphere would be a wonderful experience.

'So difficult to get hold of,' she persisted, nervously pawing my arm, 'but I'll do it! I shall invite a particular friend of his and tell him she's coming. He'll turn up then, you'll see. A little romance – rather dreadful, though, because we think she's not quite – quite – well, he *says* she's half Brazilian, of high Castilian descent, and you know what that means! Of course, he's romantic minded, and at his age, naturally he wouldn't see it.'

So Cullum Hayes came to dinner at the Coles' house in Queen's Road because of a girl, even darker than I was, whose complexion had the indescribable matt tint of lace that the light has not reached for years; its unvarying pallor kept me uncomfortably aware of the funny line half way up my neck, where the whiteness of protected skin changed into deep winter tan, the effect on a sensitive skin of three days a week hunting in a high stock, and much exposure

15

between whiles. There was a suggestion of coloured blood in the shape of her rich, over-full mouth, that smiled lazily and without meaning. She smiled frequently, speaking very little. She was a woman as perfect and empty as a beautiful flower.

Cullum Hayes was sitting by her, leaning towards her so that I saw only the outline of his shoulder and his dark red head when I came into the dim, bare drawing-room, a dull room, sparsely furnished with expensive lumps of mahogany, which had just missed the good asceticism in style that had been attempted, and was only hard and coldly refined, like a plain, unintentional virgin.

Mrs. Cole came fluttering forward, looking more than ever like a bird, half-fledged now, in an evening frock. She introduced me to her son, Raymond, a rosily blond youth, very small and dapper, who blushed, when he shook hands, with a violence that fascinated me. I had never seen such a complete blush; there was no slow rise of colour spreading upwards over the face to the roots of the hair, but a sudden flood of bright pink appearing simultaneously wherever he was visible; even his hands seemed subject to it. When I knew him better, and saw him blush on each presentation to a strange woman and every time he attempted to make an epigram, which he did constantly, the thoroughness of his blushing never lost its interest for me; though I realized after a time that it was due to habit and his complexion, not to shyness, for he prided himself on being a most self-possessed young man of the world. Unprepared for this startling suffusion, which ebbed nearly as fast as it came, I must have showed my astonishment the first time I saw it, and a voice said confidentially in my ear, 'Isn't he marvellous? If you're wondering whether he

16

blushes like that all over, you can take my word for it, he does!'

'Cullum!' said Mrs. Cole, in resigned distress, and I turned, laughing, for the thought had run across my mind, to see him standing behind me.

I was disappointed by my first impression of an author at close quarters. Strictly speaking he was not good looking; nor did he resemble my preconceived idea of a writer. I was struck at once by the restlessness of the blue eyes: he had a fair face, pointed and keen, with sharp, thin lines – much too sharp for beauty – and a charming wide smile; there was something impish about it. Even to my immature eyes he appeared incredibly young to have written quite a good novel. It was an interesting face, because it was intensely alive, but it did not occur to me then that he was attractive as a man, for he was about my own height, and I was too tall to like medium-sized men.

Mrs. Cole drew me away towards the pale, dark girl, by twining her restless fingers in the chiffon sleeve of my one precious evening dress, and pulling. I followed her docilely, afraid that she might tear the old material, and was handed over to be shepherded in to dinner by Mr. Cole, a compact little City man, whose long, white nose was banked up by a high, sloping forehead and a long, receding chin, as though Nature had achieved his one prominent feature and then sunk back exhausted.

I was placed between Mr. Cole and his son, with Cullum on the other side of the table, next to Mrs. Cole and the Brazilian girl, Paula McMillan, a silent, smiling presence. When she spoke, it was generally to Cullum, in a gently proprietary manner, and so softly that he naturally bent his head down to her.

17

Snatches of his conversation with Mrs. Cole filtered through the flow of small-talk that ran in well-worn channels on our side. He was talking very fast, gaily but always in earnest, as if the subject of the moment were important to the exclusion of everything else; and the shaded lamplight, playing down on to that flickering young face, caught feature after feature, and lip and eye and hard-angled cheek were lit up for a second at a time. I wanted to watch him, but the men beside me insisted on drawing me into conversation. Cullum was youth incarnate, with all its glamour and its splendid promise, and when they mentioned his birthday which had just passed – it was in February – I wondered how old he was, until he said soulfully: 'Twenty-two years ago I was one of the things my mother gave up in Lent. Isn't that a beautiful thought? And all my own!'

'Oh, no, it isn't!' Raymond Cole contradicted him, 'I've read it somewhere too!'

'Now isn't that bad luck!' said Cullum, unabashed, smiling amiably at him across the table.

'Cullum, my boy,' said Mr. Cole, being heavily gallant, and looking from me to Paula McMillan, 'you ought to write another book called *Two Black Beauties*, with all the material close at hand! It would be most appropriate, for Miss Sieveking here is an amateur horse-coper of note, aren't you, my dear?'

'My father is,' I said. 'I'm not.'

Raymond cleared his throat in a way that presaged an important remark.

'Man,' he said sententiously, 'is a noble animal and a friend to horses.' His blush burgeoned out again, and he subsided, looking pleased with himself.

'Not quite as good as yesterday's effort,' Cullum told him kindly. 'Have a sip of wine and try again. In a minute I'll give you a suitable cue for that sparkling saying you repeated three times last week, and perhaps they'll think it's spontaneous.'

Raymond had a passion for making or borrowing poor epigrams and bringing them into the conversation whenever possible, with an air of mingled satisfaction and self-consciousness. Undeterred by Cullum's friendly derision, he introduced several others in the course of the evening.

I was content to play the listener whenever I could. People generally listened to young Cullum Hayes, whether he had anything particular to say or not, because he had a pleasant voice and a delightful way of talking, and he evidently enjoyed his own nonsense so much that other people did too. He laughed, with a quick, backward jerk of the head, at some observation he made to the girl by his side; she frowned in a puzzled way, not understanding his play on a word, and being very much a woman, smiled at him and not at what he had said, but at twenty-two he could not be expected to notice the difference. He would be an exceptional man if he ever noticed the difference.

'But what does it matter if it's true or not,' I heard him arguing with Mrs. Cole a little later, 'as long as it's beautiful? And it is; the New Testament contains the finest short story that's ever been written – far too good to be connected with present-day Christianity, which is the world's indigestion after having swallowed something too rich for it. I can't understand why people bother whether the glorious account we have of one perfect life is historically correct or not. The beauty of the idea is the same in either case. Too much stress is laid on the importance of literal truth.'

('They always get on to religion sooner or later,' Raymond Cole remarked to me.)

'No, really, Cullum – ! said Mrs. Cole, agreeably

19

horrified. 'You'll scandalize Miss Sieveking, who may be a fervent church-goer for all we know. I'm afraid I shocked her dreadfully by telling her that I was quite a pagan at heart!'

'Oh, not "shocked," I assure you!' I said. 'And anyway I'm not an ardent churchwoman.'

It was the first time I had taken any part in the general conversation. Cullum leant forward. 'What are you?' he said seriously, 'I mean, in the way of religion?' He had an uncomfortable habit of changing the tone of a conversation abruptly from nonsense to grave discussion, disregarding everyone in the room but the person to whom he was talking.

'Optimistic agnostic,' I muttered, my voice, because I felt awkward, sinking to an unusually deep tone, a family trick over which I had no control. My personal religion, like literature, was a subject of which I was not accustomed to talk, and only an aversion from lying prevented my claiming for the moment a recognized brand of religion that would save me from questioning. In those days, having no social agility, I was always being hemmed in between shyness and a regard for truth, and then suffered out of all proportion to the situations.

'What do you mean by that?'

'Well, I don't *know* anything for certain,' I said uncomfortably; 'I can't believe definitely one way or the other, but I'm pretty sure in my own mind that everything will be all right in the end.' Why couldn't he talk of something else?

'How – "everything all right at the end"?' Cullum could be very persistent.

'Oh, I think, well, either death will mean annihilation, which won't matter to me as I shan't be there to bother about it – most people seem to hate the idea, because they don't realize annihilation as complete, but imagine an awful state in which they somehow feel themselves not existing! – or else I think death will be a melting back into the source of life, as a tree when it dies goes back into the fertility of the earth, and that's all right, too. I think Schopenhauer's "Will-to-live" is the only reason why ninety per cent. of unthinking people believe in personal immortality.'

Cullum took up the argument vigorously, chiefly for the sake of arguing, I believe. He had the faculty of focussing all his attention and enthusiasm on whatever he was doing, and once I had got over my stiffness before strangers, I became so absorbed that I was unaware that we were monopolizing the conversation, plunging deeper and deeper into youthful theology which was boring the others; several times they tried hard to cut in, but their tentative interruptions were obliterated by one of Cullum's sweeping gestures. Enjoying ourselves exceedingly, we were contradicting each other as if we had been friends for years.

'But my dear girl, don't be ridiculous,' Cullum said heatedly, 'you must see – ' and I answered – 'Oh, that's absolutely inconsistent – and you know it!' To me such talk was an intoxicating novelty, and the return to earth was a shock when Mrs. Cole rose, and I realized that for the last quarter of an hour, at least, we had been behaving very badly.

As we passed out, I hoped that it would not be long before the men joined us; I had so little in common with these two women. They would be bored if I talked about horses, and I should be bored if they talked about clothes: books, in spite of the accepted idea to the contrary, make a barren subject of discussion between strangers, unless their range of reading overlaps, which was improbable in this case.

Mrs. Cole settled herself by me on the sofa, and unaware of my hatred of being touched, pawed my arm while she chatted with her restful vigour, which allowed no time for replies; I had been thankful to it before. She had lately finished reading a book which she insisted that I must read; it was marvellously well written, quite *too* fascinating, she said, and though at the moment she could not remember the title she knew that it was by the man who wrote *The Crock* – (or it might have been *The Arrow*) – *of Gold*. Anyway, it was by whichever of these authors had also written *Fortitude*. After ten minutes of description I was no longer surprised that, as I had noticed at dinner, the attention of her family immediately strayed elsewhere as soon as she became enthusiastic over anything.

The men came in at last, and Mrs. Cole's animated attention was diverted from me to them. She led the conversation carefully to art and prepared to effervesce again with artistic appreciation. She put forward the astonishing view that unpleasant things should be left out of books simply because they occur so often in real life; and the beautiful Paula McMillan told Cullum complacently that she could not bear 'intellectual stuff.'

'You see, I'm not one of those clever people,' she said, and there was the pride of implied moral rectitude in her voice. Anti-intellectual snobbery is one of the most irritating forms which snobbery takes; it is more irritating, because more often met, than the intellectual variety.

Mr. Cole sought delicately for my views on licence in art, in which subject he was particularly interested, as was his son, who had lately come down from Oxford to go into his father's office, where he was doing well. Raymond combined an acquired decadent mind with sound inherited business instincts; and when his father discussed Flaubert's *Madame Bovary*, describing that incomparable achievement as 'spicy,' he nodded a grave approval to convey his familiarity with a work which, I discovered soon afterwards, he knew only by name.

I felt disappointedly at home with these two people, to whom art was nothing more than a convenient means of enjoying indecency in a highly creditable manner. My world was chiefly inhabited by such folk, many of them were my friends, straightforward, jolly, excellent souls, but I wanted a change.

The difference between the Coles and the hunting set with which my father's hobby brought me in contact was that the latter were freer in their speech. French on my mother's side, and brought up partly in France, where anything can be mentioned by its name at any time, and partly among riding people at Holmwood, I had no understanding of the respectability of tongue cultivated in the kind of drawing-rooms where many things may be hinted but not said.

Mrs. Cole enquired with a simulated shudder of horror whether that huge dog of mine had ever bitten anyone. 'I was petrified when the creature rushed for me,' she said. 'Simply petrified, I was!'

'Justice is too old and fat and good-natured to hurt a fly,' I told her, 'unless she sat on it by mistake.'

'What a curious name for a dog,' Mr. Cole observed. 'Why do you call him "Justice"?'

'Justice isn't a "him," but a bitch,' I answered without thinking. 'Originally her name was Sheila, but she's called Justice because she has had so many miscarriages.'

There was a moment of heavy, tense silence, before Mrs. Cole said, 'Oh, really?' in a forced voice, and

23

asked me if I believed in spiritualism, which in view of what I had said at dinner was unnecessarily crushing. Everyone stirred uncomfortably except Cullum, the only one who laughed, but he laughed uproariously. I looked at him gratefully; I think it was from that moment that I grew fond of Cullum. As his jolly laughter ended he smiled at me friendlily, caressing my hot face with his eyes.

Resumed conversation flowed back over the painful silence that my remark had caused, and I rose to go as soon as possible, explaining by way of excuse, though none was needed, that as it would take me a long while to reach home I wanted to catch an early train. My hostess's protests at my leaving so early – it was only nine o'clock – were more perfunctory than usual: I was not asked to that house again for six months, and it was only on Cullum's account that I was invited then.

I turned to say good-bye to him last of all.

'I'll see you home, if I may,' he said.

'Thank you very much, but I go by train from Victoria, and I think Mr. Cole is coming with me as far as the top of the road, where I catch a bus.'

'Oh, well, I'll tell him not to,' said Cullum self-assuredly, and nodded casually to Paula McMillan. 'I'll come back for you later,' he told her, 'it's quite early.'

We walked out of the room together, leaving Mrs. Cole nearly speechless with annoyance which she nursed, her son told me afterwards, until she saw Cullum again, when it evaporated immediately.

Outside the air was soft and fresh, and the luminous sky dark in patches above the yellow halos of the street lamps.

'I seem to have done it again!' I said sadly. 'I have an uncanny knack of putting my foot in it.'

'There's nothing uncanny about it, if you often make remarks like that!' The boy began to laugh again – it was some time before I thought of Cullum as a man and not a boy.

'But it's not only with the ultra-respectable people; if ever I meet anyone who has a mental corn of any kind I always happen to step on it,' I mourned; 'I suppose, with the best intentions in the world, I have really offended Mrs. Cole?'

'You have, you astonishing child of nature! Oh, their faces! They are the most conventional family I know, and you have shaken them to the core.'

'But why?' I asked, 'I said nothing very much worse than some of the things you said at dinner about religion.'

'Ah, but you don't understand Mrs. Cole's mentality. My remarks were on a different plane. Blasphemy, being mental, is permissible, according to her; the mildest obscenity, being physical, isn't. There are millions of people like that, you know. I wouldn't have missed that electric moment for the world.'

We turned out of Queen's Road towards Notting Hill Gate, skirting Kensington Gardens. The trees there are lovely at night, strange and expectant, like the trees that grow by chance in the more blessed places of the earth. These trapped London trees are only parodies of the others in the day time; they lack the exquisite sadness and dignity of wild things, but in the darkness they regain the indefinable quality that the light takes from them, and are full of the age-old majesty of their kind, which was the first thing to stir a sense of awed worship in me when I was a child. Trees, loved even above running water and hills, were a perpetual joy to me. When I had been away from the lovely place where I lived for any length of time, it was

25

not the people but the woods there that were most often in my mind.

Diffidently I said something like that to Cullum, and found that he understood. He loved beautiful things, and did not gush over them.

'It was the same with me and my books at home,' he said, 'when I was about sixteen or seventeen and at school. At Christmas and birthdays and so on my father always gave me books, in good bindings, and I had already quite a decent little collection. During the term I used to find myself looking forward, more than to anything else, to getting back to them and taking them down, and handling as well as re-reading them. The appearance, and the nice feeling of a good edition in my hands meant such a lot. One fine book finely printed and bound is more joy, to me, than two fine books in shabby covers.'

He talked on lovingly, about his books, as I had never heard anyone talk before. The instant sense of companionship it gave me was like the warmth of a fire to someone grown accustomed to the lack of it, who is hardly conscious of the cold until it is over; I realized then how much I had been longing for a friend of this kind.

Here at last, walking by my side, was someone else who cared for books, and realized the excellence of being alive. It was wonderful. He was the first real comrade I had found.

At Notting Hill Gate, since Cullum insisted on coming to the station, we climbed to the top of a Victoria bus, and fought amiably over the paying of my fare. He won, in spite of the advice of the interested conductor to 'Let the lidy 'ave 'er wiy, always, sir – sive you lots o' trouble in life, sir!'

'Where do you go from Victoria?' he asked.

26

'Holmwood.'

'Oh, I know it. We spent part of one summer holiday there with the Coles when I was a small youth. That was how Mrs. Cole got to know the place. Funnily enough –' he stopped and stared at me suspiciously. 'Surely this is too good to be true, but – Holmwood and your particular colouring. Were you by any chance the little girl who knocked out my front teeth?'

'Good heavens, yes! If you mean at the Dycett-Byrne's. Was it you? But anyway it was only one tooth,' I said modestly, being a stickler for accuracy even when it dimmed my glory.

'Three. One at the time, but two came out afterwards, though I dare say they were loose before. Still, you were actually responsible for their coming out.'

'What an extraordinary thing!'

'It was,' he said severely, 'I can't think what you did it for.'

'Oh, I can! I meant that it seems extraordinary to meet you again through the Coles, though I suppose it isn't really. I did it because of that puppy, don't you remember?'

Together we reconstructed one of the most satisfactory scenes of my childhood. The Dycett-Byrnes were the most important family at Holmwood, and their big annual children's party, held to celebrate the birthday of their one child, Tony, was the chief social event of the summer. As the children of one of the local hunting gentry, my sister, Olive, and I were commanded to these parties, which were in the nature of royal functions, but mere summer visitors were not invited, unless they were something special, and it was only because Arthur Hayes was a fairly well-known M.P. that his little son, Cullum, was included among

27

the favoured, and as his friend, Raymond Cole was asked too.

We were playing hide and seek in the big grounds, and at six years old I was already more interested in animals than in children of my own age. Leaving the game I wandered off after a retriever puppy into the room where tea was laid.

A small boy came in through the french window while I was playing with the puppy on the floor. There were two and a half years between us, and he must have been nearly nine, but he was delicate and rather backward, physically, and I was nearly as tall, and certainly the heavier of the two.

We looked at each other for a while, and then I went on rolling the puppy on its back and tickling its fat little stomach.

'I shall eat a cream bun, now,' he announced.

'Well, I shan't,' I said, not from any excess of virtue, but because I disliked washing my hands right up to the wrists, and I knew that the cream always spread. 'But you give me a bit for the puppy,' I ordered when he had helped himself.

'No!'

'Yes!' I said firmly, being accustomed to tyrannizing over Olive, who was three (Valérie was not yet born). He gave me a piece of bun to feed to the soft ball of black wool in my lap.

The small boy had cleared all traces of the bun from his own person when the others trooped in to tea, led by the terror-inspiring Mrs. Dycett-Byrne.

'Children! How very naughty of you!' she boomed at us. 'You had no business to come in here before tea. And you've been taking the cakes, too! Now that's very wrong indeed. I'm surprised at you, Esther!'

'Didn't!' said the other urchin, 'the puppy took it,'

and he pointed to the mat of cream on its whiskers, which the little animal was trying to clean with a long red tongue. 'He was on the chair, an' when we came in he jumped on the table, an' we took him off,' he added, with an early gift for atmospheric detail.

Something turned cold inside me, but I had been taught that one must not sneak in any circumstances. They took the puppy out of my arms and smacked it. It squeaked twice, and they put it outside the window in disgrace.

We settled down to the meal, and I ate scarcely looking down at my plate, staring fixedly at the little cad opposite whom I hated with the vindictive passion that any wrong done to an animal aroused.

He kept his eyes lowered and ate voraciously, not daring to meet my accusing gaze, but fully aware of it. He was a very sensitive child, and the tension became too much for him. He grew crimson in the face, flung out an arm in my direction and broke into anguished howling. I slipped down off my chair and was round the table in an instant, pushing aside those who were trying to soothe him.

"S all right!' I said, 'you lemme have him! I'll see to him. I'll take him into the garden. Come on, you!'

'That's a good girl, Esther,' said Mrs. Dycett-Byrne, afraid lest the example might upset her highly-strung Tony, 'take him out and comfort him, dear.'

I dragged the child, whose words were indistinguishable through his sobs, out of the room by the open window. He was crying too hard to offer any effective resistance. Those in the dining-room heard his howls gradually receding, almost dying away, and then the sounds were renewed, with piercing shrieks and a clamour of two voices. I was found with one knee on

either side of his prostrate body, magnificently aveng-
ing the puppy.

'That'll teach you – t'have – the puppy – hit!' I was
shouting, holding him down with one hand and pound-
ing him with the other.

I was hauled off and sent home at once, and so was
little Cullum Hayes, but his indignant mother, who
was not present because no parents were invited, could
not discover the name of the black-haired freckled-
faced fury who had basely attacked her dear little boy.

'You were unusually obnoxious, even for a little
boy,' I said to Cullum when we had pieced the story
together.

'I wasn't!' he protested. 'I was chivalrous enough
to try and exonerate you from undeserved blame. Of
course I know now that one should never interfere on a
woman's behalf; she always resents it. I've been
mauled about by another since then for stopping
her husband hitting her, for being "something"
drunk, he said. He was "something" drunk himself,
and I think she was sober, but she joined with him
against me and scratched my face!'

He waited with me for my train, for which I was
far too early, having left the Coles much sooner than
I had intended; and in answer to his question when he
could see me again, I told him that in three weeks' time
I was coming to London for a fortnight, and gave him
the address of the friend with whom I should be staying. I had been educated in Paris, where my mother
had lived since she left my father, and it annoyed my
young pride, reared on the excessive deference of the
Frenchmen in her circle, that Cullum asked "when"
he might see me again, not "if" I would permit it at all.

'Can't I come down to Holmwood one Saturday?'
he said, 'I'm free in the week-ends.'

I hesitated for a second, imagining this fascinating young man in the setting of my lovely English home, and then refused, obeying an instinct unreasoningly. Yet I wanted to see him again.

Doors slammed and the engine snorted; the train stirred and hung back, and as it moved forward I stretched out my hand to the window to say good-bye. Standing on the running board, Cullum took it in both his, bent his head and kissed it, and then the impudent deep blue eyes held mine for an instant.

He stepped back, out of sight, and the train carried me away. I looked down occasionally at the back of my hand and smiled, wondering if this were the beginning of a great friendship.

I suppose that he returned to Paula McMillan, who was very beautiful and not altogether white, and to whom, I learned later, he was more or less engaged at that time.

Chapter 2: *Coming Home*

IN a few days February gave way stormily to March, and quite suddenly the weather turned mild, and spring came, surprisingly, in a night. The next day, which was Saturday and a hunting day, the wet, warm ground under my mare's flying hoofs was instinct with new life, and from it rose to me as I rode the good smell of fertile earth after rain, and with that another fragrance, which is like no other scent, the heady indefinable smell of the spring itself.

It was the finest day that the local hunt enjoyed that season. From the start we had eight miles or so of straight, hard riding with hardly a check, with the wind driving into our faces, stiffening and tightening the skin and singing past our ears. Doubling back, a canny fox had taken us up over the back of Leith Hill where the cover is thick, and we had lost in the end. I was secretly glad, as I always was when a game fox got away after a gallant run; digging him out of his earth seemed a rotten business, but I only held this view through sentimental inconsistency, for I should have been loud in my complaints if the hounds had grown slack.

Hunting on Jenny twice a week, as a rule, I had to nurse her strength a good deal, so that when we came to a small hedge and ditch jump, early in the run, I was riding near the tail of the field, behind Tony Dycett-Byrne. That young man was the most pathetic rider to hounds that I knew. Exceedingly timid by nature, he hunted because every Dycett-Byrne, male and female, had done so for generations, and to break the tradition would have been unthinkable. He rode uncomfortably, with the correct, English, concave back, looking intensely conscious of where he ended and his saddle began, and was notoriously unwilling to take a stiff fence. He would go any distance out of his way to reach a gap, not for the sake of his horse, which he disliked as the instrument of his bi-weekly misery, but on his own account. I was sorry for him, knowing that he must suffer mental torture before every meet. He came off frequently.

The hedge before us was a mild quickset with a fairly wide stream on the other side, and Tony, seeing a lower place further down, made for it hesitatingly. As he came up, his mount, in the neurotic manner of a thoroughbred, took a dislike to something on the other side and stopped dead, forelegs straight out and sliding. Tony shot over the gap of his choosing, leaving his horse behind him, and the beast turned and cantered up the hedge, crossing Jenny just as I came up, and putting her off the jump. She half refused, answered to my heels as I slid forward to ease a difficult take-off, and then she lifted awkwardly and just cleared, landing with a splash in the middle of the stream, where Tony had arrived before us. She floundered badly and we galloped on, dripping mud.

It was drying into small cakes on the sodden leathers, on my habit, and even on the dilapidated bowler that I had taken off to let the wind play through my hair, now that the hunt was over and Jenny and I were coming back alone by a short cut through the Redlands Woods, where the late, slanting sunlight fell in great shafts between the trees, bathing

33

us for a second at a time, while Jenny picked her way delicately down the steep slope, over the slippery brown carpet of dead pine-needles in the long aisles between the trees. Both of us were weary, dirty, and at peace with the world.

I do not know which is the best, the suppressed excitement of the meet, when the horses are keen and fretting to be off, and there is the expectation of a good day ahead; or the hunt itself, the feel of a good horse, all fine-strung nerve and muscle, stretched out at full gallop, and the exhilaration of pace, that no machine-made speed can equal for sheer joy; or the coming home in the failing light, jogging quietly back at dusk over ground sown with memories of other great days and former hunts, to the delight of a hot bath and the delicious lassitude that follows it. All three are very good, and each seems the best at the time.

I was thinking of Cullum Hayes, as Jenny carried me out of a patch of sunlight into the gloom of a tunnel made by close-growing hazel-nut bushes, through which the light, twig-filtered, threw bright, wavering patterns on the bare earth. I was wondering if he would remember to look me up when I went to London for a visit, in ten days' time, and I was hoping that I should see him.

He had been often in my thoughts since that dinner at the Coles' house. He had given me a glimpse of the happiness that mental friendship might hold for me, and it had made me discontented with the limitations of a life which, superficially, I enjoyed to the full. With plenty of horses to ride, and my part of Surrey to ride them in, good health and friends, I should have been a greater fool than I was if I had not realized that I was fortunate. I only lacked companionship; and Cullum

34

Hayes figured in my thoughts just then less as an individual than as a kind of messenger from another sphere, to which I wanted to belong. As a means of getting in touch with it he engrossed my mind; I did not think of him very much as a person, interesting for his own sake, but simply as someone who might give me what I wanted. I lived in a green world where no man was, where no man had been at all. No one had ever mattered to me one half as much as did the people I met in books.

Early developed in some ways, because I came of a Latin race on my mother's side, I was strongly attracted by men, at nineteen, in an impersonal way. Men, and not any one man, interested me, and because I recognized it I shied away from the attraction deliberately. I was curious about the sensations that a kiss stirred in me, but I had permitted very few men to kiss me once I discovered how deeply it affected me. Through having two homes, one in England and the other in Paris, and also through my father's hobby, I had met many more men than most of the girls of my age that I knew, and I had had far fewer minor love affairs.

In my friendships with men I was still more interested in noticing my effect on them, and their effect on me, than in any of them as individuals: one part of me always stood aside and noted sensations. When I was in tantrums as a small child this impartial self, without having any control over my actions, often observed that I was behaving ridiculously and laughed at me, and this used to goad me into real fury.

I was already a little afraid of the unmeasured, vaguely felt force that made the restlessness of spring nights a call to which I was afraid to listen, and so was always half listening. Young ardour repressed

35

has the appearance of coldness. 'Fish-blooded little devil – and most deceptive looking!' one of our local gallants had said of me aggrievedly at the last hunt ball, to the next girl with whom he sat out, while she comforted his hurt pride by suffering his gallantries with equanimity. The apathetic reception accorded by girls I knew to caresses they neither desired nor disliked, passed my comprehension: in no circumstances, to my mind, could kisses be considered endurable. One either wanted or disliked them intensely.

Jenny stumbled, sending Cullum's image flying out of my mind.

Leaving the woods, we came out on to the field footpath that runs from Holmwood through Coldharbour to Abinger – what lovely sounds there are in the names of well-loved places! Jenny, moving stiffly from the withers, nobly broke into a trot as we reached level ground, and because I was very fond of her and she was even more tired than I was, I began to talk her home, as I had done many times when we ended a run many miles from Holmwood after a hard day. With one ear cocked forward nervously, in her usual manner, and the other turned back to listen to the encouraging voice, she would jog on gamely for miles, however tired she might be.

The blue sky gleamed in the puddles of the tarred surface as we crossed the high road, on to the narrow strip of common that still separated us from home, and our joint shadow stretched enormous and distorted in front of us, Jenny with a vast barrel and elongated legs, I with a tiny head. I reined in for an instant just before we came in sight of the house, deliberately enhancing the pleasure of hot water and food, which I was foretasting, by withholding myself from them a little while longer. It was a favourite trick; I used to do the same sort of thing with sweets when I was a child.

Jenny turned her pretty head and looked back reproachfully, and I pressed her gently with my knees. We squeezed through the gap in the holly hedge into the drive. Cullum Hayes, his back towards us, was standing bareheaded by the stable-gate, with the deep, mellow light that comes just before sunset touching his dark red hair to burnished bronze.

Chapter 3: *The Lie of the Land*

HE turned as Jenny's hoofs rang on the hard ground. She trotted up, stopping by the gate of her own accord, and he looked up at me with his head on one side, his eyes screwed up against the slanting sunlight that fell full in his face.

He assumed, for my benefit, the ingratiating, doubtful expression that a dog wears when it is not sure of its welcome. In his heart Cullum was quite sure of his welcome everywhere.

'But I told you not to come!' I said, smiling too, and immensely glad that he had come.

Standing close to Jenny, in an attitude of humility that his voice belied, he began drawing patterns with one finger in the half-dry mud on my riding-boot while he explained: the back of his head as he held it bent was very boyish looking, with a little peak of hair running down the nape of the neck.

'I know! But you see, I wanted to come very much, and it seemed such a waste of time to wait until you came to London when I have a perfectly good motor-bicycle. I happened to be riding in this direction anyway. And you don't really mind, do you? Consider that I came quite half the way here on the off-chance of finding you in; I think that's rather touching, myself, and, of course, very flattering to you. Aren't you going to get down? I put out my hand and you step into it, don't you? I know, from books, that something like that happens when a woman gets on or off a horse;

38

I don't remember which, but I know the attendant male makes a step out of his hand somehow; I'm not well up in anything to do with horses; I feel with Raymond Cole that they're dangerous anachronisms. What ought I to do?'

'Nothing. I only step on your hand, as you put it, in mounting, with a side-saddle, which I don't use. But if you like you can hold the head, or pointed end, of the animal – that's right.'

In England, the early morning sunshine dances on all it touches, and in the afternoon the soft, kindly light caresses, but the last golden rays rest quietly and thickly over everything. Smooth skin looks wonderful in that yellow glow. On Cullum's face just then the sunlight was like a benediction.

Meanwhile the practical part of my mind was wondering how to get the boy out of the way before I had to walk into the house. This was essential. My old riding breeches were almost worn through in the strappings; the buckskin had worn right off, and the cloth was threadbare, but habits were expensive and the season was nearly over. I had to make my old kit last out because I had no money for a new one. The fray on the inside of the knee did not show when I was in the saddle; then my habit looked fairly presentable still, but not when I walked. An old friend, Gerald Hemingway, who rode much the same course as I did and came many more croppers, insisted, after the state of my clothes had been revealed to him by my tactless little sister, that this was because I was firmly stuck to the saddle by maidenly modesty – undoubtedly an adhesive substance, he said sadly: his best efforts with so many girls failed to dislodge it.

Somehow I could not bear Cullum Hayes to see how shabbily I was dressed.

39

'Will you take Jenny into the yard for me?' I said to
him. 'She'll show you which is her door in the stables.
Just let her in and Moon, the groom, will see to her.
You won't have to wait so long for tea if I can go and
change at once – you haven't had tea yet, I suppose?'

'No, your sisters offered it to me, but I said I'd wait
for you.'

'Good. You'll find the children in the kitchen when
you've let Jenny into her stable. Walk straight in by
the back door; there's no one else in the house just
now. I shan't be a minute.'

'I've made friends with your sisters already. They've
been very sweet, entertaining me while I was waiting.
They seem quite accustomed to having strange young
men descend on them, out of the blue, asking for you.'

'Well, they aren't; but they're half-French and have
been taught not to show surprise.' I slipped off, carefully, and pulled Jenny's head round to me without
moving, 'Good-bye, Jenny, and thank you! We've
had a very good day, haven't we?' I kissed the pink
velvet of her muzzle, and she lifted her head and
nuzzled my cheek, really kissing it, as I had taught her
to do. We always kissed each other good-bye; I was
proud of her accomplishments.

She led Cullum into the yard, and I went in by the
front door, and denying myself the anticipated luxury
of long wallowing in hot water, changed in a tremendous hurry.

Cullum's explosive laughter broke out in the dining-
room as I ran downstairs. (His laugh always made
strangers in restaurants and theatres turn round and
stare at him.) Vallie, a solemn child of thirteen, with an
extraordinary deep, hoarse voice, was amusing him
with the help of our repulsively stout bull-terrier, in
whom he was taking special interest because of the

episode at the Coles'. Justice, who invariably out-witted us when we tried to safeguard her figure, was in her usual ungainly condition of promise which always fell short of performance. She was very old and had not had puppies for years. Most nice family dogs answer to several names; Father called her Creeping Misery, from the expression of her eyes, and for the same reason that I had named her Justice, Olive, my fifteen year old sister, referred to her as The Great White Hope. As I came in she waddled slowly away from Cullum on widely placed legs, and welcomed me, with a lazily wagging tail and pleased, bleary eyes. Vallie had even less sense of shyness about animals' domestic affairs than I had, and the short-comings of Justice was a favourite theme of hers; as I sat down her gruff little voice trailed away into vague obstetric mutter-ings.

'How did you find the house,' I asked Cullum, 'because I didn't give you the address?'

'I knew you lived somewhere in Holmwood, so I rode down here and asked the village policeman, who happened to be standing in the road gazing at infinity, where a Miss Sieveking lived. Chatty fellow. He asked me if I wanted Miss Esther or Miss Olive, "as, being a Saturday, Miss Esther'd be out with the 'ounds!"'

'Didn't he say anything about me?' anxiously asked Vallie, who had an admiration that almost amounted to worship for the local policeman. She always stopped to have a long talk with him when they met in the village.

'No, I don't think he mentioned you,' Cullum answered gravely, 'because he said "Miss Esther, Miss Olive, or the little one." Surely he couldn't have meant you, could he?'

41

Serious-minded Vallie regarded the whole world as a great conspiracy to make fun of her. 'He might've!' she admitted, with the air of one who has often been disappointed in humanity.

'How long had you been waiting when I arrived?' I asked Cullum.

'Hours and hours,' he said pathetically. 'Since about four. I was just going to walk up the drive to see if I could meet you when you appeared magically through the hedge from the other direction. The optimistic policeman said you were quite likely to be in at about half-past four. He seems to know all about your family.'

'Everyone in the village knows all about everyone else,' I told him. 'By this time, you are already the centre of gossip, I expect, as you've been here nearly two hours. They're probably discussing what the object of your visit could be; whether your intentions are serious and honourable, or only serious. Did you go into the garden while you were waiting? I'd like you to see the trees there, the ones we spoke of the other night.'

'Esther's got a mania for trees, and funny things like that,' Vallie explained.

'So have I,' said Cullum. 'I refused to be shown the grounds until you came back. I would rather you introduced me to them. You'll be too tired to wander about to-night, I suppose, so I shall have to wait until I'm asked again, like a perfect little gentleman.'

'If I do ask you to come again!' I said smiling reassuringly.

Olive came in with a newly-baked cake, alluringly hot and indigestible. 'I'm awfully glad you did come,' she said to Cullum. 'I'm fearfully bored on Wednesdays and Saturdays, when Father and Esther are both hunting, and I've only Vallie to talk to; I hate being alone. Father didn't go to-day, but he does generally, and anyhow he's been out with the beastly horses all day except for those few minutes when you saw him. Hunting days are horrid.' Olive was warming up to her pet grievance. 'Father and Esther come down and fuss about the time all through breakfast, then they're away all day, and when they do come in at last, they're fit for nothing but to eat for hours, and talk about saddle-galls and yawn till bedtime. If you weren't here, or Esther knew you better, she'd be lying back in the arm-chair by the fire, spilling crumbs over everything, and only grunting when any of us spoke to her.'

I laughed; 'eat for hours and talk about saddle-galls and yawn till bedtime' was an excellent description of the behaviour of most of the hunting people I knew at the end of a stiff day.

'Olive hates hunting "shop," ' I said, 'because she doesn't like horses and is always being caught by the language. Father, describing the day's run, says something about going over a "blind bullfinch," and she gets frightfully indignant and wants to know if the poor little thing was hurt. A hedge is "blind," you know, when you can't see what's on the other side, and a "bullfinch" when it's unclipped and has long sprays standing up from it.'

The blood rushed into Olive's face and she glared at me. A highly-strung child, she would sometimes take any amount of teasing in good part and at other moments resent it. Ignoring the imminence of an outburst of temper I talked on serenely. 'She really nurses a secret contempt for me because I can only ride, and not cook. I don't know if you happen to have

43

noticed how nice that cake is; it's your second slice, isn't it? Well, she made it, and she also runs the house as I'm so bad at that sort of thing.'

Cullum, very quick of perception, followed up the subject and praised her cake-making, asking her exactly how the cake was made, though the receipt could not have interested him. The next time he came, he said – with a glance of enquiry at me – would she make exactly the same sort of cake, but with cherries in it? – he loved cherries.

Olive promised and beamed. I think we had cherry cake every day that he subsequently spent at Holmwood. Both of us grew sick of it. The child adored him.

'You like cream buns, too, don't you?' she said maliciously.

'Cream buns?'

'Mrs. Dycett-Byrne's cream buns!'

Vallie exploded into giggles, and choked over her tea.

Cullum turned a reproachful gaze on me.

'So you hadn't enough sense of shame to keep you quiet about that disgraceful affair!' he said. 'In fact, at the time I suppose you were rather proud of having done it?'

'I'm still proud of it,' I said. 'In similar conditions I expect I should have a jolly good try, at any rate, at doing it again.'

Olive and Vallie cleared away, and left us discussing his book *The Chink*, which I had read since I had last seen him. It was very good indeed for a first novel, an interesting psychological study. The underlying idea, worked out in relation to all the chief characters, was the vulnerable joint in every armour, the flaw in the defence which each individual puts up against life's power of hurting. All of us attempt unconsciously to

44

protect ourselves by clothing our hearts with an outer covering of indifference. As children we are hurt easily because we care whole-heartedly for so many trivialities; the older we become the fewer grow the things that have it in their power to hurt us keenly; but however well-protected our hearts are, there is an Achilles' heel in every nature, a tender place where life can stab deepest, and Cullum called that 'the chink.' Mother-love, vanity, the desire for recognition, the inability to stand the tedium of success after the stimulation of an uphill fight – these were among the 'chinks' that he had used, writing with remarkable insight for a boy of twenty-two, and with a singularly unyouthful sense of pity.

Compassion was a salient quality in Cullum: he took the compassionate point of view whenever pity was possible, having sympathy with any kind of weakness. I had none; constitutionally I despised weakness, but in his book he showed, whenever it came under notice, that he was sorry for it, and understood it.

'I liked your character drawing immensely,' I said, 'as well as your plot.'

'Then what is it you didn't like? There is something,' he said at once, though I had made no criticism. His quickness delighted me; I was not used to people who divined unspoken thoughts, and in my voice I thought there had been no hint of the reservation in my mind.

I admitted, apologetically, that I did not like the style, which struck me as too flamboyant. Cullum's socks and ties, mannerisms, and choice of words were all rather highly coloured, but they were effective.

He defended the language of *The Chink* with parental fervour, and from my parrot-like memory for words I quoted him long passages of his book, which was full of picturesque imagery, vivid like himself, but careless. Some lines I repeated with unqualified admiration;

45

they were oases of perfect prose scattered among the rest of his clever, roughly finished work. He fastened on them and made me talk of them. He was hungry for appreciation from everyone with whom he came in contact; it was a real need with him, and he would take endless trouble to secure it.

It seemed to me incredible that I had not always known him intimately. There was all the ease of old friendship in our talk, but it held the fun of exploration too. Because I had been considered so, I had come to believe that I was reserved; but no normal young person is naturally reserved; I expanded readily enough in the atmosphere the boy brought with him.

'I know what my own "chink" is,' Cullum said. 'Most people don't. With me, it's the aching for anything that is just out of reach. If I know I can't get anything, it becomes so all-important to me that the things I have lose all their value. I am too easily satiated by the real whenever I attain it, and whatever it is, because it is instantly overshadowed by the glory of the ideal which is beyond. And when that ideal comes within reach and becomes real, the same thing happens again. I always endow the people and things that I don't know well with the qualities that I'd like them to have, and of course it isn't their fault if they prove not to have them on closer aquaintance. I wonder what your "chink" is?'

'I don't know. Certainly it isn't connected with other people, as most of the "chinks" in your book were; people don't matter sufficiently to me, in which I am lucky.'

'Why lucky? I don't agree,' he said. 'People matter tremendously to me, they're my greatest interest. To anyone who wants to write, humanity must be incomparably the most absorbing subject.'

46

'Oh, yes; interesting, if you like, to study from a distance, but not to come to grips with. It is a very different thing to observe dispassionately the emotions of other people, and to share them. I mean – it's difficult to explain – one wants to keep everyone at arm's length from one's heart; at least, that's what I feel. Most human affairs are fascinating to watch, unless one is concerned with them oneself. The less one has to do with people personally, the better for one's peace of mind.'

'But who wants peace of mind when they're young?' asked Cullum.

'I think I do,' I said. 'I don't know why, but I have always had an inherent distrust of human contacts; I don't want anyone to come close enough to be able to play on my feelings if they choose.'

'You can buy security at too high a price.' Cullum moved one hand in an impatient gesture; the other, nearer me, hung over the arm of his chair holding a cigarette. My eyes were drawn to it continually; Cullum's hands were beautiful, broad and pale-skinned, the fingers long and capable-looking. 'One has to go down into the lists and lend one's heart and interest to other human beings, and perhaps get hurt, if one wants life. Your attitude, if you could keep it up – I hope for your sake you can't – would cut you off from all the most valuable experiences a man or a woman can have. Love, for one thing. Of course, love is the greatest "chink" of all; it's so obvious that I didn't use it in that way in the book. Love delivers you helpless into someone else's hands.'

'I know,' I said, astonished at Cullum's power of dissolving shyness. 'I should be afraid of that.'

'And yet you are the person,' he said, smiling, 'whom Mrs. Cole suspects of unspeakable things, because, as

47

she told Raymond, no really *nice* girl would have mentioned miscarriages at a dinner-party among strangers!'

'I wasn't thinking, that was the trouble,' I said, 'As to her opinion – oh, well, I comfort myself by remembering that lots of highly religious people have doubts about the Virgin Mary; who am I that I should escape?'

Cullum's laughter resounded again. 'Oh, my dear, that's excellent! That's simply gorgeous. I shall tell Raymond and get him to repeat it to his mother. It'll set her foaming at the mouth with rage.'

Once more I could have hugged him for laughing like that: no one else I knew would have done so.

Time passed unnoticed while Cullum was there. I forgot how tired I was in the excitement of discussing books with a real author. It was with surprise that I noticed at last that it had grown dark outside, and glancing surreptitiously at my watch I saw that it was a quarter past seven. If Cullum did not leave soon I should have to ask him to dinner, as he had a long ride back, and much as I should have liked it, this would be exceedingly awkward to-day. Our only servant was out, and I had no idea what food we had in the house, probably just enough for ourselves, as usual on Saturday evenings. I felt that I could not ask a rising young author to put up with the sort of scrap meal that did well enough for us. But the minutes went by, and Cullum, who was enjoying himself as much I had been until I noticed the time, did not make a move to go. I gave him random answers while I tried feverishly to remember what we had had to eat yesterday; would there be any cold meat left, or should we be finishing those sardines? To my intense relief, Cullum suddenly glanced at his watch, and equally surprised at the time,

48

said half-heartedly that he ought to go, looking expectantly at me.

With an effort, I said nothing to stop him, and went out with him into the stable yard where he had left his motor-bicycle. He wheeled it out into the drive, where it was very dark and cold. I shivered. The leafless, wind-stirred branches of the trees on the common, which enclosed our isolated house on three sides, were groping like wide-flung black arms over the dark blue night sky.

'When may I come again? Next Saturday?' he asked.

He had the knack of making his impertinences sound as though they were favours. He never attached much importance to invitations; those he did not mean to accept he often ignored altogether, not purposely, but from carelessness, and naturally it annoyed many people. When he wanted to see friends he asked himself, expecting them to be pleased. It was the worst possible thing for his decaying manners, which could be charming, that as a rule they were very pleased. Cullum had more than any young man's fair share of that curious quality, charm, which is infinitely better than charity for cloaking sins.

'Yes, do come, and stay to dinner,' I said. All would be well if Olive had time to make preparations. 'But don't arrive before five because I shall be hunting.'

'You couldn't miss one day of it, I suppose?'

'Not for anyone on earth; particularly not at the end of the season, when I shan't get any more for many arid months. Come on Sunday if you'd rather.'

'I can't, I'm afraid, so I'll gratefully accept the crumbs of society you condescend to give me on Saturday. Go back into the house, or you'll get cold. I shall have to run the bike a bit before she'll start.

Her starting gear's gone wrong, so she's what you might call "touched in the wind" – Good-bye.'

Father had come in while we were talking. His deep mournful voice called to me as I re-entered the house, and I went into the study. My father, Major Sieveking, had been associated with horses all his life; he had been in a cavalry regiment before he retired and took to breaking hunters and reforming rogue horses as a hobby, and his long, sad visage had grown distinctly horse-like, as so often happens, by some incomprehensible process, to men who are always with horses. Moon, our groom, who had been a jockey, had a face even more reminiscent of a horse's; and I was always expecting the horse-look to develop in mine.

Everything about my tall, lean father was lugubrious. He was striking-looking with his prematurely white hair and bushy black eyebrows, but on his cavernous face there was an expression of settled, constitutional gloom, unless he was actively engaged in dealing with a refractory animal. If there was a melancholy aspect of any subject, Father saw it and pointed it out. Any cheerful anticipation usually drew from him the observation, 'Ah, when I was your age I thought the same, my dear. Later on you'll find – ' Unless he had some definitely dispiriting conclusion to come to, he left the sentence unfinished. His unwarranted pessimism was a joke in the family. Whenever Olive and I planned a picnic in the summer, at a time when the weather had been fine for a long while and the barometer was high and steady, Father would stand on the lawn after breakfast, staring fixedly into the clear blue sky, and saying anxiously in a voice that presaged disappointment, 'I do hope it doesn't rain!'

'I suppose,' said Father sadly, as I came over to his desk, 'that this young man of yours is staying to supper; we've run out of beer, and there's no whisky, either.'

Father could hardly have escaped hearing Cullum's very noisy motor-bicycle departing, but as we were short of drinks he chose to take it for granted that there would be someone extra to dinner.

'No, he's gone,' I said. 'It was very awkward; he stayed late and I felt I ought to ask him, but I couldn't get hold of Olive to find out what there was to eat.'

'I daresay there would have been enough,' said Father, now that he knew that Cullum had gone. 'Is he interested in horses?'

'Not a bit. Why did you call him "that young man of yours," Daddy? He doesn't belong to me; I've only met him once before.'

Father gave his short, stifled chuckle.

'When I saw him for a minute earlier this afternoon he asked me so indignantly why I allowed you to go in for such a suicidal game as hunting. He seemed concerned about it; I thought that was certain proof.'

'And I suppose you told him, for his comfort, that I was a thoroughly reckless rider?' I suggested. 'Or did you fall back on "Well, well, we must hope for the best?" ' This was the saying he brought out at all times, whether it was appropriate or not, in a manner that denied all hope. It had become such a habit that it crept into his conversation when he was in one of his absent-minded moods; he said it once to my aunt, when her impeccable husband, his brother, passed into a supposedly better world: ('Gone to his Maker! Well, well, we must hope for the best.' His voice conveyed the slenderness of that hope: and my aunt had no sense of humour.)

Either of the remarks that I suggested would have

been typical of him, and he was one of those characters, satisfactory only from the artistic point of view, who are always being typical of themselves. In family life it is intolerably irritating to know almost for certain what someone is just going to say, and then to hear them say it, time after time.

For once the guess was wrong. Father had not made either of those answers; he had gone one better. 'I told him,' he said lugubriously, 'that personally I would rather die hunting than in any other way. Still, one can't arrange these things to one's liking.' He shook his head, evidently expecting heart disease or pneumonia to get him in the end. 'Well, well – '

Afterwards I asked Cullum about this conversation, thinking that Father must have been joking, unusual as this would be, but what he repeated to me was exactly what he had said to the astonished young man. Father was only happy when he was with animals; he had a genius for managing them. Besides breaking in young hunters he travelled all over the country buying, without a warranty and for ridiculously small sums, horses with bad reputations, and he sold them again eventually, cured of evil tricks, at prices that represented a very good profit.

Our financial position was curious. We entertained, and always kept good horses for our own use. There were ten horses of various kinds in the stables just then, and I think no one outside the house guessed that we were very hard up, living up to the last penny of Father's army pension and hobby-income combined. I paid subscriptions to two hunts out of my small dress allowance, and there was never enough left over for my clothes, which were rather disreputable.

I left Father and toiled slowly upstairs, feeling my weariness now, to collect the clothes that I had left scattered on the bathroom floor in my haste to be with Cullum when I came in.

We had no gas or electricity in the house, and too tired to light the lamp, I fumbled around the floor, hitting myself against the corners of the mass of miscellaneous furniture with which the bathroom was filled. It had done duty in different parts of the house for years, and had finally come to rest in this Sargasso sea of a room, into which drifted all superseded domestic relics like our old rocking-horse, and broken baby-chairs, that no one liked to burn though they were too battered to give away.

I suddenly got up from my knees and gave up hunting for a lost sock and my gloves. I felt for some unformulated reason that this was a red-letter day, a wonderful day, and it was not fitting that I should bother myself just then about a sock, which had a hole in it anyway, and dirty gloves. There were other things in the world that mattered so much that trifles did not count any more. Cullum Hayes was coming down again in a week's time, and he was the first intellectually interesting person I had met. What did socks matter, or gloves?

Olive was full of him at supper.

'What did you think of him, Daddy?' she asked.

'He seemed quite intelligent,' said Father, and then added the inevitable qualification to his approval. 'Of course, I only spoke to him for a moment – '

It was a good thing that I had not asked Cullum to dinner. We were finishing up the sardines, and those four portions of sardines on toast could not have been made to look like five, even by Olive's talent in that direction.

Chapter 4: *'Your Face my Quarry was—'*

I woke to the sound of rain in the garden on the Saturday when Cullum Hayes was to come again. Outside my window a blackbird was singing gloriously from the slender top shoot of the deodar tree, bending it with his light weight. He was often there, and as he was spoiling the tree, Father threatened to shoot him, only refraining because, he said resignedly, 'Some other wretched bird will only take his place if I do.'

Father's brute, the Lepper, gave trouble as usual while he was mounting. We had a queer collection of rake horses in the stables just then, jibbers, surly ones, and bolters, but the Lepper, father's regular hunter, was the worst mannered beast in the stables. He was the one horse that Father had not been able to tame sufficiently to re-sell and as the animal was a well-bred beast and a marvellous jumper – hence his name – Father, who could ride anything, kept him for his own use, noticing every hunting day with sombre satisfaction that it cost him a greater effort each time to mount quickly: as he had done easily a few years ago. Swinging into the saddle before the beast expected it was the only way to mount the Lepper, who reared as soon as he felt any weight on stirrup or saddle.

'Scent'll be good to-day,' I said joyfully, after he had pointed out his increasing stiffness.

'Yes – if we find, of course. It will be sickening if we get nothing of a run after turning out on a miserable day like this.'

'But why on earth shouldn't we find?' I said impatiently, though I knew by experience that it was no use arguing against Father's unfounded gloom. 'How many poor days have we had this season? Not one, for a long time!'

'Ah, that's why. One mustn't expect a run of good luck to last for ever, you know; it never does. It's about time it broke. Well, well, we must hope – Look out, Esther! Keep her off!'

Jenny, who had been boring her head up and down restlessly as we rode, had wheeled and tried to bite the Lepper, for whom she had a strong dislike, which was shared by most people and horses; he was an incorrigible kicker. I had made no attempt to stop her, though I had seen that something of the sort was coming. I did not want any more of Father's despondent philosophy, which I knew by heart, on that excellent morning. The Lepper, prevented from retaliating, began to buck, and to keep the peace I rode on ahead to the end of our drive, which Gerald Hemingway, riding down the Mill Road, happened to be passing at the time. I had half-expected this apparent coincidence.

'Well, isn't this a bit of luck, meeting you here!' he said, with a good show of surprise.

'No, not from the look of Gracious Lady!' I said, eyeing his mare. 'It takes you about two minutes to get here from your house, and she's not only steaming but actually dripping with rain already! You've been riding up and down waiting for us for some time.'

' "Us?" Oh, damn, is the Major coming too?' he asked. 'I hoped you'd be the only one out. – Ah, hello, sir!' he called, infusing fresh cordiality into his voice as Father appeared, 'I was just asking Esther if you were coming!'

I looked at him and laughed. The inflection of his voice had entirely altered the meaning of the words.

Lightly and openly, with his hand on his heart and his tongue in his cheek, Gerald made love to nearly every girl he knew. I was always kept posted of the progress of his affairs, which succeeded each other very rapidly; his affections were never very seriously engaged, but for the first few days of every little amour he usually believed that they would be, this time. If the attachment ended with a sharp break, instead of petering out as most of them did, he was down-hearted about it for at least an hour, sometimes for as much as two days. He never gave his heart sufficient time to heal between spasms, it suffered mildly from chronic comminuted fracture.

We had known each other all our lives. The Hemingways were our nearest neighbours, and because we had played together as long as either of us could remember, Gerald had never treated me to the attentions, often fervent by habit rather than feeling, which he paid to the rest of his little flock. Only lately had I begun to wonder whether his attitude to me was not losing the frank good-fellowship that had always been between us. Little things, nothing in themselves but significant in accumulation, had set me hoping that Gerald 'wasn't going to be a darn' fool.'

He was a tall, good-looking youth, curiously loosely built, and a wonderful natural acrobat. His long arms and legs seemed to be insecurely fastened on to his body, and whenever he did contortionist's tricks for my amusement I felt that he might come to pieces at any moment. The dangerous circus-riding that we practised together as children, both of us frightened, but each egging the other on, used to turn poor little Olive, the unwilling audience, cold with the continual apprehension of seeing one or both of us dead at the feet of our exasperated ponies.

'Oh, by the way,' he said, as the three of us cantered over the sparkling Holmwood common, bright in the hollows with masses of golden and silver palm, 'the Dycett-Byrnes visited us from on high for tea yesterday, and Mrs. D. B. of course discussed everybody she knew; she always does, the old cat. When it came to your turn she didn't scratch as much as usual, she only said something about so much riding being very bad for any girl, but Tony piped up on his own account – he is the most insufferable pup! He said condescendingly that you were fairly good across country – (*fairly* good, mark you! and this from Tony, of all people!) – but that it was a pity that someone couldn't teach you to ride like a lady! I was so flabbergasted that I couldn't think of an answer until it was too late.'

'Tony Dycett-Byrne said that! Oh, the nasty little human catapult!' I said, thinking of the way I had seen him shot out of his saddle the previous week. 'He's always cloying-sweet to my face, too. I think something must be done about this, Gerald! Heaven knows I have little animosity against the poor little chap, a seat in the saddle like his is just about enough tribulation for anyone, but I'm not going to stand patronage about riding from that abject little gap-hunter!'

'Confounded cheek! Intolerable!' said my father, much more indignant because his daughter's riding was in question than he would have been if only her character had been impugned.

'I knew it would ruffle your feathers a bit, Esther,' said Gerald. 'I only told you because Tony is getting so impossible that I thought it was time he heard a few home-truths from someone.'

'Never fear! He shall,' I said. 'This is too good a

57

chance to miss. Tony's airs have been storing up trouble for him for a long time.' I was feeling more than usually full of spirits that morning, as excited as Jenny, and grateful to the lordly youth Tony for providing me with an outlet.

'If you need a second,' said Gerald, 'I claim the privilege of an old and trusted friend to nurse the sponge.'

Tony was waiting on the further side of the crowd of horses on Beare Green, which is, by local tradition, the last place where a wild bear was killed in England. It was a small meet, the steady downpour had discouraged many people, but the Dycett-Byrnes hunted and went to church conscientiously in all weathers. Wild with expectation, Jenny danced and sidled round the outskirts of the crowd. I let her out a little, and she cantered mincingly towards Tony, heading as if we should pass directly in front of him. As we drew level I lifted her on her hind legs and swung her in a half turn, an accomplishment that had taken us three months to perfect together, and would have taken longer if I had ridden aside, like a lady. We brought up sharply right under the nose of his nice horse. It shied violently, and he lost one stirrup, clinging in an undignified position to the pommel of the saddle until the beast quietened.

'Oh, Tony, do be careful!' cried the comely, stout Miss Hapliss, though she must have known it was unnecessary; Tony was always as careful as circumstances permitted. Her obvious interest in him was a joke all round the Holmwood; she was ten years his senior.

'Whatever did you do that for?' he asked me peevishly, disregarding her efforts to help him, and feeling gingerly for the stirrup with his toe. 'You might have had me off!'

'Thus understudying every hedge in the district!' I
said. 'I wanted to talk to you. You shouldn't be such a
dare-devil, Tony. Fancy riding such a nervy horse! I
hear you made a flattering remark about me yesterday!'
I tried to get out of earshot of Miss Hapliss, on the other
side of Tony, so that I could tackle him alone, but she
caught the unaccustomed coy note in my voice, and
staring at me resentfully, moved closer.

'Oh, did I? Really? I'm afraid I've forgotten,' said
Tony airily, and apprehensively.

'Now that is unkind of you! Oh, Tony! You said I
was fairly good across country! I was awfully pleased
when I heard about it; on my honour, I was!'

'Oh, that!' He was sufficiently relieved to be complimentary. 'Yes, I may say I think you are. Quite
good.'

There was a muffled burst of laughter from a big,
dark Scottish youth who had just arrived, Carlisle
Jamieson McDonald, whose people had lately settled
in Capel.

'How sweet of you, Tony. Then, as a fair offer, if
you'd like to teach me to ride like a lady, I'll teach you
to ride like a man!'

In the next few seconds of silence, Miss Hapliss' round
pink face grew white with indignation, while her
protégé's turned red.

'Well, I never! Of all the uncalled-for rude –'

'I don't know what you mean, Esther!' said Tony.

'Naughty, naughty! He does!' chanted Gerald from
the background, like a Greek chorus.

'I suppose you're trying to be funny, Esther, but I
may say you aren't!' said the victim. 'Not a bit. Not
at all. No.'

Miss Hapliss who could never be kept out of anything
in which Tony was concerned, broke in acidly. 'This

59

is all quite beyond *me*, but if it's a question of *riding*, personally I, for one, should hate to take *my* jumps looking as if I was half asleep, as *some* people we know do, and I'm sure Mr. Dycett-Byrne would too!'

'I may say I certainly should!' said Tony gratefully.

'Good,' said Gerald impartially to Miss Hapliss. 'That's a very well-taken point. Esther doesn't moon across country as if she didn't notice the hedges, with a rapt, far-away expression on her face, doesn't she? Still, why not call Tony, Tony? You do generally, and we always do. Don't let's make this little chat unfriendly or stiff or anything.'

'But you don't like taking jumps anyway, do you Tony?' I asked, still with a pleasant smile. He and I had scrapped since we were children. 'If you took them my way instead of yours the only difference would be that your coming off would then be certain, instead of only probable.'

'I still don't know what you're referring to,' Tony said loftily, 'but all I can say' – with a dark glance at Gerald – 'is that if people repeat what other people say, they can hardly expect people – '

'But which?' asked Gerald.

'Which what?' he said testily.

'Which people?'

Young McDonald's subdued laughter became audible again.

'I hardly think it's worth going on with this stupid discussion,' said Miss Hapliss. 'See, there's dear Mrs. Dycett-Byrne. Shall we join her, Tony?'

He followed her thankfully.

'Wh-what was it all ab-bout?' asked McDonald, who stammered very badly, after the other two had moved away.

Gerald told him.

'B-but I'd not wish my w-worrst enemy taucht riding by either of you two, Hemingway! Everyone isn't equally anxious to p-p-prove that they're among those whom the g-gods love!'

Through a gate the hounds poured into the first field, a surge of sleek, dappled bodies, pennants waving and keen heads held low. As we moved away to the coverts the all-informing knowledge that I should see Cullum Hayes again in the evening slipped into the back of my mind, not out of it as all other matters did, and rested there, colouring the whole day with its own delightfulness.

Normally I did not think at all when I was hunting, save automatically, to judge the ground before us and find the best way for Jenny. I was far-away in mind, as Gerald had noticed; but everything was different that day. Lines of a sonnet of Wilfrid Blunt's came back to me while we were waiting by the coverts.

'To-day, all day, I rode . . .
And once, when checked, a thrush sang, and my
    horse
Pricked his quick ears, as to a sound unknown.
I knew the spring was come. I knew it even
Better than all by this, that through my chase
In bush and stone and hill . . . and Heaven,
I seemed to see and follow still your face.
Your face my quarry was. For it I rode,
My horse a thing of wings, myself a god.'

I was going to see Cullum again; very soon, now!

A fox sneaked out on the side of the copse furthest from the place where Gerald and I were waiting, and galloping after the rest of the field I looked back before I reached the first little hedge, and saw that he was the only rider behind me; the foot followers were out of sight. I knew that he would not ascribe anything I did to 'showing off.' Spring madness was in my blood, and I stood up in the stirrups and put Jenny at a low place, standing while she took the jump and landing back in the saddle on the other side. It was Gerald who had taught me that when we played follow-my-leader on ponies long ago.

The head of his hard-spurred bay mare, Gracious Lady, came up on my left.

'Don't do that again, you little idiot!' he shouted.

From sheer bravado I kicked clear of the irons and hitched my legs forward in front of the saddle-flaps to take a better hold on Jenny; there was a little ditch ahead.

'Esther! For God's sake, Esther! Don't!'

I looked at him in surprise. Gerald, who had dared me over and over again to take these slight risks, was white of face, and for a moment I imagined that he was ill.

We were over the narrow stream before I could find the stirrups, but afterwards I rode on more soberly, until the joy of the great game went to my head and made me drunk with motion, oblivious to everything but the calls of the moment. Jenny was in a mood to take in her stride whatever I put her to, and Father and I rode side by side. The Lepper was in like fettle; he never baulked at anything, either he cleared each jump with nearly a foot to spare, or, on his superior days, he disdained the obstacles, galloping steadily at, and on to, and through them, leaving a trail of demolished fences. It was nerve-racking for the rider but convenient for timorous spirits who followed in his tracks. Tony Dycett-Byrne was one of the few people who had a real liking for the Lepper, but the brute did not smash him a path that day. We rode across Henfold, towards Newdigate, over a stretch of country where gates and gaps were rare, and Tony was thrown, respectably, by his horse stumbling.

When he came off my conscience pricked. I was too happy that day to feel vindictive for long, and Tony had achieved a fall that was no disgrace, for once. Pressing Jenny hard, I worked my way through the field to Miss Hapliss, who rode so well herself that her infatuation for Tony was incomprehensible.

'Tony down last field – not much hurt,' I called, knowing that she would welcome a chance of ministering to him, and that he would be glad of her sympathetic and admiring attendance. He never remounted once he had come off and so had an excuse for getting out of the rest of the run. Miss Hapliss unobtrusively drew out of the field and turned her horse back.

We killed one fox after a check, hounds chopping him in cover; – a horrible business; hunting is an abominable sport which deserves, on all moral counts, to be firmly put down. May it never be! – we found another and lost it, and then one old questing hound picked up a fresh scent, threw up his head and bayed, on the note that always made my nerves tingle, and the others, whimpering, spread fan-wise round him. They gathered on the new trail and gave tongue in a deepening chorus, landing us at the end of the run in my favourite, rarely trodden copse near Rusper, where pale, small wild daffodils were flowering.

Gerald and I rode home together, as Father had business in the neighbourhood.

'Why did you make such a fuss about those two little jumps this morning?' I asked, after we had ridden a mile with hardly a word spoken, though Gerald was not taciturn by nature. 'You've never minded my doing that sort of thing before; you do it yourself. There was no one to see.'

'Possibly. But since I obviously dislike you doing that sort of thing now, please stop it,' he said.

'All right, I will, when you're there. But we'll have a little less of this Lord-of-Creation-ary air. You know it never has worked well with me. Remember I'm not Julianne!'

Julianne was the latest and meekest of his loves, and regarded Gerald as a god. 'How is she, by the way?'

'Oh, she? I dunno. All right, I expect. I haven't seen her for some time. Why?' His was the slightly aggrieved air of a man who is uncomfortably reminded by Nature of an indigestible previous meal. He may have been hungry for it at the time, but once it is a thing of the past he feels that he should be allowed to forget it. This was Gerald's usual attitude towards his decayed love affairs.

'Oh, I merely wondered if that little affair was finished yet. Evidently it is. I suppose she got monopolizing like the others? It *is* hard luck on you that women will insist on taking your devotion seriously, and then expect to have control of all your thoughts and actions. Women are such fun to chase and so awkward to handle when captured, I suppose? It's tragic!'

Women's chief fault in Gerald's eyes was their strong mental possessive instinct, their hankering to order the lives of anyone for whom they care, or who appears to care for them. It is a rare woman who does not want to know all the comings-in and the goings-out of her lover, when he is not with her, and to exert some influence on his mode of life.

'Yes, it's sickening,' he agreed. 'Why have nice women this secret itch either to be made slaves of, or else to make slaves? – oh, always for the man's own good, so they think! "I'm sure you ought to change your wet socks, dear. Do change your wet socks, dear. Won't you change your wet socks, dear, just for my sake?" – Ugh!   It's this blessed maternal instinct, always prompting them to interfere. As soon as they see you're interested in 'em they start wanting to prove to you, or themselves, or the world, I don't know which, that they've got power over you. If you haven't got a moustache they want you to grow one, because they say it would suit you; really I think they want it as a sign of their dominion. If you have a moustache they ask you to cut it off. Same reason.'

'Well, at any rate you've preserved your moustache, if not your heart, intact from hundreds of affrays.'

'I've jolly nearly lost them both together over and over again!' he said.

'A close shave! It would be a great pity, for your moustache would take so much longer to return to normal.'

'You know, if I could find a decent girl who wouldn't regard me as her property just because I admired her eyes,' Gerald said, 'well, I honestly think I might stick to her!'

'Now I know why I remain an evergreen, if not a bloom, in your young affections, while the other faded flowers get thrown away!' I told him. I was anxious to keep the conversation on this light level. 'I must be a great comfort to you, Gerald. Knowing you as I do I can be relied on not to believe an affectionate word you say, nor to care in the least what you do.'

'Oh, *you* can, I know,' he said, without elation, giving Gracious Lady an unnecessary cut with his crop. The amusement had suddenly died out of his voice.

We were riding home faster than usual. It was past

65

six, and I was afraid that Cullum Hayes had been waiting for me a full hour already.

Jogging through the dripping Henfold woods, where autumn leaves still fluttered and tapped, I pictured him standing there among the trees through which we rode, seeing in imagination the alert blue eyes in that curious sharp featured face looking out of the shadows between the trunks.

Pulling off my gloves, I accidentally dropped one, and had dismounted to pick it up before Gerald noticed it.

'Oh, sorry,' he said, 'I'd have got it – ' He slipped off, too, and held Jenny as I walked back.

'And that is so damnably like life!' he said moodily when I rejoined him. I was not thinking of him at the moment, and as I sought hurriedly in my mind the remark to which he referred he caught me against him, hurting me with the pressure of his arm.

'Gerald, have you gone crazy?' I said. 'Let me go! Let me go at once!'

'You see, you are just the one person that I want to care! Because I love you, Esther! Dear girl, you know that's true, don't you? I think you must. Before God, it is true! Other women haven't mattered a damn; it's been you behind them all the time; only I've always known that I was nothing at all to you except a friend, and that you'd only laugh if I told you, and I couldn't face that – '

'Will you let go of me immediately! Gerald, you're hurting my arm!'

'I don't care,' he said wildly, 'I've been wanting to tell you this such a long time, I will tell you now! You've been unapproachable simply because we knew each other so well; you knew what a fool I've been over other women; there seemed nothing that I could say.

66

There *is* nothing I can say, except that I love you, and that the others have been just episodes to me; they never mattered very much. But you've always mattered.'

'I'm sorry, my dear,' I said, 'You see. I don't care for you like that. I'm awfully fond of you, but – oh, you understand, don't you?'

His hand, lightly touching my face, brushed my hat off. He pressed his face against the coiled thickness of my hair, crushing me until I could hardly breathe, and then forced my head back, kissing the curve of my throat above the stock with hard lips.

He was whispering broken love-phrases, telling me of the faint smell of my hair which had pleased him when we played games together years ago, of his first boyish desire for me, and the suppression of it, and of the way in which it had been diverted into many different loves that had appeased but never satisfied him, and had now returned to me, certain of itself at last. And while he spoke I could think of nothing but that he was stealing minutes from the time I could spend with Cullum! Only the other self, that always stood aside and listened, was paying full attention to him, recording impressions; all the rest of me was straining to get away, to go to Cullum.

He lifted a flushed face and looked down at my mouth, and I turned my face aside, and, with my hands against his shoulders, pressed him away from me, begging him to let me go.

'I will kiss you, though!' he said, and caught both my wrists in one hand as he bent over me.

'Gerald, don't! If you love me – please, oh, please!'

For some reason I was terrified lest he should kiss me; instead, he took his arms away. I remounted, to end

67

the situation, and after a second's hesitation, he did too, and we rode on for a few paces in silence.

'I'm sorry,' he said. 'I knew how it would be. I'll try not to bother you more than I can help.' He would not look at me as he spoke.

He dug his heels into his tired mare and galloped on up the road out of sight beyond the bend. Had I wanted proof that Gerald cared, this would have been enough. It was an untarred flint road, and he, too, had been brought up to worship his horse's feet. I could not imagine myself galloping Jenny on that surface under the stress of any emotion.

I pressed on home, forgetting Gerald entirely in a few minutes.

'Well, anyone called to see me, Mrs. Barrie?' I asked, coming from the stable into the warm kitchen. I was so certain of the answer that I said it carelessly.

'No, miss,' said our cook-general. 'Did you have a nice day?'

'No one! No one has come? Are you quite sure?'

'Oh, yes, Miss. 'Bin in all the afternoon, I 'ave, because Miss Olive asked me to take to-morrer afternoon off instead. She's bin expectin' someone to supper I think, bin popping in and out, makin' cakes and things. I don't mind 'er, bless 'er; because she does think of keeping my clean kitchen clean; not like you, Miss Esther, comin' straight in from the rain and lettin' all the wet on your clothes mess up my clean floor! You run upstairs and 'ave your bath, dearie, and don't mess up my nice floor.'

Olive, with a tragic face, came out into the passage to meet me.

'Esther, he hasn't come!'

'So I hear! Oh, well, never mind.' My voice

sounded flat with disappointment, but Olive was too woebegone to notice.

'Oh, it's all right for *you!*' she said, 'you never care about anything! I took all the trouble to make a really big cherry cake. And got a lovely dinner ready, too.'

'There's been no 'phone message or anything? Well, I'm sorry the wretch has wasted your time, but it doesn't really matter, does it? I expect he's found something better to do. After all, it's a long way to come for a few hours, and he mayn't have liked the look of the weather. It has been a rotten day, come to think of it. Come up to my room, there's a dear. I must have a new dress for the hunt ball, second week in April. I can't wear that old blue one again. The people who'll be there know every stitch of it by heart, except those new ones at the waist where I tore it on Tuesday. I don't want to borrow from Janet again. If you can make me something wearable out of what we've got between us, you can have my white jersey.'

I wandered about the house disconsolately during the earlier part of the evening, unable to rest or to settle to anything. The telephone rang, and I raced into the hall.

'Is that Esther?' asked a man's voice. But it was Gerald's voice, and it sounded very miserable.

'Sorry to disturb you, dear – I say, you don't mind my ringing you up, after – this afternoon?'

'No, of course not.'

'The trouble is, I keep wondering if this is going to mess up everything. Things are rotten enough as they are without that. You won't let what I said make any difference to the friendship we've always had, Esther? If I can't have anything more, I must still have you to talk to. You aren't fed up with me altogether, are you?'

It occurred to me then, with a warm glow of vindicated pride, that here at any rate was a man who would not treat my invitations, as Cullum Hayes did, as matters of no importance.

'Come along round to see me!' I said in answer. 'Come now!'

'Esther! You really want me to?' he said eagerly.

'Yes, why not?'

In the depth of my own disappointment I did not realize into how great a hope Gerald would transform the least friendliness that I showed him just then. I opened the door to him, and his arms closed round me.

'My dear, you do want me a little, don't you?'

'No, not in that way.' I lifted my shoulder, with his hand on it, and rubbed my cheek against his hand. 'But you're a very nice person, Gerald.' I rested my head back against his arm, and closed my eyes, smiling; bitterly resentful against Cullum Hayes; thinking only of him, that he had not troubled to come. With a low, low, soft sound in his throat, Gerald tightened his arms round me and kissed my mouth.

I let him make love to me for a few minutes, refusing his kisses sometimes for the sake of hearing him laugh triumphantly before he re-settled me in his arms in such a way that I could not take my mouth from his. Suddenly I revolted from it all, and would not let him touch me again. Physically, his passion had left me unstirred, but it had satisfied some mental need.

Chapter 5: *The Weaving of a Spell*

THE next day, Sunday, Moon sent the expected message that he was laid up again with a bout of the 'rheumatism' which regularly attacked him once a month, after pay day; it had occurred nearly every Sunday in the days when he drew his wages weekly. I had to do his work, and was glad of the physical preoccupation, which obliterated the memory of the disappointment and the queer impulses that had ruled yesterday.

I tried once more to bully Olive into helping; if she had been willing to ride we might have sold more horses locally. That fragile looking child on horse-back could have convinced anyone that her mount was suitable for women or children to use, but she would not go near the animals, and people argued on the Holmwood that the way a horse behaved when the Major was on it was no indication of its usual manners, and I, though a very inferior imitation of Father in that line, was considered too old a hand at the game to be any more reassuring.

I was out on the common with him all the afternoon, coaxing two clumsy two-year-olds over the low gorse-topped hurdles we had put up in one of the rides, until at about six o'clock the light, though it was still full day, lost the first clarity which is essential for judging distances.

Making the round of the stables, I fetched an apple from the loft for Jenny before saying good-night to her. She caught the smell of Osiris, the stallion I had just left, and pressed her nose into my hands, where the scent still clung.

'Love-hungry, my dear?' I said. She was then in condition. She nuzzled and blew, and dribbled apple-juice enthusiastically over my sleeve.

'All right,' I said, 'wait a few days; a marriage has been arranged and will shortly take place between you and the gentleman of your choice, though I can't think why you fancy him. Osiris isn't even half-blood! You've no more sense of social caste over this sort of alliance than men have! It's incomprehensible!'

I looked about, hoping that there would be something else that required to be done, and found it. The desire for immortality, which is in all of us and takes strange forms, had urged the milkman's boy to cut his name deeply into the pillar of our stable yard gate, in huge letters. It is strange that this repellent human weakness for carving names in unsuitable places springs from the same blind instinct which produces great works of art. Nearly everyone craves to carve his name indelibly in some medium. It is more than the desire for self-expression, it is the innate, unconscious longing to cheat death the extinguisher by any means, however humble. Seaside trippers carve undistinguished initials on breakwaters, in preference to writing them in the shifting sand, that something may remain, though they do not intend to return to the place; and the milkman's boy had chosen the stone of the pillar rather than the more perishable wood of the gate itself. He was known to me, by report, as being 'that set on' our cook's daughter, Daisy, though she would have none of him, and in chalk he had written under his name, 'Daisy Barrie is a fool.' In order that this subtle form of love-making might have the intended result, which was that Daisy should hear his public opinion of her at second-hand, and be piqued by such indifference, I drew Mrs. Barrie's attention to it before I rubbed it out and started cutting out the name, with a chisel, and filling in the hole with cement.

Footsteps behind me in the drive made me look up.

'Cullum!' I said delightedly. He had his left arm in a sling. 'What is the matter?'

'Nothing serious. Sprained wrist and a torn ligament. I had a bit of an accident on the bike yesterday when I was starting out to come down here. The other cyclist got most of the damage but then it was entirely his fault –

I nodded sympathetically. Without his mentioning it I should, at that period, have taken it for granted that the other party in the accident was to blame; I had not had, as yet, any experience of Cullum's hair-raising driving.

' – only the policeman couldn't see it. He couldn't have been looking at the time. I had a lot of bother about it, and what with that and getting my arm done up, I couldn't get down yesterday. I'm awfully sorry.'

'It didn't matter a bit,' I said. I felt that it never had mattered at all. The disappointment of the previous day was wiped out of my memory by the supreme fact that he was here, now. I knew that for supper there were adequate remains from last night's preparations.

'Last week you suggested my coming to-day instead of yesterday,' said Cullum, 'so I thought there'd be a chance of finding you in if I came down by train, to explain why I didn't turn up when you expected me.'

'You said last week that you couldn't manage to-day.'

'Well, Father has one of his usual Sunday gatherings

73

of tremendously old and eminent political people, all talking "shop." I ought to be at home, doing the polite son of the host, but to-day I simply felt I couldn't. Parliamentary "have-beens" are very depressing. Each time they mention by accident anything that has the remotest bearing on modern conditions and the problems of to-day, they all raise their eyebrows, and then the air is full of the rustle of decaying laurels, stirred up by the shaking of their heads. What are you trying to do with that wet cement? Fill in that hollow?'

'I'm not "trying to do" anything,' I said. 'I'm doing it!'

'Oh, I see! Well, you'd better let me finish the job, even though I'm one-armed. You're making a mess of it.'

'I'm sorry I'm in such a mess myself,' I said. 'You see, I didn't know you were coming – '

The boy laughed, happily slapping on cement with a trowel.

'You look hot, grubby, untidy, and perfectly charming!' he said, 'that's a feat. Few people can. It isn't too late to see the grounds, is it? I've wanted to go over your garden since you talked of it when we were coming away from the Coles.'

When he had finished we went out into the garden, I still in the dirty stable kit that he would not let me go and change. Fortunately they were not my hunting breeches, but a cheap pair that were shabby all over, but sound. It seemed my fate to be caught by Cullum when looking my worst. I was embarrassed, too; hoping he had not noticed that I had inadvertently called him Cullum.

'Oh, this is beautiful! I don't wonder that you are so fond of it. And I love this green-blue evening light that you get after sunset; it doesn't seem to come from any special part of the sky,' he said, looking upwards beyond the high surrounding wall of oaks, bright red-brown now with unopened buds. 'You do, too, I remember.'

I could not recall when I had told him that.

It was growing late, and creeping up from the ground came that gloom in which the outlines of big objects are more distinct than they are during the day, but the details are lost. Branches were cut in filigree against the radiance that still shone above the tree tops.

As we walked through the little coppice at the bottom of the garden, I could not clearly see his face; he was only a deeper moving shadow and a voice beside me in the darkness of the trees. The transforming magic of coming night had touched them all; alive and waiting, in the strain and whisper and surge of spring dusk, they shut us in together, weaving a tent of darkness round us. An oppressive feeling of suspense brooded over the garden that evening. There was an extraordinary feeling of still excitement; we had not spoken for a long while. I said the first trivial sentence that came into my head, to break the overpowering hush. There was not a bird singing anywhere.

He did not answer at once, but stood, listening to something, probably the very faint swish of the wind among the leafless larches and the deeper sound it made in the evergreens, and then he turned to me. Where we had stopped by mutual impulse the trees grew further apart, and I could see his face. It was glowing with intense gladness.

'But this is extraordinary!' he said in a low voice. 'I've dreamed all this over and over again – this place, and you, and your last remark about the gum from that fir tree getting into your hair when you used to climb it! As a recollection it is far more vivid

75

than my memory of anything that I've seen lately. It's one of a series of recurring dreams that I've had at odd times – all my life, I think; anyway, ever since I can remember. I had forgotten them, because they didn't seem to mean anything, but they're coming back to me, one by one, as we live them over again. One of them was of us standing here. I know the particular shape of those trees over there so well!'

' "Of *us*?" ' I said, softly, because something in the surrounding quiet made one speak very quietly.

'Yes. You see, you were in all of them. I've been hoping you'd remember, too. I've met you in dreams for years, and I recognized you, not quite at once, but suddenly, when we were on the platform at Victoria waiting for the train. It seemed so marvellous that I couldn't say anything. You'd been puzzling me the whole evening, because I felt there was something familiar about you, and it wasn't a recollection of the little girl who went for me at the Dycett-Byrne's; I never dreamed of you like that; you were never a child in my dreams even when I was a child, you have always been grown up; at least, as grown up as you are now. I've always seen you among trees, too. Here sometimes, because I remember that big tree with no branches for some way, and then one that bends down nearly to the ground and up again. You have sat in that crook very often?'

'Yes,' I said wonderingly.

'And read there?'

'Yes.'

'I used to see you in another place too. I shall know it again when I see it. Those were always the best dreams. By the way, you know when I said about your loving the greenish after-sunset glow in the air? I learnt that in a dream. You do love it, don't you?'

76

'I always have,' I said, staring at him, with my hands pressed to my hot face, in amazement, 'but this is very strange; the strangest thing I've known. Are you quite sure that I was the person you dreamed of? It might have been someone else, someone like me; dreams aren't generally very clear.'

'These are, and I don't know anyone else like you. You don't share those dreams, then? I hoped that perhaps you did. You don't remember at all?'

'No. I'm sorry.' I felt oddly apologetic.

'Well, even so, it's wonderful, Esther! It's an Adventure!' he said in an awed, happy voice. 'A great Adventure!'

By unspoken consent we put the subject aside and did not refer to it any more that night. The queer discovery was too precious to be examined and handled in talk; it was as if this incomprehensible link was something apart, something so delicate that it would not bear long discussion. I hid it away in my mind to think over later, when I was alone.

Cullum and I wandered all over the big garden and the three paddocks, and out on to the common by Four Wends pond, where four roads meet, and the hundreds of frogs coming up from the bottom of the water, now that spring had woken them, made the air vibrate with the harsh purring sound that they kept up incessantly. On the gleaming surface of the pond, that had drawn to itself all the light from the surrounding land and air, I could just make out their heads, protruding in couples; they would be goggling up, I knew, with that look of unutterable, conscientious boredom with which frogs, for three days at a stretch, answer the call of the spring. ('Three or four days! Oh, why wasn't I born a frog!' as Gerald used to complain.)

How gorgeous in its variety life seemed! Amusing

77

and glorious by turns, sometimes both at the same time. For me, the coming of Cullum had made all things perfect.

The earth was in a love mood, and walking back to the house by dew-wet paths, I wondered suddenly if Cullum, too, was aware that all the insistent essence of life around us, and in us, was crying out to him to kiss me. I was almost certain that I wanted it myself, before I thrust the thought away – Cullum was talking of adventure in general, and Cullum on Adventure took one's entire attention; it was his great subject.

'Adventure – the unexpected – you find it at every turn of existence if you look for it,' he said. 'I can't understand how anyone can be so unimaginative and limited in their interests as to commit suicide, for instance, when there's always the possibility that something magnificently exciting might happen to-morrow! Of course, the truth is that most people don't want anything tremendously exciting to happen to them; it would "upset all their arrangements" as they say, and people are slaves to their own arrangements, particularly their arrangements for meals. The number of people there are who don't do things that they really want to do, because it might interfere with a meal-time! They daren't miss one, even for their own pleasure! Half the people in the world are moored to a mutton chop –' The boy gesticulated indignantly with one hand.

' "Moored to a mutton-chop" is good,' I said approvingly.

'Well, they are. They waste so much time by putting off starting to do something, simply because there isn't time to finish it before the next meal-time! Most of the people I know who have cars are like that. On the most gorgeous day they won't drive into the country before they've debated for hours where they can have lunch if they do, and then they spend the whole time worrying whether they'll get there at the time they made up their minds they would. That *is* being moored to a mutton-chop. I'm always urging people not to get into ruts. Getting into a rut is the worst fate that can happen to anyone; it makes adventure in daily life impossible. What is the fun of living if you know to-day exactly what you will be doing this time to-morrow, and the next week, and a year hence? You've lived through all the interest before you get there.'

It was Cullum's preoccupation throughout his life to avoid forging any chain of habit that might bind him to a settled existence. I do not know why it should have been so, for with his nature there was never the least danger of it.

'When I've got the money,' he said, 'and I ought to make enough by my next two books, I'm going to buy a fairish big sailing-boat – something of the East Coast fishing smack build that will stand any weather, but of about fifty tons, and ketch-rigged – and drift about the world, writing. I want to collect beforehand a small voluntary crew of people who are all interested in writing and – oh, that will be the life!'

He painted word pictures of the places he intended to visit, seeing them sun-drenched, starlit or dark, according to his fancy; and then of the glamorous things that his jolly company might do in them; he gave reality to his sketches by putting in occasional technical details of boats, of which he had a good deal of knowledge, and by touching with local colour the spots he knew best through books.

Cullum was always effective when he talked. The enthusiasm in his face as he spoke of wild but just prac-

79

ticable plans, working them out on the spur of the moment with his brain a little ahead of his tongue, coloured his pictures for those who heard him, and even the listeners who laughed at his projects fell into the trap of discussing them with him, and after that, for a little while at least, they seemed perfectly feasible. It was almost impossible not to take his idea seriously for the moment, he was so thoroughly in earnest himself.

'If the crew is to consist largely of young writers, I suggested lightly, "why not, as a side-line, kidnap editors and publishers who turn down work, written by any of the ship's company, which the crew in council has decided is good work? Get them aboard the lugger and make them do the dirty work.'

'Oh, we will! Piracy up-to-date! I think they shall learn by heart the work they refused, and before we put them ashore without a copy of it, they will be forced to sign a contract promising to set it up in type immediately they get back to their offices. They'll pay for all necessary corrections themselves, which will make it very expensive for them if they haven't learned it properly.' He added ruefully that on his own account he had already a list of editors who had basely qualified for this experience.

'Quite seriously, and rotting apart,' he said, 'I am going to get a boat and go wherever the wind blows and life isn't too mapped out in advance, and of course you will have to be one of the party.'

I was not asked whether the distant prospect appealed. But naturally it did; I was nineteen.

'Three years ago I had two glorious months in a small tramp steamer trading with Iceland,' he said later, at supper, helping himself absent-mindedly, to Olive's delight, to the cherry cake that appeared inappropriately at that meal. 'That was a wonderful business.

The greatest two months of my life! Pater knew the owner, so I went just as I had always longed to go, as an extra deck-hand, not a passenger. I wasn't paid, and the men knew it, so there wasn't any jealousy about "a toff buttin' in." They merely thought I was amiably mad for choosing to work my passage there and back, and said so. The cold on deck, when we got up north, went through you like a sharp, physical pain; you ached with it; and down below there was such a stink of sweating humanity that you could hardly breathe. The men were about the roughest one could find; splendid fellows; I was heart-sick at losing such friends when I left the ship. The skipper was a hard-bitten case, too. He was always cursing the modern regulations that insist on decent treatment for the sailors. "Pampering the men! Can't do anything with them these days," he used to say. "The Board of Trade will make the skipper go round kissing them all good-night one of these days." His face used to be a study. They say he'd been a perfect terror in his youth. Oh, I must tell you about him and the sea-lawyer! A "sea-lawyer" 's a fellow who's always arguing about sailors' rights; one of them in the fo'c'sle can ruin the temper of any ship. We had one called Smithers, and he complained to the skipper one day about some trifle, and the Old Man came raging to the bo'sun when I was standing by.

' "Fifty years ago a man who took that liberty would have been kicked down the bridge-ladder faster than he came up it!" he said. "A captain daren't touch his men now-a-days, a *captain* daren't!"

'The bo'sun sucked his teeth and grunted. Tiny little cockney he was. The skipper went on fuming – they'd sailed together for years – "Daren't touch his men, *a captain* daren't, not a *captain!*" and the bo'sun went on sucking his teeth, and you could see they both understood each other.

'The next day, the chap who'd made a fancy complaint came up with a real one. His face was a mess, one eye bunged up and a cut lip and so on, and he said that without provocation the bo'sun had set on him half an hour ago when they happened to be alone together in the fo'c'sle. He was a hulking great chap, very unpopular. In size he'd have made two of the bo'sun. The rest of us knew that the fun was going to start, and we managed to find work that urgently needed doing, close at hand.

'The skipper said it was a very grave charge indeed, and called the bo'sun, and told him without moving an eyelid that he hoped it was not true, as Smithers stated, that he'd knocked the man about that afternoon. The bo'sun swore by all that's holy, and much else besides, that he'd been in the galley all the afternoon singing hymns with the cook!

' "Singing hymns?" ' asked the skipper, looking curiously at the bo'sun.

' "Singin' 'ymns, sir!" said the bo'sun, looking firmly at the skipper. "If you'll ask the cook, sir –"

'We were all hugging ourselves with joy, and word was sent along for the cook, a most blasphemous chap. He came, and was asked whether the bo'sun had been with him all the afternoon.

' "Yessir, all the afternoon. We bin singin' 'ymns together."

'So the skipper turned to the man whose face had been badly battered and said gently: "You see, my man! No one's been hitting you. You've been dreaming, that's what it is! Get along forrard!"

'And the chap who'd "dreamed" himself into a black eye and the rest, just went off and did his work in a dazed sort of way for a bit. Nobody paid much attention to him in the fo'c'sle afterwards. Oh, those were days!'

He stopped.

'Go on!' said Olive breathlessly.

Father was out, and she, Vallie and I were listening entranced, afraid to miss one word of Cullum's, though his ability as a story-teller lay not so much in his words as in his own animation, and the slight explanatory gestures that he used unconsciously. He had, in a lesser degree, the wonderful gift which I believe Chesterton ascribes to Dickens; Cullum, too, could make things happen again, for his hearers, and make them happen better.

He talked, to amuse Olive, of the seals that he had had a chance of studying on the Faro island beaches on that trip.

'Fascinating, they are. Each old-man seal with his wives inhabits his own bit of beach. I used to watch them for hours. There's no visible boundary between each seal's particular domain and the next one's, but they all know just how far their own territory extends, and you'll see two old-men seals go flopping along, towards each other, each to the limit of his own recognized ground, and then they'll carry on what is obviously a friendly conversation, but if one of them moves an inch over the invisible line, the other is on to him in a moment, and there's a tremendous fight. The young males can't have wives of their own until they're big enough and heavy enough to beat one of the old fellows and steal his, but the wives want to flirt with the young ones, so they go out to sea to catch fish, and it will happen, apparently by chance, that the young males are bathing out at sea at the same time; and as long as the old husband is snoozing on the beach they'll

83

carry on a little affair, playing about together in the water, but the instant he looks round, the wives are industriously catching fish, pretending not to see the young seals hanging round. Then the old seal dozes off again, and they go on with the flirtation. Eventually they try to find a stretch of unoccupied beach for a little surreptitious love-making, and if the old seal catches them at it he comes lolloping along at a tremendous pace, in great indignation, and then the fur flies, and the young seal gets a jolly good beating.'

'Does the husband turn on the unfaithful lady too?' I asked.

'No,' said Cullum, 'I believe man is the only animal that does that, in such cases!'

'Animals usually have a certain amount of chivalry towards females,' I said. 'In spring, when they were drawing a covert, I've seen a vixen, very heavy in cub, slink out very slowly, because she simply couldn't make much pace, right under the nose of two old dog-hounds. They looked round to see if the huntsman was in sight, and then they sat on their haunches and looked silly, glancing at each other appealingly. They weren't going to run her if they could help it.'

'That's the first decent thing I've ever heard about hunting!' said Cullum.

'It only happens with dog-hounds,' I said. 'If a bitch-pack had been out, they'd have been on to her in a second, of course. No mercy between female and female.'

Cullum made a grimace of distaste. 'It beats me,' he said, 'how you of all people can take part in that disgusting and unfair form of sport, where all the strength, safety and enjoyment is on one side, and nothing but long misery and agonized exhaustion before death on the other. Fox-hunting seems to me nexcusable.'

'But it isn't all fox-hunting in this part of the country,' I said, in weak self-defence. 'There's stag-hunting two days of the week.'

'Chasing captive beasts! Can one imagine anything more contemptible!'

Olive was enraptured. He began a homily on the horrors of hunting, with which my mind thoroughly agreed. Spirit and flesh were divorced in me over this question of hunting; but the flesh won two or three times a week.

'The civilized woman,' he said, and paused impressively.

'But why drag in a fabulous animal?' I interrupted to avoid being convinced again of the wrongness of what I intended to go on doing, in any case. 'There are no civilized women! Not when they're excited, anyway. And one is naturally excited by hunting.'

He laughed, and giving me up as hopeless, reverted to the more satisfactory habits of the seals.

He did not offer to shake hands with me when he hurried off to catch the last Sunday night train to Town.

'Good-bye, dream-partner,' he said, in the soft, charming voice that made everything he said, even casual remarks, sound caressing.

'Good-bye, Cullum,' I said, glad that I need not touch him. All at once I had grown pleasantly ill at ease because he was so near me.

After Cullum had gone I wrote to Janet Keene, the friend with whom I was going to stay in Town, mainly in order to fill in the time before I went to bed, for I should see her in a few days' time; but the disinclination to settle down to anything, which had come over me the previous day, when he did not appear, came back as soon as Cullum went. When anything bright is flashed before one's eyes and withdrawn, a dark spot appears where it shone. Cullum's absence made itself felt as definitely as his presence; an empty mental space persisted for a while in places that he left.

I described him to Janet as well as I could, hoping that she would not mind if he came to see me when I was with her. I wanted Janet, the one friend for whose opinion I cared, to like Cullum. She loved young people and collected them round her, playing second-mother and adviser to a little court of them, with a graciousness and tact that had made me a devoted admirer in the first hour I spent alone with her. She had a marvellous knack of extracting confidences from unwilling people without direct questioning; it was difficult to keep oneself from telling things to Janet, and she received confidences so charmingly that after a time one did not try. Janet was the only person, before Cullum's coming, to whom I had admitted, shamefacedly, my bookish ambitions. She could not enter into these, for all her interests were personal, dealing with people and not ideas, but she encouraged me to talk of them sometimes. She dealt sympathetically with the egotism of all her youthful satellites, earning their adoration in return, because she satisfied youth's imperative need of unburdening itself of its views on itself occasionally. I stopped keeping a diary when I became a friend of Janet's. She was even kinder to me than to any of the other young people who swarmed about her flat, and I accepted her preference gratefully, as I accepted the dresses she lent and sometimes gave me, without hurting my pride, a feat which no one else could have accomplished.

'You are the daughter I ought to have had,' she told me once. 'It's amusing to watch you going through the same stages of growth as I did, and you take them just as seriously!'

Janet at thirty-eight had the good looks of her youth crowned by a serene maturity that made her manner queenly. She was always beautifully dressed. Naturally some of the very young men who confided the more creditable of their early love affairs to her, went on to give her their views on love in the abstract, and so ended, inevitably, by believing for a short time that they cherished a hopeless passion for her. Janet mothered them firmly through this difficult period, patting them on the cheek soothingly when they tried to kiss her. I never tired of watching the delicate way in which she handled those helpless bewildered youths, the sacrifices to her unsatisfied maternal passion. (Janet was a widow, and her only child had died young.)

I could not tell even Janet of the link, forged in dreams, that Cullum had found between us. I wanted to keep this strange, delightful secret to myself. My mind was dancing with it.

Lying awake in bed that night I played with the idea, growing hot and disturbed at thought of what this might mean. All things lovely and fantastic seem credible on spring nights; what might it not mean?

It was so still in my room that through the open window I could hear Jenny whinnying in the stables, and Osiris answering her across the yard. My room overlooked the stables, I could always tell my mare's high whinny from that of any of the other horses, and she and Osiris had called to each other so often these last few nights that I was beginning to recognize his deeper tone as well.

Urgent life, drowsy in autumn, asleep through winter, was awake and possessing the earth; the horses were troubled by the spring.

87

I slid out of bed and knelt at the window, where I could catch the sound of rustling straw as the horses moved restlessly in the stalls. Twice I heard a heavy thud, muffled by the thickness of the stable doors, as Jenny reverted to her old bad habit of kicking the partition. If she went on with it, she would be lame in the morning, I knew.

It was eerily still. Tenuous, unmoving clouds covered the moon, but the light percolated through, spreading itself dimly over a desiring world. There was a feeling of ancient savagery abroad, of unconquerable forces stirring. Mare and stallion whinnied again, wanting each other in this night of earth's excitement. Leaving the window, I felt hurriedly for shoes and a coat, moved by an impulse I did not wait to define.

Each board creaked as I crept downstairs, and I felt the black shadows of the house closing in like living presences behind me while I groped my way to the back door, whispering reassuringly to Justice who was chained there. If she had not recognized me, and had barked, waking the household, I should have had to explain what I was doing, and I realized suddenly that the explanation would sound idiotic at that time of night, or, indeed, at any other time, to practical people. Running my hand along the dresser shelf I knocked down a cup before I found the stable keys. The noise echoed as if the house were empty. Outside, it did not matter so much that the key of Jenny's stable grated loudly; no other bedroom looked this way. The straw crackled in the warm darkness as I went into the stable and then nothing moved for a few seconds. I knew that she was straining her head round to see the intruder. I took a deep breath to steady myself; Jenny, being nervous, was likely to kick if she could not make out who it was. I talked to her and edged into her stall, feeling along the twitching body till I reached her head. She let me slip her halter and turned round of her own accord, squeezing me painfully against the partition and luckily just missing my felt-slippered feet with her hoofs. I could only trust to luck to avoid being trodden on until we were out in the yard, clattering over the cobbles.

'I say, Shades of my Ancestors,' I appealed, knowing that on Father's side they had been Scandinavian horses and cattle thieves, 'give us a hand, and for goodness' sake don't let this noise be heard!'

My estimation of them went up that night. Stout fellows they must have been to get away with strange horses by night; it is exceedingly difficult, I found, to move a horse quietly in the darkness, and this was a horse that knew me well. Jenny was trembling, and starting at every shadow, and it seemed to my anxious ears that we were making a tumult of sound.

I let her into Osiris's loose box, knowing that she was too eager to lash out at the stallion then, as blood mares do.

'You fool, Esther!' I whispered, laughing at myself as I went back to bed, where I shivered luxuriously in returning warmth, 'what did you do that for?'

No reason that I cared to recognize came forward to defend the impulse; but I dropped to sleep happily and was up two hours before anyone else, to return Jenny to her proper stall. I was glad that she had had Osiris when she wanted him, in a night when it seemed wrong that anyone should control the desire of another creature. She was officially mated, in the usual cold-blooded manner, two days later. Moon and I were, so to speak, best man and bridesmaid at the ceremony and when Moon was not looking I punched her in the ribs, coarsely.

Chapter 6: *Knowledge*

JANET and Cullum liked each other immensely when
they met. Their faces, as they talked, making friends
eagerly that first evening in Janet's flat, were very
pleasant for me to watch. The faces of one's friends
when they are happy are lovely, and these were the
two people in whom I was most interested: that they
should please each other seemed a natural part of the
new excellence of life. They were amusing to watch,
too, for both of them had the same need of appreciation
from every acquaintance, and that evening each was
unconsciously intent on extracting from the other the
little tribute of admiration that they required from
anyone they met. Janet, always unsatisfied until her
graciousness had added a new touch of deference to a
man's manner, was making herself especially fascinating for him. I had seen her do it too often to think
that her desire to charm at first sight was anything more
than habit. Janet needed admiration as a plant needs
sunlight; she rarely failed to obtain it. She was a big
woman, finely made, and carried herself superbly.
Her delicate face was rather immobile; with clear cut
features.

Cullum talked to her of his work, repeating with
naïve self-complacency the complimentary remarks of
his publishers in the interview in which they had discussed the publication date of his next novel.

Cullum's mind was of all ages at different moments,

and rarely of one age for long. He seemed older and wiser than his years sometimes, in the quiet moods that came on him rarely, and suddenly. At those times the nimble face, caught in repose, had a look of wistfulness that I grew to resent later on, for it meant a loneliness beyond my healing, when the boy's restless soul showed itself for a moment in his eyes. Under his gaiety and companionableness lay an unexpected streak of Celtic perversity. Cullum, endowed with a gift for attracting friends, was by nature a lonely person; it was true, as he said of himself, that he was always sighing, more than most artists, for the beauty that is just out of reach. But all that evening with Janet he was as young as the spring seemed, almost like a child in his frank pleasure in his own achievements. *The Chink* was a very good first novel, and he saw no reason for pretending that he did not know it. I do not think that he felt self-conscious at any time in his life.

Once I saw Janet smiling in her most maternal manner at something he said, as a mother smiles indulgently at the quaint pride of a child, and the blood crept indignantly into my face. At the Coles', Cullum had once shown the same boyish good opinion of himself; it was one of the traits that had attracted me; it was so open; he was evidently still surprised at himself for having done as much as he had; but on this occasion I wished that he would not make it so apparent; but I need not have troubled, for his jolly self-satisfaction appealed to Janet just as it had done to me when I was in no way concerned with the impression he made. The cause of the change in my attitude lay there. After he had gone Janet expressed her approval of him so whole-heartedly that I was reassured.

'He's got both brain and decent manners. Wonderful!' she said. 'I like his "I-come-conquering" attitude towards the world. All young people should have a touch of unconscious swagger about them. Yes, he's very nice.'

Her face took on a thoughtful expression. Janet always wanted to play providence to her friends and arrange their lives for them; whenever she introduced any man to any girl her mind automatically jumped to put one and one together and make three. She did not consider, in her tireless efforts to organize romances among her friends, whether these affairs were likely to turn out happily or not; her instinct was simply to promote them at all costs. It was part of that universal womanly passion for interference in the lives around her, of which Gerald complained. Actuated by what she believed to be anxiety for her protégés' welfare, Janet in her heart was as ruthless as nature, if, luckily, not so well equipped for enforcing her designs. In one or two cases she had succeeded in marrying her friends to the partners she chose for them, and the results had not been markedly happy, but that did not seem to weigh on her conscience, nor to deter her from further benevolent activities. Still, the individuals concerned were probably no worse off, on the whole, than they would have been had their choice been made without her assistance.

'He must come again,' said Janet. 'What a waste such lovely hair is on a man! That touch of dark red, and the wave that I suppose he's ashamed of – The colouring is rather like Miles Marston's but he's not quite as good-looking as Miles.'

'Cullum really isn't good-looking at all. Nor is Miles,' I said.

Janet had selected Miles Marston for me some time ago, and had done her subtle best, but we remained obdurately uninterested in each other.

92

'Oh, my dear, Miles is very good-looking! He has wonderful eyes.

'His ears stick out,' I said, 'and artistically speaking, they obscure his eyes. Be a dear, Janet, and don't chuck Miles at my head this visit! You know I don't share your liking for very young men; I have no protective instinct; they only annoy me.'

'I should think Miles is older than young Hayes!' protested Janet, loath to relinquish a pet plan.

'Yes, I think he is, but then Cullum is the only man under twenty-five that has ever interested me at all. Miles is still in that aggressive stage of comparative innocence when he tries to impress on one what a dog he really is, by exaggerating the number of times he was "tight" in one week. I'm not old enough myself yet to be amused by boys whose mouths are wet with mother's milk, like Miles'. He thinks it's beer, but it isn't, it's mother's milk. If you throw him at me any more, I shall tell him so, and that will finish everything.'

While I was staying with Janet, Cullum stretched her permission to drop in whenever he felt inclined into an invitation for a late tea, after he left the office, every two or three days. He came to see us both. Janet and he remained as pleased with each other as they had been at first. Cullum slipped easily into the intimacy of an affectionate, but rather respectful son, which was the attitude Janet liked: he was always quick at realizing what was expected of him.

No work was done on Saturdays on his paper, and on the first Saturday of my stay we three drove into the country in Janet's tiny two-seater car, with Cullum hunched up on the floor among our feet, wedged uncomfortably between the lunch basket and the door, half of him in the body of the car, and half on the step.

Janet was not one of those people who are 'moored

to a mutton chop,' and we had a picnic meal of lunch and tea in one, some time in the afternoon, at Liphook.

'Go away, you children, while I get it ready. You're more bother than you're worth, both of you,' she said, when first of all Cullum broke a cup in getting the basket out of the car, and then I irritated the Primus stove into a miniature geyser of gushing, flaming paraffin.

Cullum and I wandered off under tall elms, still leafless, which held a rookery full of spring commotion.

'Mrs. Keene is a wonderful woman!' he said enthusiastically. 'She is like a chameleon in the way she seems to change her whole appearance, not just her clothes, to suit the places she's in. To-day, down here, she seems part of the country, all health and energy. But when I saw her first in Town I thought she was one of the most exotic-looking people I've ever seen, obviously delicate, and incapable of doing anything more strenuous than being admired.'

'I love that trait in Janet,' I said. 'She has the knack of fitting perfectly into any scene.'

'Your personality never changes,' said Cullum. 'That's what is so restful about you. You give one a feeling of being always the same, and always rather – what's the word I want? – rather intangible; immaterial in some way. Even in London I feel that there's a cool wind that no one else notices blowing round your head! You don't give the impression of belonging entirely to this earth. At least, you're of the earth, very much of it, but not in a human way; you might be a tree-spirit. If there are any nature-spirits I'm sure they have faces like yours, which always looks a little amused, as if you had some secret joke that you were hugging to yourself. In London you are so utterly

out of your element that I half expect you to drift
through a wall and disappear one day. I kissed your
hand, the evening of the Coles' dinner-party, because
it looked so long and wispy that I felt it couldn't be
real. Mortal men have a right to kiss nymphs when they
catch them in disguise.'

As an appropriate answer I threw back my head
and whistled a long drawn-out owl's hoot. A pair of
white owls had nested all my life in the rafters of our
loft, and by hours of practice I had learned to repro-
duce their unearthly hooting. I gave the female's call.
Every rook in the trees above us shot into the air,
cawing excitedly as they circled round, looking for the
intruder.

'Oh, good Heavens,' exclaimed Cullum. 'I knew
there was something eerie about you. That wasn't
an imitation, it *was* an owl's hoot. You've sent creepy
thrills tingling up and down my spine. Of course, you
were born among those evil old trees at Holmwood;
they're beautiful, but they're sinister with age; I expect
you're a changeling. Tell me, as a matter of interest,
do you throw a shadow by moonlight?'

I looked all round with a frightened air.

'Sh!' I said mysteriously, with a finger on my lips.
'You mustn't ask me that. We aren't allowed to tell.
Please don't give me away, or they'll send a mumbling
priest to abolish me with book, bell and candle, and
then I shall dissolve altogether and become part of the
crying of the wind. Kind sir, don't give me away, and
I'll show you all the secrets of the woods. I will give
you immortal youth, and the spell for binding human
hearts. Only, don't give me away!'

Even in childhood I had never had anyone to enter
into make-believe with me, as Cullum did.

The birds were settling down after their alarm, and

95

I hooted again. They rose instantly, and far away an owl answered.

Janet called to us, and we returned to the car. After the meal, Cullum insisted that I should repeat the performance for her.

I whistled the call when we reached the trees again, and the rooks flew up, seeming a little less perturbed than they had been at first, but when I repeated it hardly any of them stirred, having discovered the trick by this time. Instead, a white owl floated on silent wings over the tops of the elm and swooped down towards us. All the rooks, and there must have been several hundreds, rose in one body and launched themselves at him, pecking and banging him about the head with their wings. Dazed by the blinding daylight, the deluded male owl wheeled and fled, with the rooks pursuing him out of sight.

It was rough luck on him, but he got away safely, so paying lightly, on the whole, for that most expensive mistake, a love-blunder.

'Esther's positively uncanny!' said Cullum, as we walked away.

'Perhaps she is,' said Janet. 'Certainly I can always feel her eyes digging into me when she looks at me, even if I'm not looking her way. Yes, I can, really, Esther! Those unwinking eyes, planted nearly on opposite sides of your head, have the most disconcerting stare. Grey eyes are so cold. If you were a detective and I were a criminal, I should scream and confess at once if I found you watching me in the way you seem to watch everyone.'

'I shouldn't dare confess anything to Esther,' said Cullum. 'I should be too afraid of getting exactly what I deserved! There is more justice than mercy in her.'

'No, I protest!' I said, 'I don't know why everyone gets the idea that I'm one of the hard people whom nothing touches. I can forgive most things except weakness and stupidity.'

'If you can't forgive weakness and stupidity,' said Cullum, 'you can't forgive much; nearly all failings – nearly all crimes, too – are due to weakness and stupidity.'

We were smoking lazily, now, sitting on one of the fallen trees, in that comfortable state of inactivity produced by a large meal. None of us felt like exertion of any kind, and so the talk was desultory, but Cullum suddenly woke up and became vehement on the need for tolerance; intolerance of any kind always roused his indignation. The subject seemed to be often in his mind, as though it held some personal significance for him.

'People have no right to judge harshly those who are different from themselves. People do wrong, as the world calls it, because they were born with a kink in them; they can't help it, it's not their choice,' he said earnestly. 'No one who is normal willingly does things that every sane man condemns, and so it follows that a man who commits not only the big crimes like murder, but lesser things, stealing and so on, is insane on that particular point. He isn't really responsible. It isn't altogether his fault. Don't *you* think so, Mrs. Keene?'

Janet assented vaguely, and I returned to my own point.

'Yes, possibly, but by stupidity I meant slow-wittedness. I can bear with most things except that.'

'Not you, my dear!' Janet said. 'Don't claim understanding as your strong suit. I don't believe you're capable of putting yourself in anyone's else place;

97

you're far too certain of yourself to make allowance for any failings that you yourself don't possess.'

For a second I was hurt by her tone. Janet was not in the habit of belittling me in any way before other people. On other occasions it would not have troubled me, but I did not like it when Cullum was present.

'Esther thinks I've wasted my life,' Janet said to him, 'because I weakly fell in love and gave up my career!'

When Janet made fun of any of her protégés she usually did it so gently that they enjoyed it themselves, but just then the caressing undernote seemed lacking from her chaff. The faint sense of unhappiness it gave me passed before I was fully aware of it. Nothing that Janet said could offend me, and I admitted the truth of her last remark; I did deplore the waste of her gifts.

She had the voice of a great singer and at twenty-six she had given up a half-made career in order to marry a Captain Keene, putting aside the probability of fine achievement as an artist, though they were to live in London and she could have gone on with her work, because she wanted to be this man's wife, and possibly the mother of his children, to the exclusion of all other interests. They had had one boy, who died at three years old, and her husband had died four years before I met her. She was then thirty-two, and her health had been injured by the coming of the child. She would have been at the height of her career had she continued it; already when she married, having won her hearing after five years' hard work, the sweets of the profession were within reach, but she had given herself no time to try them, and now it was too late to start again. The incoming tide of new talent soon washes out marks on those shifting sands, and her name had been forgotten. The influential people who had recognized her ability were men of the past, and she was not strong enough to go again through the crushing preliminary struggle.

Fortunately, it was not necessary for her now to earn her own living, but it had always seemed to me the abuse of a trust, in some inexplicable way, for anyone to possess great talent and not to use it. Yet from the individual point of view she had been wise; the happiest women are those who fulfil the natural vocations of women and want nothing more; but there is more in life than happiness; contentment is not a compensation for everything.

'Esther can't see why I gave up public work when I married, but you can't combine two things when each claims all your enthusiasm and intelligence. You can understand that, Cullum, can't you? I think you're more human than Esther is yet. If I could have divided myself equally into singer and wife I shouldn't have been of much use as either, and singing meant much too much for me to go on with it less than half-heartedly. How can there be any choice between sometimes singing the part of a great lover, and living it all the time? It's like choosing between glass and diamonds.'

'Yes,' said Cullum, evidently much impressed; Janet in her exalted moods was remarkable. 'I think you have chosen the better part.'

'But in this case it *has* been taken away from her,' I reminded him, 'contrary to precedent! And what's left?'

'My dear,' Janet said, 'I have all my memories! Six years of happiness! Do you suppose that any career I might have had would have been worth that? Of course not, child! And the success of my married life was worth infinitely more to me because I gave up a great deal for it.'

'But when there's no necessity for it, self-sacrifice becomes nothing more than moral self-indulgence,' I said, 'rather a morbid form too: some women have a craving for it; and besides – but oh, well, never mind. Anyway, it's done now and can't be undone.' I knew from experience that it was useless for anyone to attempt argument with Janet; she could always make it look futile by meeting reasoning with rhetoric. My affection for her did not prevent me from feeling a little over-awed by her; I liked being with her, but her self-possession, which seemed to me boundless, made me feel my insignificance. She dealt with everyone who disagreed with her in the patient, pitying way in which she dealt with obtuse shop assistants or waiters. I envied her that firm but kindly manner which swept all opposition aside, as being somehow irrelevant.

'I'm not surprised you tread on people's mental corns, as you say,' Cullum observed to me, 'if you always feel bound to state the truth as you see it with such uncompromising vigour!'

He made a good story, for Janet, of that uncomfortable episode at the Coles' in which Justice figured; the story was much better than the original happening.

'Well, it's so difficult with that sort of person to know what you may say, and what you mayn't,' I complained. 'They have such nasty minds. Why, for instance, is it permissible in society for a woman to have a breast, but not breasts? You can decently mention anyone laying their head on their mother's breast as long as you don't disclose the horrid fact that she has two! Why should one be respectable, but not both?'

'Ah, there's the subject for an article,' said the journalist in Cullum at once.

'My idea!' I warned him.

'But you don't want it, do you?'

'Yes, I do, or I may do. I shall have to be a journalist too,' I said. 'I want to get a job this summer. I'll have to do something for a living; I can't go on being a kind of head stable-lad all my life, and there's no other work that I'm in any way fitted for.'

'Oh, good,' said Cullum. 'I'm glad you're thinking of journalism. You'll have to live in London.'

Those were wonderful days for me. Happy, I did not measure the extent of my happiness; deliberately I kept myself from examining its causes, aware that this was an intermediate stage. Change in some form would come; I did not want to realize what the change would be; the excellence of the moment was enough. There was a feeling of expectation, of transcience, in these days that slid so fast into one another.

Cullum had not arranged the long-suggested introduction to his people before I had to leave Janet, to be home in time for the hunt ball at Reigate.

I regretted leaving London more because it held Cullum than because Janet lived there. In the last fortnight I had learnt to consider his arrival as the best happening that any day could hold. The expectation of seeing him had lost none of its keenness since that hunting Saturday at Holmwood, when he had not arrived. My liking for him as an individual was growing. His brain produced for mine, which had been starved of companionship, an apparently endless supply of mental toys to play with, and they delighted me. There were his own out-of-the-way, extravagant ideas on all sorts of subjects to be discussed, and curious theories of which I had never heard; there was pleasant accord between us on some points, and best of all, in my estimation, long heated arguments on the innumerable subjects on which we disagreed. All these things seemed very important at the time, because Cullum entered into them whole-heartedly.

The hunt ball, to which I had been looking forward, did not come up to my expectations, though it had all the features of the one that I had enjoyed immensely the previous year, but virtue seemed to have gone out of them. We danced decorously at first, less restrainedly later on, and noisily after midnight; I was again amused at the ball-room solicitude of the men who bumped into me and enquired anxiously whether I was hurt: most of them, at different times, had seen one or other of Father's beasts bring me crashing down at a jump, and had ridden on without even looking round to see if I was badly injured or not; but for that one night they behaved as though I had suddenly become a fragile flower.

I danced chiefly with Gerald, because he was the best dancer there, and also with the Scottish youth, Carlisle Jamieson McDonald – because he gave me no choice. He was the lad with the stammer who had spoken to us after the affray with Tony Dycett-Byrne. I knew him by sight as a rough but tenacious rider; a thruster who hunted with great determination. Except at meets I had only met him once before. He had bought a hunter from Father, and I had ridden it over to Capel to deliver it to him. Young McDonald, coming into the study into which the servant had shown me after the groom had taken the horse, caught me prowling round the room, looking longingly at the books with which it was lined. Some of them were very dull, the kind of books plodded through by the industrious young of the Scottish race when they set out to educate themselves, but I saw one or two that I coveted. The McDonalds, simple, unpretentious folk, had unexpectedly come into money a year ago, when they had immediately satisfied their characteristic national ambition to get out of their beloved country, and away from their esteemed compatriots – a desire innate in most Scotsmen, and far more comprehensible than their public complacency over everything Scottish, with which it accords so ill.

Seeing that I was interested in books, the son told me that they were his, and asked if I would like to borrow some. I accepted eagerly, but before I had time to mention which of them I had set my eye on, he started a weighty discourse, lengthened by the stammer, on the books which he considered had had the greatest influence on his life. I did not care at all about the particular works that had made young McDonald what he was, but he would not let me choose what I wanted, and forced on me the ones that he appreciated.

He took them down from the shelves, and just as he was going to hand them over to me he stopped, and looked at me dubiously.

'I th-think I w-will juist put my name in th-them firrst!'

He rummaged in his pockets, found a pencil, not indelible enough for his purpose, rejected it in favour of ink, and wrote not only his name but his address on the fly leaf of each book.

'Therre,' he said amiably, 'ye see, one neverr knows –'

No explanation, however tactful, could have excused his doing that in my presence, but it did not occur to him to try to extenuate the insulting act. In peace or war the Scots never seem to know when they are doing the impossible: in which lies the secret of their universal success. I had always been conscientious about returning borrowed books, because loving books, I realized their value to their possessor. It is not generally the people who love books who do not return them, but the people who are indifferent to them and consider the loan of them so trivial a matter that they forget about it. But the three books which Carlisle Jamieson McDonald lent me on that occasion I kept for an unconscionable time, not because I liked them, for they were very dull, but out of revenge. No doubt this little affair confirmed both of us in the mutual contempt which the Scots and the English usually feel for each other.

I hardly recognized him in evening dress at the hunt ball when he made his way purposely towards me through the crowd, at the end of the dance during which I arrived, a little late.

'I have b-b-b, I have been k-keeping several dances to have w-with you,' he announced.

'Oh!' I said, so taken aback that I could think of nothing adequate to say, 'how, er, how kind of you.' I had no intention of dancing with him.

'What numbers have ye free?'

I knew nearly everyone in the room, and I expected to pick and choose my partners.

'Let me see. Oh, yes, number twenty-eight,' I said, thinking that McDonald's dancing was sure to be execrable, and that I should probably be gone by the time number twenty-eight came round.

Before I realized what he was doing, he had taken my empty programme out of my hands.

'Ye can spare m-me a few, I see. I am glad I caucht ye in time,' he said, and wrote his name, in full, that there might be no possible error, against seven dances.

The English part of my upbringing had unfitted me to deal with the paralysing directness of Northern attack. I gave in with the helplessness of this Scot-conquered race, and looked round wildly for Gerald. Cullum was not deficient in self-assurance, but in his case, impudence was deliberate. This over-whelming fellow had no idea that he was overwhelming.

'Oh, well, you can't possibly dance all those dances with the bounder,' Gerald said decisively when I told him. 'Just cut them, that's all.'

But one could not cut Carlisle Jamieson's dances. Wherever I was sitting out the interval before one of his dances, he came hovering, smiling reassuringly if he caught my eye, to convey that all was well, he had not forgotten. He came forward with the first bars of music, saying, 'Ourr dance, I think?' and I found that he danced remarkably well.

'I do not c-c-care for dancing very much,' he said, 'but it is an ac-c-c, it is an accomplishment all should have. That is why I l-lairnt it. I am glad ye do it well. That hunter your f-father sold me is most satis-factory. Major Sieveking is so thorough in his worrk, he would b-be Scots, no doubt?'

'He would not!' I said promptly on Father's behalf. We came in contact with a good many of McDonald's compatriots through horse deals, and Father and I were agreed in resenting their tacit assumption that any good thing probably comes out of Scotland. 'There is a little taint of Scottish blood in the family, but not much.'

He seemed puzzled.

'Arre ye not proud of it, then?'

'No,' I said, 'why should I be?'

We were dancing at the time, but he twisted his

head round and stared at me, looking as if he did not like to believe that I had really asked that incredible question. Once before I had received that withering glance from one of his countrymen, when I had questioned the literary value of Burns.

'Do ye mean ye d-don't l-l-like, *that ye don't like the Scots?*' he asked, as though the possibility of this extraordinary contingency had just dawned on him.

'Well, this is getting a bit personal, isn't it? I'm glad the horse is all right, though. He used to be scared of standing water; does he give any difficulty now when you meet it?'

'But, tell me now, d-did ye really mean that ye d-don't like the Scots, as a race?'

'Yes, if you will have it!' I said. Having known many Scottish people I knew that this astounding fact would not penetrate all at once into his brain, and we danced on for some time while he digested it.

'Then ye have not met many,' he said, with the air of one who solves a mystery.

'Oh, yes, I have,' I said, 'you are the third McDonald I've known and, so far, the only one who hasn't made me wish that the massacre of Glencoe had been more complete. You dance well, you see.'

'*Well!*' he said at length.

He pondered during another long silence.

'B-but you must admit they are a g-great people!'

'A marvellous people!' I agreed, 'only I don't like their virtues. I don't like their lack of the superficial graciousness – often false perhaps – which makes life so pleasant in France, for instance. I particularly loathe the bumptious patriotism that they can't keep quiet about. I don't like stolid worth, or clannishness. I don't like their patient, dogged way of shouldering themselves up in the world, never minding what they throw aside in order to "get on." In fact, I do not like the Scots!'

We waltzed half round the big hall before he spoke again.

'Och, ye're pulling my leg!'

'Oh, heavens,' I said in despair. 'Now that is the typical attitude of the people whom I do not – '

'Ye have s-s-said that before!'

'I know. But you aren't able to believe it even yet, are you?'

'Well, I cannot understand it. Will we sit out a while? Thought I fear ye will not f-find me a c-c-congenial pairson if ye do not like ambition – '

'I didn't say that; I said –' I began, but he waved me aside, continuing:

' – for I have made up my m–mind that one day I will get into p-p-p, get into parliament. Ye have noticed the impediment in my sp-speech?'

('Truly a wonderful people! What could I say?)

'Oh, well, perhaps – perhaps just a little.'

'It was f-far worse three years ago. I am getting over it, with b-breathing exercises in the mornings, and reading to m-myself aloud. My people arre quite humble, but a man can do a great deal for himself – '

'Yes, I suppose so,' I said, still at a loss to know how to treat this extraordinary outspokenness.

'Miss Sieveking –' He hesitated, and then went on with a rush, confidentially. 'I would be honoured if you would g-g-, if you would g-give me yourr society sometimes. I have often obsairved you. You, and y-young Hemingway also, have the air which I would like to have. The deefinite social g-graces, like dancing, I can have myself taucht, but the manner of life I can only l-lairn by obsairving those who have it. It is essential, if I am to r-rise as I want, that I should have

107

it. I would like fine if sometimes you would come to tea at ourr house, and p-p-perhaps, one d-day you would let me come to yours?'

It was the most disarming speech I had ever heard. I thawed completely.

'Of course I will, if you like!' I said cordially to this single-minded youth who longed earnestly to be a gentleman, not as an end in itself, but because it would help him in his career. I saw that all this conversation was funny, yet I had no inclination to laugh at him now. There had been a saving note of diffidence in his voice at the end.

'Ye are verry kind! Noticing you, I thought long ago, I know no w-w-w-, no woman who would be a g-greater help to any man in a big poseetion!'

I was past being embarrassed by his frankness by this time.

'Oh? And what made you come to me instead of Gerald Hemingway, since we both of us have the same "air" as you call it?'

'B-because I find it easier t-to ask f-favours of a woman!' he said.

I smiled. I liked people who recognized their assets, whatever they were, and made no show of not knowing them. Carlisle Jamieson McDonald's handsome, hard-looking dark face, erring on the heavy side, would be his best social lever in life, and he knew it. I foresaw that he would always find it easier to obtain what he wanted through women, though except as a relaxation, in which rôle they would be essential to him, they would count, with him, as little but stepping-stones.

'Ye won't have to m-mind my asking, Miss S-Sieve-king," he said during a later dance, 'but are ye en-gaged to young Hemingway?'

'No. Has anyone been saying so?'

'No, no. But ye are often together; I juist liked to ascairtain.'

From this, among many other sayings that evening, including his expression of satisfaction that I danced well – "an accomplishment all should have" – I gathered with much amusement that this staggering young man already had me in view as a suitable wife. He admitted long afterwards that it was so. He had weighed in his mind the assistance that I might give him in his early years, against the greater advantages that he might obtain elsewhere if he waited, and all things being calmly considered, he thought, at present, that the balance was in my favour. But McDonald was cautious; he said nothing more definite for a long while, and bided his time.

Until two in the morning I danced, and ate, and talked, and laughed, exerting myself to be entertained, to throw off the feeling of dissatisfaction. I found myself wondering, even while I assured myself that I ought to be enjoying this affair, why I had looked forward to it so much. To Gerald I was unfair, turning irritable when he scooped me unexpectedly into his long arms and kissed me while we were sitting out, though I had once let him make love to me, without protest, and he could not be expected to know that I had changed. Without wishing to, I tried in thought to compare Gerald's love-making, easy and practised, but without finesse, with the unguessable ways in which Cullum might do it. But I did not know at all how Cullum made love. Except on that first evening when he kissed my hand he had never touched me deliberately. For some reason we never shook hands now when we met. It was just 'Hello, Cullum!' 'Hello, Esther!' and then we stood and smiled at each other while the world brightened imperceptibly round us. It was as though we were afraid to come any nearer to each other. And when he left we said good-bye in rather the same way, only then the radiance faded. I thought that he actually avoided contact, and wondered if this was only my imagination.

'I don't understand!' Gerald said, with his head between his hands. 'If you were anyone else I'd say you were playing the old, old game of keeping the man uncertain, for sheer love of cruelty; "playing" the poor fish – haul in, reel out, haul in again, and so on – only I know, thank goodness, that you wouldn't do that. Why have you suddenly grown changeable, Esther dear? I could understand well enough that you might not have any use for me at all, but why do you sometimes seem to want me, sometimes not?'

'I don't know!' I said unhappily.

There was no one else in the little room where we were sitting out. He took my hands and kissed the palms of them.

'You can't think,' he said, 'what it's like to come to the one thing you really want in life, after lots of aimless drifting and waiting, and to find it doesn't want you!'

'Oh, my dear, don't!' I said, and put my hand on his arm. 'I'm so sorry, Gerald, but what can I do?' I wanted to comfort him in some way, but I could not bring myself to kiss him now.

'Esther, do you care for anyone else?'

'No,' I said, believing it. And instantly I grew aware that this was not true. Knowledge like a flame leapt in my mind. The Hunt Ball only seemed dull to me because Cullum was not there!

I sat very still for a few seconds, staring fixedly at the floor, realizing . . .

'At least, I am not sure, Gerald!' I said, in a hushed voice, and then;

'I believe I do.'

He stretched out his hand towards me, and then drew it back –

'Oh, God! And I'm not the man!'

'No,' I said absently, too dazed by the amazing new glory of the world to think of being kind to him – 'Oh, no, it's not you!'

Chapter 7: *Paris*

IT was a glorious spring the year that Cullum and I fell in love with each other. He came down to Holm-wood every Saturday, and together we used to tramp for hours through my lovely county. The casual visitors, who take away only an impression of picture-postcard prettiness, which Surrey shows on first acquaintance, never find her secret heart, hidden in her woods, between her hills, in places where cowslips and wild daffodils and rare little orchids grow undisturbed, spring after spring, beside her quiet streams. Surrey is a wanton with many lovers, generous in her variety, but she keeps some of her lovers, quietude in untrodden places which the crowd never finds.

It seemed only natural that Cullum should be a good walker, for I loved it, and we shared a liking for so many things. There were still days when we tramped together through shining dampness among half-clad trees, urged to talk a great deal by our growing con-sciousness of each other; when we were easily made awkward by a silence, while earth steamed into life all round us, under the strengthening sunshine. And there were other, rougher days, of bowing saplings and wheeling birds blown high across a windy sky. Sus-tained conversation became difficult, then, when our voices were carried away by the singing wind, and we hardly talked at all. Those were the days when the sense of companionship was deepest, and I was at ease in his company. At other times I was beginning to be afraid of him, with the woman's happy shrinking from the untried mate, when she first recognizes that she must give everything to this man one day. We were deliciously uncertain of each other, full of reticences, and yet confident that something tremendously good lay ahead. Our conversation sheered off any subject that threatened to lead us on to a discussion of love in any personal sense, as affecting us individually, and at our ages most subjects seemed to be by-paths to the tacitly forbidden topic.

I knew that I loved Cullum, knew in my heart that he loved me, but I was not sure what I wanted to happen, or if, indeed, I wanted anything to happen that might alter existing conditions. To both of us just then, I think, love unexpressed but gloriously apparent seemed sufficient in itself. Certainly I did not want to marry Cullum. Marriage did not enter my head; the child of an unhappy union, I looked on marriage as a stupid, rather sordid business, the common-place tomb of the high adventure of love. From the little that Cullum let fall about his own people I gathered that they were not very happy either, but I did not know what his views were.

The first time that I saw him after the Hunt Ball at Reigate I was afraid, before he arrived, that everything in some curious way would feel different, but when he came he was full of a startling short story which he said he had just written, beginning, 'Men, who are lice on the body of God –' (naturally it was never published; I do not suppose it was even written) – and I was reassured.

We did compare our opinions of marriage that Saturday, when we were picking bluebells, in Henfold woods, for Cullum to take to his mother. This was diplomacy; it seemed that lately she had several times expressed a wish to see the cause of Cullum's sudden partiality for Holmwood, which he ascribed to the scenery, and she, being the adoring mother of an only son, did not. He told me that she always eyed with distrust anyone in whom he seemed interested. I thought she had better be propitiated with flowers beforehand.

We were alone in a rustling house of trees, in which the floor was a blue and green mosaic of bluebells and their leaves, rarely flecked with white where anemones danced in the light air, and the walls were oak trees with gleaming new yellow-green foliage, and great beeches down whose smooth trunks twined, like snakes, long dark streaks of dampness.

It turned out that Cullum felt much as I did about marriage: all sensitive youngsters view it at some period as the anticlimax of romance.

We saw that love is a fine and fragile thing, too delicate in its first keenness to remain unblunted by the friction of everyday life; both of us found close at hand examples of what a few years of constant intimacy makes of love; killing it sometimes, or changing it, if not into the slightly affectionate mutual contempt, and compromise, which is called 'getting on together all right,' at best into a calm acceptance of one another that seemed to us a poor travesty of the passion that must have preceded it, the dull echo in a dry shell of the splendour of breaking seas.

'Mrs. Keene is the only person I've met,' Cullum told me, 'whose married life seems to have been really happy.'

'Janet's husband died young!' I said. I had often wondered if it would always have been the same had Captain Keene lived.

'I recognize the necessity of holding two people together after inclination has ceased to do so,' said Cullum, 'for the good of the state which depends on the family, and the safety of children, and so on, but individually it is simply degrading that two people should stay together for social or economic reasons; for any reasons, in fact, when they don't even like each other any longer. That is enslaving Ariel to Caliban. It's horrible, however expedient.'

To the cleanness of our youth it seemed a particularly nasty form of prostitution, which no amount of blessing from any church could gloss over.

It must have been early May, because the bracken was just coming back to the common, when he said, 'It's only the unsatisfied sort of love that lasts, it seems. Love is always sentenced to death by its fulfilment.'

He was lying full length, face downwards, on the high open ground between North and South Holmwood, playing with the small green loops of the young bracken with his fine hands. I was sitting by him, and in the long silence that had passed before he spoke I had been wishing that he would not injure the shoots that were still bent double, by freeing the tight-curled, brown-powdered fronds from the clinging earth before their time. I knew that they only turned black and withered; unlike Janet, I did not believe in trying to help nature.

'I know,' I said, feeling my blood beginning to beat fast. 'And I wonder if it's worth it – the fulfilment? No summer is ever quite as glorious as the spring makes you expect, and people like my father say that life never comes up to its early promises; even in little things it's the same, no coffee tastes quite as delicious as it smells when it's being ground, does it?

I've sometimes thought that love – somehow I don't believe fulfilment could be –'

It was difficult to find the right words.

'Consummation couldn't fulfil the glory of desire?'

I nodded, hot under his eyes. 'Not for me.'

He sat up, looking at me intently. 'Nor for me. Not for any artist!'

I dropped my eyes involuntarily, feeling little burning sensations tingling through me.

'Girl,' said the voice that I had come to love, 'I want you more than anything on earth! Do you want me?'

'Yes, Cullum.'

Did I want him! Many times, while I was with him and when I was alone, at nights, I had longed for him, almost faint for a second with the desire for his kisses, which I could only imagine. Love, feeding on itself, had grown greatly. Cullum obsessed me; all of me, mind and body.

I dared not look up; his hands were gripping my shoulders.

'Let's keep things as they are, and be the masters of love,' he said softly, and did not kiss me. 'It'll be very hard, but it will be worth doing, for then we'll hold love, always.'

Stirred beyond speech, I nodded again, agreeing with his wisdom and never doubting that our strength was equal to whatever we intended to do.

Walking home with him to tea I hardly saw that the earth all around us was wearing the bloom of the year's first possession. That is the worst of being a lover; in amazement at the incredible fact of the other person's existence one is blind to the beauty of the lovelier perennial things; and that spring would have been as strangely wonderful to me if the white mist of may blossom had not lain thicker on the hedges than in any year that I remembered.

Vallie, leaping up and down in a state of wild excitement, was waiting for us at home, waving a telegram from Mother.

'Esther, you're to take me over to Paris!' she shouted as soon as we were within ear-shot. 'As soon as ever you can, she says. Will that be to-morrow? She's sent heaps of money for the tickets. Oo, isn't it lovely?'

She seized one of Cullum's hands and one of mine, and swung them up and down.

I felt the ground grow solid and prosaic again under my feet. The magic of the afternoon was dispelled at once.

'When shall we go? To-morrow morning?' Vallie asked. 'What time shall we start? We can go to-morrow, can't we?'

'Oh, yes, I suppose so,' I said, 'I suppose we must.'

Mother always issued her invitations imperiously, and we kept ourselves ready for her sudden summonses.

'But, Esther, don't you want to go?' asked Vallie, surprised at my lack of enthusiasm.

'Yes, of course; only not just now. Oh, *damn!*'

Formerly, visits to Paris had been pleasure un-alloyed to me, but at that moment I hated being called to France when all my interest was centred round my English home, and Cullum. It seemed to me that together we had thrown a fragile bridge from earth, as I had always known it, to an unfamiliar place, full of unthinkable glamour – earth as he showed it to me. And resting on nothing solid, surely that bridge might crumble away before I returned if I left England now, interrupting the spell, since it was only built as a dream is, of intangible material.

Cullum's tragic look met mine.

'How long does this mean you'll be away?'

'Can't say. A fortnight, three weeks, a month – I dunno!'

'But need you go?'

'Oh, yes; there's no getting out of it.' I looked again at the telegram. ' "Esther to bring Valerie at once." '

It might have been a parting for years from the seriousness with which we both took it.

'I'll go now, because you'll want to pack,' he said.

Vallie was fussing round us, so we said good-bye as two normal people might have done, though both of us were keyed up to a fine pitch of nervous exaltation. Very little had passed between us that afternoon, but it seemed to us that something definite had happened.

I did not mention, before he left, the time of the train by which we should start in the morning; though there was only one good one, and while Vallie and I were travelling to London by it, I kept wishing that I had done so. There would be barely three quarters of an hour between the arrival of our train at Victoria and the departure of the Sunday boat train to Newhaven, but if he had known, I thought, perhaps he would have come all the same. In the circumstances, that was out of the question.

We steamed into Victoria, and he was waiting on the platform. He came up to us, his face lighting up with a rather shy smile, and explained that he had reckoned on this train being our best connection.

He gave me flowers, so much less sensible, so far more precious than the chocolates which the practical Gerald had provided. Vallie and I were very glad of the chocolates before the journey was over, but

118

Cullum's roses were in the way all the time until they were left behind accidentally at Dieppe. I had a real sense of loss when I found that they were gone; I loved their charming unsuitability; they were typically his gift.

In Paris I became again the light-hearted, careless individual that French environment always brought to the surface in me, and I enjoyed myself superficially to the extent of an enormously increased capacity for pleasure because, being with my French mother, I had become chiefly French again. The French preserve beyond childhood the child's ability to be happy out of all proportion to the cause, and probably this is partly why the English, as a race, disapprove of them. It is not so much their methods of extracting pleasure from life which offend the Anglo-Saxon since, less openly, he employs them himself, but he feels resentment against the Frenchman for obviously getting more enjoyment than he does out of doing the same things, and for doing them with much more zest.

In the first days of my visit I missed Cullum less than I had expected; the days were full of things in which he had no part. Every particularly interesting happening made me think of him for a moment, and wish that he could have been there to enjoy it too, so completing the pleasure of the minute; and when I was in bed my mind always turning to him, and I wondered what would happen when I went back to England. But there were hours when I did not think of him at all.

I had that good time which my father had wished me, when we started, in a manner which showed that he had little confidence in the wish being fulfilled.

He and my mother were on terms of benevolent indifference. She had left him seven years ago, and love, worn out, had not even bequeathed them animosity in dying.

My mother's history was one that could only have belonged to a Frenchwoman. She had been extremely pretty as a girl, and at eighteen she had been married, not against her will but without much say in the matter, to an amiable and rising young solicitor from Marseilles, with whom she had hardly spent five minutes alone before the marriage. She lived with him contentedly for several years, until she met my father, who must have been an exceptionally handsome man in his younger days, and they fell wildly in love with one another. My mother was a French protestant, and her first husband, though a Catholic, was a slack one, who recognized the necessity for divorce. They had several arguments over her unfortunate preference for another man, which, he conceded with French commonsense, was a matter over which she had no control, and for which no blame attached to her. Then, in order that there might be no slur on her name, they came to London, and he went away to an hotel and gave her cause for divorcing him, with his usual amiability.

A respectable time elapsed before she married my father, who retired from the army soon afterwards because, in those uncharitable days, Mother was not well received by military society in the small garrison town where he was stationed. Leaving his regiment seemed, at the time, a small price to pay for marrying her, and they had a short period of ardent happiness together.

At the end of five years, Olive and I were all that remained to them as evidence that their consuming passion had ever existed. Born in the year of their first possession of each other, while Father was still the ardent lover, I was altogether his child, as Olive was Mother's; she came four years later, when the woman's interest in the man had waned, and was centred on herself as the expectant mother. Olive was so like her in every way that she irritated Father by her unreasonableness and excitability. Because Vallie was afraid of his dourness, and Olive could not get on with him, I tried to show myself more in sympathy with that lonely man than I really felt. At least we shared the love of horses; Mother and he had hardly an idea in common when desire had gone.

Like a violent tide receding, love left them suddenly stranded on the barren shore of their dissimilarity of taste. My mother liked music and town life; Father's inclination, as well as his hobby, tied them to the country, where they lived for two more years, in an atmosphere of daily irritation over trifles. The coming of Vallie, resented by both of them, finally broke their strained mutual endurance. The last strand snapped, as usual, over a small thing. My father wanted the child called Muriel, after his sister, whom Mother loathed, and Mother, too nervy to differ persuasively, made a flung challenge of her natural determination to have her third child, at any rate, called by a French name. With the surreptitiously baptized Valérie she went back to her own people in Marseilles as soon as she could travel.

Three years later, Vallie was sent back to us; Henri, the solicitor, as amiable as before and only a little stouter, had written and suggested that she should rejoin him. After all, he pointed out, they had both outgrown the instabilities of their youth by this time, and they had always suited one another well. He missed her very much, and was still quite devoted to her. Altogether, why not? The arrangement seemed particularly convenient as my mother, being highly sexed and therefore very religious in the intervals of passion, had come over to his faith, which she embraced with more fervour than he had ever shown, and consequently they could both disregard her divorce and second marriage. The marriage with my father was annulled and she rejoined Henri in Marseilles. Later they moved to Paris; the city pleased them both, and there no one knew much about their former affairs. They went through the civil marriage again. So, having suffered a 'mariage de convenance,' broken away from it and been disappointed in her own choice, Mother returned of her own free will to the man whom her parents had selected for her.

In order to sever herself from the past as completely as possible, she refused on principle to understand a word of English, which she knew well, and would not even speak it with Olive, Vallie and me, her only links with the other life, when we came to visit her in turns.

I asked her jokingly one evening, while I was brushing her beautiful dark hair, whether she considered us legitimate or not, since she did not now recognize her marriage to my father. The question shocked her. Mother had a strong, though flexible, sense of morality, and she had always had the law on her side to uphold her respectability.

'But naturally!' she said, 'since I was not Catholic at the time and the marriage with your father was accomplished in England, where divorce is permissible.'

'Ah, but that only applies to England, then. The question is, what are we when we come to France or stay in any Catholic country, where your second marriage wouldn't hold good?'

'*Mon Dieu!* Esther, you should have been the daughter

of Henri, with the taste for legal nastiness that it seems you have!'

'Niceties, dear!' I corrected in English. 'I think it's a charming notion to have one's legitimacy altering with the frontiers and with the religion of the inhabitants of any country we visit. I wonder what we should be considered in Switzerland, for instance, where they are half and half, Catholic and Protestant? I believe there are more Catholics than Protestants, so I suppose we should be two-thirds illegitimate!'

'*Je ne comprends pas ce que tu dis*,' she said stiffiy. 'And in any case, everyone here imagines that you are children by a former marriage, one which was unfortunate and so not to be mentioned.' This was the main issue of the case, to her.

'Well, so we are.'

'Yes, yes; but of course I convey that it was a marriage without any – '

'*Arrière pensée*,' I suggested.

'Exactly, *chérie*. In effect, before I met *mon brave Henri*. Decidedly I am sorry for my mistake, the good God knows that no one could be more so, but there is nothing in it for me to be ashamed of; only it would be so complicated for people to understand. They are so stupid. That is why I do not ever explain.'

Somehow she had managed to reconcile herself with her conscience, the more easily because of the survival of her reputation, by which she set great store. It is possible that in exceptional circumstances the facts of her life might have been those of an English-woman's, but no one except a Frenchwoman could have preserved, through all that she had undergone, that air of well-shielded propriety which made it seem absurd to connect her name with anything irregular. Mother, at forty-three, had an expression that was

123

almost virginal; strangers found her unapproachable. Her august manner could have sprung from nothing but genuine self-respect. On the vagaries of the rest of the world she turned a forgiving but uncomprehending eye. Few are so intensely respectable in later life as the woman who at one time nearly missed respectability altogether.

Her first and last husband, Henri, was short and fat and rapidly going bald, but he made up for the diminishing of the hair on his head by crowding as much as possible on his face. Each time I came over to Paris, his eyebrows looked thicker, and his great semi-circular moustache more luxuriant. The foreign male upper lip is much more fertile than the Englishman's; I disliked this lush growth and dreaded the inevitable kisses when I arrived and left his house. Henri embraced openly all the women whom he had a shadow of excuse to salute in public, and kissed in private as many of the others as would allow it. To my mother, who remained curiously unaware of his frequent infidelities, his marked attention to every woman she brought to the house was only another manifestation of his invariable amiability, the quality in him which she most esteemed. The finest proof of it, in her opinion, was the obliging way in which the dear man, desolated, as he said, but quite resigned, had gone away with someone else so that she might free herself without scandal. Knowing her husband as a philanderer better than she did, I imagined the piquancy of being fortified in an intrigue by the gratitude and approval of his lawful wife must have taken the edge off the first keenness of his sorrow.

His attitude to me, his wife's child by another man, was extraordinarily affectionate. He even persevered valiantly with a one-sided flirtation with me, in the

face of unaltering opposition, and regretted that he
and Mother had no little girls of their own like me.

'Well, you can't expect everything,' I said in English,
which he liked to practise when we were alone, 'you
two have money, and rich people very often have no
children. Capital doesn't go with Labour!'

He was enchanted by this idea.

'Assuredly, Esther, you are not half English! That
is impossible for one who has such charming thoughts.
Though I give you that at times you do show a trace
of being English. This little dottiness of letting unsuitable air into the house, for example! Air, of course,
is good, but one must treat it like a food and have
enough, but too much is bad; it must be fresh, certainly, but not crude and raw. But I have noticed
that the Britisher distrusts comfort. He will not have
it. To hear him, you would think great comfort was
dangerous for his soul! Warmth is comfort, and so
he talks of cold baths in winter – oh, my God! – and
he takes long walks. Good food, too; that is also comfortable, and so, see, his cooking is the worst that can
be found! Love! Ah! – Henri rubbed his plump hands
and turned his eyes upwards – 'that is the supreme
comfort, and so to make it possible for himself and his
wife to have it with self-approval he calls it a sacred
trust, a participation in the great art of creation, his
"duty" to his wife, or the State! Yes, I *have* heard an
Englishman call it all these things! But in France
we say that it is a supreme pleasure, and so does not
need that one should justify it at all! Always the
Englishman must excuse himself whatever he does. If
he does a kind act he excuses himself for it; he gives a
penny to a beggar-child and says, as if it is a crime,
"Oh, I only do that because I have too many pennies
in my pocket." '

125

The whole household was concerned over my appearance. The maid who attended on me, a luxury unknown to me elsewhere, politely lamented the disappearance of the beautiful complexion which no doubt I had inherited from Madame, though it was now buried under all that disfiguring sunburn. *Quel horreur!* the brown terminated itself so abruptly, too! If only it had stopped at the chin, or the shoulders, or even the waist, Mademoiselle in evening dress might still have been presentable, with a little care. But halfway down Mademoiselle's neck! And she with such a long neck too! Mother wondered aloud how she had ever produced such an unbecomingly lanky child, and Henri bemoaned my enormous appetite, which was not at all suitable for a young girl. It was not, he explained, that they grudged the food; they would have been only too happy to see me eat more, had that seemed humanly possible, if I had shown that it was not wasted, but no; I had nothing to show for it, except sinew in unnecessary places.

'In England, I am supposed to have quite a decent figure,' I submitted meekly.

'But how can that be,' argued Henri, spreading his hands fan-wise, 'since the figure is not there? Nothing but meagre curves where a certain generosity is so becoming in a woman? Decent? *Ma foi!* yes! By all means, "decent"; there is nothing indelicate in a good skeleton, and one can see by your collar bones that you have that.'

Vallie's round green eyes had been roving from one to the other with a puzzled expression. Her face cleared, and her deep and husky voice broke in, suggesting: 'Perhaps Esther has a worm inside her, like dogs have, and it eats up all the food!'

The theory appealed to her as explaining everything, and she enlarged on it seriously until Mother made her stop because Henri was getting a pain in his side from laughing. Mother had developed a great fondness for Vallie, her unwanted third baby; though Olive, who was French in her ways, remained her favourite. I was too like my father to please her now, but she was very kind to me while I was in France, taking me to the opera, and to several dances, and driving with me about the enchanted streets of Paris.

The intoxicating wind that blows round the boulevards blew irresponsible content into me. I was perfectly happy until Cullum's first letter arrived, when I had been a week in France.

I picked it up from the hall table when I came in alone one morning, and stood for some time holding it, wondering if this large, square writing were his; and then I went upstairs very slowly, to my room, and took off my outdoor things and put them away, contrary to habit, before I opened it, eagerly and yet almost reluctantly, because I knew that it would disturb me.

'Esther, come back!' he wrote. 'I didn't realize that all this last month or two – I don't know exactly when it started – I'd been looking at the world through the rose-coloured spectacles that you must have lent me. They're gone, with you, and the whole world's plain and grey, and most of the people I meet have grey minds and grey faces, only that I don't see them much, even when I'm looking at them. All I see when I'm sitting alone, supposed to be working for this unbearably grey firm, are the slim, hungry lines of your lovely body, when you sat near me on the grass last Saturday, and I ought to have kissed you. Why didn't I! What do theories matter when someone like you is within reach!

'The memory keeps coming between me and the things I should be doing, and I get savage over it, half with the want of you, half with myself for being such a fool, such an astonishing fool, girl! I have the unsatisfied love I've longed for and dreamed of, the never-lessening hunger that I thought would make the ideal spur for my work, and now I can't work!

'In my mind there is nothing worth writing about now, except the beautiful and most confusing lines of the narrow brown-red lips in your dear, brown face. And I might have kissed you! When I looked at you, you couldn't keep your eyes on mine; you were trembling, did you know that? I was close enough to feel it; you, a wild thing from the woods, were mastered, were mine for the moment, afraid of me, and I let you go, because I am still as afraid of great love as I believe you are. Between us we possess this thing, which the whole world yearns for. One day I shall be sole owner of it, for you, and all you have and are, will belong to me in spirit.

'How you have drawn the radiance out of everything I used to love! There's no intrinsic worth now in any beautiful thing I see; it is nothing but a background for my imaginings of you. Rotton poor imaginings, Esther – one doesn't need to call you "darling" or to use any of the ordinary endearments, the sound of your name is a caress in itself – because they only have your likeness, not your glory. I can't recall now just where your glory lies; only I know that it is there.

'You will think I'm mad, writing to you like this, and you'll be right; I am mad; all lovers are mad. And I don't think that, having caused this madness, you can cure it; and thank God, I don't believe you want to! No, not "thank God." Love's a pagan thing, a gorgeous, brutal thing, as you'll find when you come back to England. The first time that you dare let me see you alone, my woman, I am going to kiss that lovely mouth of yours as I don't think it has been kissed before.

'I still believe that love, to live, must remain unsatisfied, but it must be fed, and I am starving for the sight and touch of you. When are you coming back to me?

'I love you, Esther,

'CULLUM.'

I had always loved Paris, but after his letter arrived, the happy city became merely a place of waiting, where I had to stay for another week, counting the days, not wanting them to pass too quickly, because they were filled with such glorious impatience. The instinct to delay the coming of anything for which I longed ardently was even stronger in me than it had been in the days long gone by when, if I was given an apple, I used to polish it and put it down, and not look at it for a few moments, enjoying the thought that the whole pleasure of having it was still to come. But I knew more or less how the apple would taste; the taste of this strange rich fruit, love, I did not know.

I cannot remember how I answered Cullum, but his next letter arrived the evening before I was to take Vallie back to England.

'My dear, do you mean this?' ran part of it, 'I know you do, and yet I daren't let myself believe it. Your incredible, adorable letter came by the last post yesterday and as I read it I realized the absolute impossibility of behaving like a rational being before my family for the rest of the evening, and of talking about humanity in general, which seemed engrossing yesterday, with my cynical father. It's all so trivial now before the colossal fact that You and I are We,

129

because we love. You love me. My God! I felt that the only hope of not going raving mad lay in violent exercise. So I ran. I ran all through Knightsbridge, across Hyde Park, and for miles along the Bayswater Road. People stared at me, and I knew that they were saying, "Ah, he's evidently in love with Esther Sieveking." They'd know, you see, because, quite obviously, loving any other woman would be inadequate to account for my condition.

'I walked home solemnly winking at every star that I caught solemnly winking at me. . . .'

For hours I did not sleep after I went to bed, the last night in France. Cullum was too vividly before my eyes. I thought of the way his red-brown hair grew down in a little peak at the nape of his neck; his nicely shaped head looked very boyish from back view because of that piece of hair. There were his fine hands and the intense blue of his eyes to remember, and the way his head jerked back before his tremendous laughter, showing the soft skin of the throat. One does not love people at first for what they are, but for little details of appearance, and mannerisms that are peculiar to them; even Cullum's occasional, unconscious show of conceit was delightful to me, in memory.

I thought of kissing his mouth, until the knowledge that I should do so soon brought me actual physical discomfort, from a queer kind of apprehension. I wished that I might have a few more days of waiting, in Paris, because suspense seemed better than being faced with the fullness of the time.

We went home early in June. I slept late the morning after we arrived, and before I was up Mrs. Barrie called through the door that 'the young gentleman' wanted to see me.

For years 'the young gentleman' had meant Gerald Hemingway; I was not expecting Cullum until Saturday; this was Thursday, so I called back:

'Tell him I'm not dressed yet. Ask him to come round later.'

'I did say you wasn't up, Miss, and Mr. Hayes said he'd wait.'

'Mr. Hayes! Oh, tell him I'll be down in a minute.'

When I was ready I hesitated for a few seconds outside the drawing-room door, afraid to open it, and longing to go in.

Cullum did not move from where he was standing when I entered, and so I had to go right across the room to him, and we faced each other, finding no adequate words, while the first shyness of love grew between us. He made a slight movement towards me, and then drew back.

'My dear!' he said, 'I'm somehow afraid to touch you, here. There is the atmosphere of too many other people in this room; I want you alone, out of doors. Let's go. Anywhere. The Redlands.'

'In this drizzle – is it raining? I didn't notice.'

We went across the common, waist high in wet bracken, between clumps of golden gorse, and both of us, I think, forgot that it was raining, though we spoke only of everyday matters.

I asked him how he had managed to come to me on a week-day, and he told me, with pride in his own cleverness, that for two days beforehand he had complained in the office of the recurrence of old pain in one ankle, the result of a dislocation of bone when he was at school which had never been properly attended to. He had gone about his work with an air of forced cheerfulness, minimizing the trouble, between uncontrollable winces. The previous day he had suggested to his Editor that as he had to see his doctor about it at eleven-thirty, it was hardly worth his coming in the morning, and anyway, could he have the day off if anything had to be done immediately? Naturally, he was given it.

'But is there anything wrong with your ankle?' I said. The story, with full details, sounded convincing as he told it, but he had never mentioned this before.

'No, but how could I have worked to-day, when you were in England again?'

It passed from my mind at once that he had won us this day together by lying; though dishonesty was then an almost unforgivable sin in my eyes. It was too wonderful to be with him again for anything else to matter.

'Somehow I don't want to make love to you in rooms,' he said, after we had turned off the main track and were climbing the steepest part of the hill. In the Redlands heights, half a mile above Folly Farm, there is a clearing, and the trees that surrounded it frame a view of half Surrey, and Sussex to the limit of the higher, far-off South Downs.

Cullum stopped there and turned to me.

'Come here!'

I hesitated and he held out his arms to me.

'Come here, Esther!'

I went to him and we kissed; I had not known that a kiss could mean so much, and afterwards I buried my face in the damp shoulder of his coat, to escape his eyes.

'Oh, girl, there are raindrops shining like a crown in your hair!' he said inconsequently, passing his hands over my bare head. He turned my face up to his with one hand under my chin. All the surging life in me seemed to meet at my lips, and join his, leaving me an empty shell in his arms. Cullum, whom I loved, was no longer a man to me, but Love incarnate, and I was conscious of no feeling save the touch of his hands, and his mouth.

'This is the place in which I have often dreamed of you,' he told me.

Chapter 8: *The Flaw*

THE days when we were not together ceased to count. Absent in spirit, I drifted through them towards the intense emotional reality of the week-ends. Gerald Hemingway came and went; I rode with him sometimes to pass the time, and the Scottish lad turned up every few days, and was touchingly grateful for my strictures on brown shoes with striped trousers, and for his initiation into the curious English reticence about money, from which most of his race are immune. Probably the legend of Caledonian meanness grew up through the clumsiness with which Scots mismanage their generosity. They are not careless with their money, but they are as free-handed as most people once they are convinced of the worthiness of the call on their pocket; only they cannot give gracefully. The Frenchman pays for a woman's railway ticket as though her acceptance of this small tribute had crowned his day with pleasure, but the Englishman does it furtively. He mumbles, 'How much?' if the woman is within earshot of the ticket-office, and he covers the coins with his hand when he pays, as though they were obscene. A Scot, with no sense of money-shame and a keen sense of the value of money, is capable of remarking on the exorbitant price of railway fares on the way to the station, and reckoning out what the ticket will cost, in order to have his small change ready. If the woman is not of his own sensible race she feels moved to insist on paying for it herself, and looking back on the incident she blames the man for not having managed it better. The Englishman and Frenchman may also wonder beforehand what the price will be, but they do not wonder aloud.

Carlisle McDonald took me about in his small car in return for my social bullying, and I taught him, when we had tea out, not to let me see the bill. I had begun to like his downrightness, and the remarkable simplicity of his shrewd, sound mind. But none of these things really mattered, because Cullum was not with me. Nothing counted unless Cullum was there.

Saturday was the crown of the week, the pinnacle to which the other days were the successive steps. When it was very hot we spent it lazing about the garden or on the cuckoo-haunted common, but more often we went expeditions on Cullum's much-enduring motor-bicycle Zoroaster, which he had bought third-hand from a friend, as a battered piece of wreckage after an accident. He had tinkered it up marvellously, being an inspired but erratic mechanic, and it certainly went, with him, which it would have done with few other people, but it constantly shed parts of itself by the way, when we were far from home. Cullum always succeeded in coaxing it back into working order; I could give no active assistance, being too wedded to horses to be capable of a sympathetic understanding of engines, but I could supply hairpins admiringly. By the end of June it seemed to me that Zoroaster must be largely held together by my hairpins.

The recklessness of Cullum's driving, which nothing I said could moderate, made every excursion a desperate adventure. He had a passion for breaking his

135

own time records between the various little Surrey towns, which all show such a strong family resemblance: Guildford, Godalming, Reigate and Redhill – groups of beetle-browed houses straggling along each side of one main street which widens in the centre of the place, where it divides round a monument or Town Hall. Between the towns lie the folds of Surrey's mantle of stately trees, in sheltered valley and softly curving hill; but Cullum was consumed by speed lust, and we hardly saw the country, except when we stopped for picnic meals.

This was my part of the land, and the sense of possession was strong in me; not the sense of owning but of being owned; I belonged to it. Every particle of Surrey's varied soil – chalk, clay, sand, and the light brown loam – had a claim on something in me. Is there anywhere a more gracious ground, and where else do trim holly-hedges attain such height and thickness with age? The six-foot wide walls of holly reached nearly twenty feet in height at the end of our drive; I was particularly fond of them because I had once been bucked off on to the top of one by an Australian horse of Father's, and the hedge held me, saving me from any damage except scratches.

Into my new love for Cullum was absorbed my worship of former gods; this little part of earth and the good things that grew from it; books, ideas; the beauty of easy movement and young strength carelessly displayed.

'Help me, instead of watching me with that cat-with-a-mouse expression!' Cullum exclaimed aggrievedly one day, while he was trying to lift Zoroaster over a ditch into the concealment of a clump of bushes, where we wanted to leave it for a while. I went to him at once, but, like violent movement arrested in bronze by a sculptor, there remained in my brain the indelible impression of that second: Cullum as I saw him then; the interplay of strong, controlled muscles seen through the thin shirt and breeches, as the wind moulded the light material on his vigorous body, finely unconscious in its pose; and the sunlight streaming over back-flung head, taut flank and straining shoulder. Two memories of Cullum stand out in relief from my other memories of him. Both are sunlit. This is one of them.

'I'm so amazingly happy that I feel something is bound to happen soon to spoil it,' I said, a little while later, lying with my head on his arm by the side of Mag's Well, up Coldharbour way, when he had bathed my eyes in the dank water to make them beautiful, according to the old tradition of the well. 'This is already much more than any mortal's fair share of happiness and things always seem to be evened out pretty well in this life in the end. One pays for one's good times with lean ones. *"Plaisir d'amour ne dure qu'un moment: chagrin d'amour dure toute la vie."* '

His fingers ran through my hair, playing with the strands that the wind had whipped loose.

'Nothing is coming to spoil this, except, eventually, old age. I promise you that. I've not had to pay in kind for any of the pleasure I've had, and I never shall. That's very clearly marked in my horoscope. I am supposed to die young, and so escape the law of compensation. I should like to have your horoscope cast; it's interesting. So far, all that mine has indicated has come true.'

'Your family goes in for horoscopes and suppressed complexes and egos, don't they?' I said. 'Don't you yourself think that all that sort of thing is rather rot? Mrs. Cole talked a lot about her ego – I'm sure it's cracked. I should think most egos are. She should take a little salt with it and boil it; that's the proper thing to do with cracked eggs, and I expect it would be ideal for egos too.'

He pulled a piece of my hair viciously, and I yowled like a cat until he let go.

'You intolerant child! Why will you condemn things that you don't understand, just as the whole stupid world does?'

It was the old subject on which we often had little disagreements. To distract his mind from it I turned on my elbow, leaning over the beloved face and brushing it with my lips, playing with it as a butterfly plays with a flower. When I hovered over his mouth he closed his eyes; but I drew back, my senses swimming. His arms wound round my shoulders and waist, forcing my body against his and my head down.

'Kiss me! Kiss me, Esther, you devil!'

I settled lightly on his mouth and rested there for a moment without moving, and then the still contact changed into hungry, lovers' kisses.

We were both breathless with emotion when we let go of one another and lay still; I with my head still on his arm, holding the hand that lay on my shoulder. Cuckoos were answering each other all round us, breaking one another's intervals with their calls. One sang nearer and nearer, and came to the tree above us, calling with his head and tail jerking up towards each other at every cry, in the odd manner of cuckoos. He was so close to us that we could hear clearly the four or five very soft rising notes that sometimes fill in the time between the louder calls. He flew away when Cullum spoke.

'Promise me that you'll try to make allowances when I fall below your unyielding standards!'

138

'You!' I said, smiling at the idea. 'I don't pray generally, but there was a feeling of something so big and benign in the garden when I was out there late, yesterday evening, that I did pray, vaguely, to be worth you!'

'Oh, don't, Esther; that hurts!' he said, and turned his face away.

We fell into long drowsy silences.

'This is the most wonderful love that a man could have,' he said after a pause. 'You feed my soul with beauty, keeping my flesh hungry.' Said by anyone else, that would have sounded stilted; from Cullum it came naturally; he was simply thinking aloud, and not altogether of me, I knew, at such times. The writer's mind was playing with ideas and noting them for future use. 'If you gave yourself to me you'd be robbing me of something precious, of that hunger. I want to see you always clad in the double glory of your own loveliness and my want of you. If I knew you more intimately, you would still be as beautiful, but I should be too close to you to see it. In both of us, if we were always together, insignificant little traits which aren't really an integral part of us would come to the fore and hide us from each other. That's what happens in most intimate friendships. If we were married I suppose that after a time the adventurousness of your mind, the way it leaps to meet mine at any new idea, your humour, too, would be less important than the trivial fact that you're hopelessly untidy, for example, and I'm naturally orderly in mind. Funnily enough, the things I love most in you are qualities that wouldn't make us happy in everyday life; it was your straightness, rather a hard kind of straightness, which attracted me from the first —'

I looked at him uncomprehendingly. One did not

139

love anyone for being straight, I thought, any more than one loved them for having baths. One took that sort of thing for granted.

'Your idealism which has no use for the second best; I love it, but it means that if you can't reach what you've set your heart on, you won't compromise with the next most satisfactory thing; it's all or nothing with you; but when two people of strong temperaments come together they must compromise continually, unless one sinks his or her individuality completely in the other. And I love your clear, sharp mind which has absolutely no subtlety in it; talking to you is like looking down into deep but perfectly clear water; it sometimes seems shallower than it is because it's so transparent. And I must have subtlety in the people I am with continually; I don't like it, but it's a mental stimulant that I need.'

I resented this charge of lacking subtlety. We argued over it until Cullum suddenly broke off in the middle of the discussion with one of his lightning changes of mood, saying:

'Oh, before I forget, I must tell you my latest poem, which I wrote in the bath this morning. It mightn't be considered strictly "nice" by some people, but then you, being perfectly natural, make everything "nice," as a child's mind does.'

He rattled off:

'Travellers on the Continent
Who feel a certain discontent
Because the French show lack of vision
In railway sanit'ry provision –
Remember, as the poet says,
"Kind hearts are more than *cabinets*." '

140

'I got the information about the scarcity from a friend just back from France,' he said, when I had appreciated it.

'You haven't been to France yourself?'

'I've never been out of England,' he said.

I sat up and stared at him.

'But the trip you told us about, the sea-lawyer, the Faro islands; seals, and all that?'

'Oh, my dear,' he said and laughed, 'you didn't take that seriously, did you? I was romancing to amuse Olive – having a sort of author's practise.'

I was dumbfounded. I did not know how to take this; I had had no experience of people like Cullum.

'I never thought you were being taken in too. Doesn't that prove what I was saying about your mind, you dear thing?'

'I suppose so,' I said slowly. Looking back I could not remember whether he had given any indication that he was only excercising his imagination, or not. It seemed to me that he had not.

'Don't frown, sweetheart. Really, you ought to have seen through that!'

He was annoyed for the moment that I did not enter into the spirit of the joke. It worried me at the time, but it was soon forgotten; for the afternoon was glorious.

'Look here,' he said, 'I dislike your being wasted down here all the week among teeming hordes of objectionable young men.'

'The teeming hordes consist of two – Hemingway and McDonald, whom you've met, and neither of them is objectionable!'

'Oh, well, there seems to be dozens, to me. One's always coming or going when I arrive or leave, and we snarl and gibber at each other in the hall. Only mentally, of course. Actually we say 'Hello!' and exchange banalities. But anyway, I wish you could come to London more often. For one thing you must be presented to the Table. Three of us always lunch together at the Marlborough Restaurant in Fleet Street; Raymond Cole, who is amusing when he's away from his home circle – he goes in for being aesthetic – and an exceedingly brilliant chap, "Ropes," R. O. Pace, studying medicine. Between one o'clock and two, every day, we pull the world to pieces, seeing, of course, exactly, what is wrong with it. Ropes has heard rumours of you, started by Raymond, and he says you must be produced for inspection; I want them to see what I've found. I know a man in the Cameron Press, which is just across the way from us; they produce hundreds of cheap periodicals and he said they had vacancies in their staffs. You'd like a job in a publishing house, where you'd have a chance of writing for the firm's productions, wouldn't you?'

'Oh, Cullum, I'd love it! Do see what you can do!'

Because I knew little of its meanings, the word 'Journalism' was written in letters of gold, instead of in slabs of bread and butter, across my imagination.

'All right. It will be something very small to begin with. I was talking over the possibility of it with Janet the other day.'

'I didn't know you'd seen her?'

'She wrote some time ago and asked me to look in any Wednesday or Thursday I liked, and I sometimes do. It's a relief to be able to talk of you, to someone who's fond of you too. She agreed that working in a crowd of all sorts and conditions of people, like the Cameronians, would be an excellent experience for you. Unfortunately we're over-staffed already on my paper, or I'd get you in there.'

I knew that Cullum was in a junior position because he was often nearly as short of money as I was, but he always spoke grandiloquently of his employers' immense regard for him. From his conversation one gathered that only the Editor's haunting dread that one day Cullum might leave the paper tempered his joy in that young man's co-operation. It was simply his way of expressing himself, and if I laughed at him for it, he laughed too. His readiness to see a joke against himself was one of his nicest traits. But he was an invincible optimist; every week, according to himself, he was on the point of securing either a valuable first edition, dirt cheap; or buying at par, through a friend in the inner ring of Finance, shares that would be paying twenty per cent. next year, though Throgmorton Street was not yet on to it. Any friend of his who was connected with wireless or patent paving, positively *was* Wireless, or was famed internationally as the Man Behind Paving. And in his reports they, like himself, were always just about to achieve something startling. He had a marvellous enthusiasm for life, and the failure of one hope never shook his confidence in the next. Cullum liked liking things, which was the reason why so many people liked him.

Because he believed in each future windfall implicitly when he told me of it, he generally made me believe too, but I was so eager to be a journalist, working in Town, that I doubted the possibility of realizing the dream. In this I was wrong, as it turned out. For once, Cullum's scheme bore fruit.

I received a telegram from him one morning in the following week, telling me to take the first train to Town and ask at the Cameron Press for a Miss Leslie.

Painfully nervous, I was interviewed by this kindly, wizened Scotswoman.

'You look very young; are you turned nineteen yet?'

'Oh, dear, yes,' I said, intimating by my manner that I had been nineteen for years.

'Have you typewriting?'

'No, I'm afraid –'

'Shorthand?'

'Yes, a little.'

I knew the rudiments of it, but it still took me much longer than long-hand.

'Mmm! I wanted someone who knew it well.'

'I can take down letters at ordinary talking speed,' I said. As a child I had had an abnormal memory for words, which I was then only beginning to lose. I could still repeat word for word, like a parrot, about half a page of a novel immediately after it was read aloud to me, and a great deal more if I could take notes of one or two words in each sentence.

She asked if I had done any writing myself, and I told her of that one astonishing acceptance from the *Little Review*, which did not impress her at all.

'Och, that's not the sort of work that counts!' she said, as contemptuously as the Editor of the *Little Review* might have done of her productions; and my heart froze.

I was feeling certain of being turned down, when she said:

'Sieveking? Is that not a North-country name?'

Far back it was a Scandinavian name, and the slight trace of Scottish blood in the family came only from inter-marriage and settlement in Scotland, but I had a sudden gleam of intelligence, and did not explain. For the first time the clannishness of the Scots appeared to me as a shining virtue.

I remembered that my father was born in Scotland, and told her so.

Her manner changed its impatient efficiency for personal interest.

'Was he now! From what part does he come?'

I told her. By good luck it happened to be her own locality, and I was given a job at a salary of two guineas a week. Later I learnt without surprise that a large majority of the people in the Cameron Press were at least partly Scottish, and so are quite half the inmates of Fleet Street.

After the interview I wandered about the neighbouring streets, lost in beatitude, until Cullum was free, and then together we rushed off to Janet. She hugged us both, and was properly delighted, promising to find a lodging for me at once, as the job started on the following Monday.

Mrs. Barrie was the first person I saw at home.

'Most gorgeous news!' I said.

'There! I knoo it would 'appen! I was only saying so to Mr. Barrie last night.'

'No, you weren't,' I said, 'because you don't know what it is now.'

'I think I do, Miss Esther! And shan't we all be pleased. Such a nice young gentleman. You're engaged to Mr. Hayes, now aren't you, dearie?'

'No, heavens, no! Much more exciting than that. I've got a job in Town in a publishing firm, and I start on Monday, and I'm going to be a journalist!'

I seized her by her two fat hands, and spun her round.

'Miss Esther, Miss Esther, don't! You'll make me fall. Oh, Miss Esther, stop! Well, I'm pleased if you are,' she panted, 'though I mus' say I 'oped for something different. Oh my! You 'ave 'urt my bad leg, dearie!'

'I'm so sorry,' I said, sympathetic because I was happy, 'I forgot all about it. What really is the matter with it?'

'I don't know, Miss. But the pains I get! Something chronic. And they come sudden, just like that, as you might say!'

'Well, why don't you get the doctor to look at it when he comes to-morrow to Miss Olive?'

Olive, with tonsilitis, was quite certain that she was dying. Olive was almost certain that she was dying whenever she had a severe cold.

Mrs. Barrie drew herself up and looked at me, over her enormous chest, as if I had insulted her.

'They'd 'ave to give me chloriform, Miss, before I let anyone but Mr. Barrie look at my legs!' she said superbly, and became even more dignified when I laughed and suggested that if she ever married again, it would have to be an anaesthetist.

My family took the great news quietly. Father, thinking that I should be in Janet's care, agreed that it was a good start. Then the gloomy side of the arrangement struck him.

'Shall have to get a boy to help Moon in the stables,' he said. 'More expense. Probably drink, too.'

'Why should he drink?'

'Ah, they do,' said Father vaguely, not to be deprived of the comfort of his forebodings. 'Or have heavy hands,' he added as the only conceivable alternative.

Gerald made a valiant pretence of sharing my enthusiasm when I told him I was going to London, coming back only in the week-ends. I squeezed his arm gratefully, and the gaiety went out of his face.

'It's going to be damnable to think of you in Town,' he said moodily, 'continually with that literary chap, Hayes, I suppose. You can't understand what a fool jealousy makes of a man, and what hell it is too.'

'No. I've never had to go through it, you see. Poor Gerald! I don't think I could know that sort of jealousy, I've got too much colossal and unwarranted pride, pride of the arrogant sort that makes one feel "Oh, if you prefer someone else to me, have 'em and be damned to you! You're not worth bothering about!" The very proud and the very humble are both immune from jealousy, for different reasons, but you've got a decent nature and are midway between the two, that's what's the matter with you!'

'Perhaps!' he said. 'Well, my dear, I know this isn't Tuesday, but I claim a "special permit" to-night as I shan't be able to pester you on future Tuesdays – ?'

Gerald, in spite of anything I could say, persisted in expressing his devotion, until half desperately and half as a joke I had forced him into an agreement not to mention love except on Tuesdays evenings, when he always had supper with us.

'Well, I suppose I can't stop you saying anything you want,' I said ungraciously, 'but it won't do any good.'

'No, you can't stop me!' he said. 'I shall go on offering you my irritating affection until you marry someone else, and then I expect I shall pester you to let me be your lover! I don't deserve you, but I do want you, Esther!'

It would not have occurred to Cullum, I thought, to consider whether he deserved anything he wanted, or not; he would have taken it for granted that he did.

Chapter 9: *The Cameron Press*

My work at the Cameron Press was exciting at first, because it was strange and varied. I was engaged as a 'junior,' under the sub-editress of the *Office Friend*, one of the group of four papers edited by Miss Leslie, the faded, elderly Scots-woman who had engaged me. They were written to appeal to the less educated class of office-girls and they had quite a big circulation. Their serials, their chief feature, generally dealt with a lonely typist who supported a little, coughing sister, and was pursued by many men, either her employers or members of that sinister body, the aristocracy. In the illustrations the rich young man about town, who was always the villain, had only two expressions, either he gloated, in the first part of the story, or looked baulked, towards the end. The heroine's innocence always baffled him; it would have baffled anything.

Badly printed on cheap paper, those productions of Miss Leslie's must have strained many of the eyes that read them, in ill-lit trains on the way home, and in bed after work, but they brought romance into drab lives. There was sound reasoning in the way Miss Leslie coached her authors; each reader must be made to feel that the dramatic troubles and final rewards of the heroine in *Her Secret Ordeal*, (or, *Alone in the Baronet's Bathroom* as I once called it and was snubbed by the sub-editress) might easily have happened to her had circumstances been only a very little different: they might happen yet. In the light of this possibility, every reader's own intrigues with the office boy or a fellow clerk were transformed from the prosaic affairs which they probably were, into romantic adventure, and their walks-out together, full of nudges and giggles and commonplace back-chat, became 'rambles, love-crowned, among the envious stars,' as the *Office Friend* put it. If the office boy proved fickle, the reader had the consolation of believing that hers ranked with the great tragedies of modern life, as reflected by her favourite literature. Something similar was sure to have happened to the heroine of the current serial, and though at the time the heroine, too, had thought that her heart was dead – 'crushed like a bud that has not yet bloomed,' the writer told them – it was all for the best in the end. Their letters, telling Friend Betty all about it, were sometimes printed in the column called 'Advice Corner,' with the real names suppressed and noms-de-plume substituted, such as 'Wistful Birmingham,' or 'Blue Eyes, of Eastbourne.' This was very consoling. The idea of confiding in an unknown sympathizer, who expressed her longing for confidences every week, attracted the type of girl who read Miss Leslie's papers, and thirty or more of these letters came in every day to the *Office Friend* alone.

I had to sort out each week a certain number of them that were interesting enough to print, and my selection was submitted to Miss Bullen, the sub-editress, for her final choice. When the letters needed answers by post I took down the replies, supposedly in shorthand, and Miss Leslie dictated to me all the correspondence connected with the four papers. After the first few days she found it saved time and trouble, and was quite as satisfactory, if she only gave me the gist of what she wanted said, and left me to write the letters, but to the end of my time at the Cameron Press Miss Bullen dictated every word of the simplest letters, unwilling to delegate the smallest part of her responsibility and authority. She was jealous of any trust bestowed on someone younger than herself.

My memory for words stood me in excellent stead, and I needed it. For the first few weeks it was a tremendous tax to remember, word for word, a large number of letters at a time, with only the essentials jotted down, and hanging over me was the fear of losing the job if the extent of my ignorance of shorthand were discovered. I knew enough of it to appear to be writing shorthand, if the squiggles I made were not examined too closely; most of them were abbreviated longhand words. My evenings were too taken up with other things for me to study shorthand in them. By the time that Miss Bullen found me out I was, luckily, too useful to be sacked.

Efficiency as a secretary was not my aim in life as it must have been Miss Leslie's when, twenty-five years before, she had held my post. In her case, it was efficiency, not for its own sake but for the good of the paper, that she set herself to attain. I gathered from what she told me that from the moment she joined the firm, her paper was to Miss Leslie as the hive is to the bee; loyalty to it was her ruling emotion; she would as cheerfully have worked herself to death for it. The acquisition of the three other papers in the group meant only an enlargement of her loyalty; the *Office Friend* was her favourite, the centre of her existence.

She was one of those countless middle-aged women whose youth has slipped away in conscientious work, without providing them with any absorbing interest outside the sphere into which they have drifted. They are the backbone of most big firms, because the work which they once did in order to live becomes at last their main reason for living. They devote all their energies to it. Both Miss Leslie and Miss Bullen wore habitually that fretful, anxious air which such women acquire, suggesting that they have mislaid something, but have forgotten what it is. I wondered if it was life. Miss Leslie, well over fifty, was already resigned to doing without whatever it was that she had lost, but the other, brisker, harder and ten years younger, was sometimes bitter, and always sharp when she noticed a lack of her own single-minded devotion to work in the younger people in the office. To her, the *Office Friend* was an achievement, an absorbing business proposition, a financial success which she had helped to build, and she was immensely proud of its circulation; but to Miss Leslie it meant more than that. Not only her mind but her heart was in it. Her papers were her children – she would have loved them had they failed.

I often heard her interviewing one of the authors who wrote our serials. In a business-like way the two would discuss the price per thousand words the total length, and work out together the 'curtains' at the end of each instalment. When the first instalment came in Miss Leslie would read it with as much pleasure as any of the girls to whom it was designed to appeal, and if she had stipulated that there must be pathos in it, there would be tears in her eyes when she handed it over to Miss Bullen.

'Beautiful work. So human!' she would say, blinking happily.

The human touch was not in Miss Bullen. She would skim through it with her thin eyebrows drawn and her pale lips invisible, nodding thoughtfully at every telling point, and would answer that it was good selling stuff, or, on the rare occasions when she differed from Miss Leslie, that in her opinion it would not be much of a draw.

Besides dealing with readers' letters, typing the office correspondence, keeping the files, index, manuscript and address books up to date, counting the words in each instalment of the serial and making tea in the afternoon and blank dummy copies of the paper each week, I did all the odd editorial jobs after a time, any reference work in the library, saw that the galley-proofs came up in time and cut and fitted them into the pages. I earned those two guineas a week.

The Cameron Press was called the nursery of Fleet Street. Its policy was to catch young people, work them as hard as possible on the minimum pay, and when they slacked off, finding that they were giving very much more than they were getting, to let them drift away to better paid positions, replacing them with fresh youngsters anxious to secure what training they could in the hard trade of journalism. Except in the case of heads and sub-heads of departments, like Miss Leslie and Miss Bullen, there was something wrong, a lack of ability or ambition, in everyone over thirty who was still in the Cameron Press.

I had a wonderful moment of proud excitement when I was told for the first time to write something for my paper. It was found in an hour of stress on press day that the instalment of the serial had not panned out as long as we had expected. There were three and a half inches blank at the bottom of the page.

'Miss Sieveking, run through the last column and find a place where you can put in two hundred words, and write them,' said Miss Leslie.

'I'll do it!' Miss Bullen said at once.

'No, she can,' said Miss Leslie firmly.

Glowing with pleasure, I found a piece where the heroine thought – 'I will go to him now, and explain all,' and then it said that 'Midway to her room she paused, and then mounted the marble staircase with firmer tread.'

I cut into the last sentence, after 'paused,' and for two hundred words, nearly all unfinished sentences ending with three dots, after the manner of famous novelists uncertain how to end the phrase, I held her hesitating at the foot of those marble stairs.

> 'No, she would not humble herself to him, and yet. . . . She tossed her head back with a defiant gesture. . . . What did it matter what she did? Who cared? Was she not an outcast, a nobody, friendless and alone, without a soul to mark her struggle between right and wrong? And yet! . . . Even he to whom she was going had said – Ah, the thought of his last words to her on that memorable occasion. . . . What was it he had said? She could not bear to think of it. . . .

(I could not remember what he had said myself, and there was no time to look it up.)

> 'He was wrong; he was unjust! There had never been any other man in her life. . . .'

I brought this in because the anatomical significance of the word 'life' in the *Office Friend* stories always interested me. 'There had been two men in her life,' or 'No man had ever entered her life,' we used to print, always meaning that she had had, or, in the second case, had not had, lovers.

This, I found, was only a hundred and three words done, and I had run dry. The printer's boy was already standing at my elbow waiting for the sets, and the idea of her trusting old mother came to my rescue. I gave her nearly a hundred words of heart-clutching memories of country roses and fowls and Mother, so poignant that it was all I could do to get her up the marble stairs at the end.

To the readers it was probably rather a dull passage, which they skipped in order to reach the meatier parts; to me it was an epoch-making composition, for it made me, I felt, a journalist. I was no longer a dabbler, as I had been when the *Little Review* accepted my verse. Now I had written something to order in a weekly journal received in thousands of homes. It seemed to me that this was a far, far better thing . . .!

I told Cullum about it jubilantly when we met for lunch. He laughed unsympathetically, having filled space on a much bigger paper for two years. That day he was full of a note he had just received from R. O. Pace, the eldest member of the unofficial lunch society to which Cullum referred constantly as 'The Table.' So far I had not been presented to it; women were generally excluded, it seemed.

Cullum had been lunching elsewhere, with me, for a week, and Ropes had written on the back of a menu:

'MY DEAR HAYES,

Your chair remained empty all last week. Raymond and I looked at each other with surprise at first. And then uneasily. But we did not voice our suspicions. "He'll turn up on Monday," we said, with assumed heartiness. Raymond, in possession of a clue he did not share with me, was the first to lose heart. The chair remained empty yesterday.

It gapes at us again to-day. The doubt was too much for me; I have just raised my eyebrows meaningly at him and he has nodded back, confirming my worst fears.

To-morrow, with infinite tact, whichever of us gets here first will see that there are *two* empty chairs for you.

So bring her along.'

A different writing, Raymond Cole's, had added, 'Don't give the fourth party the idea that this invitation is permanent, but only for to-morrow.'

Cullum explained, as we walked up Fleet Street, that the aesthetic Raymond believed in keeping everything in separate mental compartments as much as possible; the woman-interest must never be allowed to overflow into intellectual or work-interests.

'Quite right,' I said. 'I didn't think, from what I saw of him, that young Cole would hold such an intelligent theory. When I'm doing something in which you have no part, working on the *Office Friend* or coping with Father's horses on Sunday, I try not to think of you at all; because it interferes with what I'm doing.'

'And do you manage it?'

'Never for ten minutes at a time,' I admitted cheerfully. 'You creep into everything I do, but that doesn't alter the rightness of the theory!'

'I say, haven't you got any gloves?' Cullum asked.

My carelessness about clothes, on all but very special occasions, worried him as much as his taste for unusual tints in socks and ties displeased me. I could not afford good clothes at all times, and was not sufficiently interested in them to make the best of the second rate, giving myself what I considered unnecessary bother for an inadequate result. It was, again, a matter of compromise, which I could not manage.

'Forgot, and left them in the office,' I said.

'Well, look here, you must have some if we're going to the Table for the first time. You'd better buy some.'

'I can't. Pay-day is to-morrow. I've only got just enough money left for lunch.' (We always paid our own.) 'Anyway,' I retorted childishly, resenting his criticism, 'if I'm not wearing gloves, what does it matter? You're keeping your head unnaturally still because your collar's too high, and that's much more conspicuous!'

'It isn't,' said Cullum, hotly. 'It's a very good collar. Matter of fact, it's one of my father's, because I couldn't find a clean one of my own this morning. Dear, I'll stand the lunch if you'll get some gloves. You see, Ropes' fiancée came up some time ago, and she was awfully well dressed. She always is, and I do like that.'

I nodded understandingly, wishing for his sake that I, like Janet, had the means of being always perfectly turned out, to the smallest detail. It would be worth taking pains then, to be the type of woman he most admired, but I saw no use in the half-and-half effect which was all I could possibly achieve with the money I had.

'All right, Cullum. I'm sorry!'

I touched his hand for a second, and we smiled at each other, not seeing the lunch-hour crowds in Fleet Street.

I liked Raymond Cole at the Table in the Marlborough Restaurant better than I had done in his home. The other man, Ropes, I did not like at all. He was a big, rough-featured man, whose pince-nez were continually slipping sideways, one lens resting against his right eye, and the other, which was cracked through all the years I knew him, straying between his other eye and a point half way down his blunt nose. He adjusted his glasses as we came in, but hardly looked at me, fixing his eyes on Cullum's neck.

'This is mine!' said Cullum complacently, pushing me forward, 'isn't it a nice one, Ropes?'

'We'll see later on,' he said, pulling out one of the empty chairs for me, 'meanwhile, put it down here.'

After one or two remarks to me in a slow, quiet voice he ignored me altogether for a while, listening to the other two, who had plunged into argument as usual. He stared at Cullum's collar with a look of puzzled fascination, until Cullum grew conscious of it and broke off in what he was saying.

'Is there anything wrong with my neck, Ropes?'

'No. Go on. Raymond is all wrong, you say, in his hope of regulating life into two parallel lines of mental and physical, with a gradually straightening curve of conduct traced out between them, inclining more and more to the mental? This is most enlightening. You got to "stagnation, which is the Little Death." Well?'

I disliked his air of lofty amusement, but the other two did not seem to mind. I found them immensely entertaining. It was always worth while listening when Raymond, who professed to be searching for a methodical system of life that eliminated chance, argued on the aims of existence with Cullum, who had hopefully carried a sword-stick about Fleet Street until the others chaffed him out of the habit, and would have owned a gun-stick if the price of a really good one had not put it out of his reach.

In Raymond's eyes, the highest purpose of human ingenuity was the stabilization of life, security: to

Cullum, the chief merit of civilization was that it let
the world down at crises with an endless variety of
unexpectedness.

While Cullum talked, without his customary jerky
gestures because the points of his collar jabbed his
neck when he forgot and moved his head quickly,
he fingered his collar nervously under Ropes' persistent
gaze.

'I wish I could recollect,' said Ropes' gentle voice
plaintively in the first pause, 'what it is that keeps
reminding me of a donkey looking over a white
gate?' Detaching his gaze from Cullum's neck he
blinked at the ceiling through his lop-sided glasses,
and began to talk of something else.

Nothing more was said on the subject, but Cullum
bought another collar on the way home, and I never
saw him in a high one again. At the time, he joined
in the laughter against himself. Ropes was the one
friend to whose judgment Cullum readily deferred.
One humorous, sarcastic comment from him effected
more than any amount of remonstrance and per-
suasion from other people. Had he cared to exert it,
Ropes could have wielded a strong influence over the
younger, more volatile character; but he did not care.

Both the others, I noticed, treated Ropes, the
quietest member, as head of the Table, asking his
opinion on any hard-argued point. 'As Ropes says,'
Cullum often began, and then brought out some
fantastic theory of his own.

'I never did,' Ropes would contradict lazily, but
he smiled at the boy, of whom he was evidently fond,
in what I considered an objectionably patronizing
manner.

'Mother complained the other day,' said Raymond,
who was dressed with extreme, quiet care, 'that you

and your gentleman's snappy suitings were as bad as spring sunlight for making wallpaper look shabby, Cullum.'

'Your mother – Oh, Lord!' exclaimed Cullum, standing up to pull out of his hip-pocket a crumpled, stamped envelope. 'She gave me this to post when I was leaving on Tuesday, because it had to go at once, and it went clean out of my head! Oh, good Lord!'

'Is it addressed to a Miss Grainger?'

Cullum looked, and nodded.

'Mother's been fussing and complaining for three days because she hasn't had an answer! It was to ask the woman to stay last week-end with us, and Mother couldn't understand why she didn't turn up, or write. She must have forgotten she gave you the letter, or she'd have guessed that it hadn't been posted,' said Raymond, candidly.

'What am I going to do?' asked Cullum in consternation.

'Own up and tell the truth for once,' said Ropes nastily.

I said: 'Let's see the address. I've never heard oi "Begham, Hants." Before posting it now, you might write round the envelope in different sorts of indelible pencil, as postmen do, "Not known at Little Pegham, Try Bingham." "Not Beggleham." "Not known at Begginham," etc. I don't know if there are such places, but they sound all right.'

'But would they deliver it?' asked Cullum, taking the suggestion seriously.

'They'd have to,' said Raymond. 'And then this rather impossible woman would simply write to Mother saying that the letter was delayed in the post, and that something ought to be done about the scandalous way in which the postal service is carried on, and that she's sorry to have missed the visit – which is all to the good. I find her a very trying creature.'

'My guardian angel, Esther!' said Cullum, waving a stump of blue pencil towards me and setting to work.

'No, Cullum; you can't really do it!' I said. 'I was only fooling. Look here, it's not – oh, I don't know; but don't.' I wanted to say, 'not honest,' but was prevented by the schoolgirl fear of being thought priggish. Instead I finished, 'it might get a perfectly innocent postman into trouble.'

'I don't suppose there are any perfectly innocent postmen,' said Cullum. 'One of them once got a housemaid of ours into trouble; we will avenge her!'

Raymond lent him a mauve indelible pencil, and between them they gave the forgotten letter sufficient alibis to account for a week's wandering. I sat by uncomfortably, ashamed to protest again, and Ropes, who could have stopped it easily, remained silent, watching with his superior smile. The subsequent history of the letter was exactly as Raymond predicted.

As Cullum and I were leaving Ropes adjusted his errant glasses again and studied me for the first time.

'Bring her again!' he said to Cullum.

Cullum was greatly pleased.

'You know, you've scored,' he said as we walked back together towards our neighbouring offices. 'I didn't expect as much as that from Ropes. He's not much more enthusiastic than Raymond about women's intrusion into men's friendships. He only brought his own fiancée once, because she insisted on seeing what we were like.

'I can't imagine a man like that being engaged.'

'Oh, I think he's devoted to her, but I must say she wasn't what I'd expected him to choose; but then, in a way, I expected to be surprised, before I met her. A man's taste in marriage is the one thing his friends can never foretell, however well they know him. She's very feminine and charming and silly, in the nice sort of way that a lamb is silly: she chatters a lot without saying very much. I should imagine that Ropes' feeling for her is mostly physical. He must be rather an intense sort of chap from that point of view, and she'd appeal chiefly to his senses.'

'Pretty?'

'Yes, very, with the kind of piquant, childish prettiness which I'm glad you haven't got. I find prettiness boring. You know, I *do* love you, Esther!' he said in a clear, conversational voice.

'Sh!' I said indignantly. 'For goodness' sake don't shout it!'

The elderly man who was hurrying past us in the street turned round and smiled at us so benignly that we smiled back.

'How much do you love me?' I asked gaily, measuring off space with my hands. 'As much as that?'

Cullum considered it gravely, and shook his head.

'Like that?' I said, bringing my hands closer together.

'No, the other way. Several yards more.'

'That's quite a lot!' I said.

We talked nonsense all the way back, and parted some distance from the Cameron Press because I wanted to avoid the knowing facetiousness with which the office people treated any friendship between a man and woman that happened to come under their notice; but evidently some fellow-Cameronian whom I had not recognized – there were five hundred of us – had lunched in the Marlborough restaurant. A girl who had a job like mine on another of Miss Leslie's papers came into our department in the half-hour interval in the afternoon, when the work of the whole Cameron Press was dislocated by tea and biscuits.

'Been hearing all about your giddy goings-on, Sievie!'

Among the girls in the office, everyone was known by a twisted form of their surname.

'Oh, really?'

' "Oh, really," yes! Some little bird saw you out to-day with three men!'

She gave me a playful push which spilled my tea over the pile of letters on my desk. This meant an hour's work wasted. She was one of the dreadful type that Cullum called 'slap-and-tickle' girls.

'Brownie from the *Girl's Sporting Mag.* it was. She was sitting quite close, too; she kept trying to catch your eye, but she says you were so taken up with one of the party that you didn't see her even when you looked right at her. You must have got it badly, dear! Does your friend often lunch with you?'

I flushed with annoyance, but knowing that her curiosity was prompted by good-natured interest, I could not resent it openly.

'Yes,' I said.

'Jolly nice for you! You are lucky; Brownie said he looked awfully gentlemanly.'

('Oh, how Cullum will enjoy that!' I thought.)

'Have you noticed Mr. Saunders of the Pay Office?' she went on sociably. 'He's very gentlemanly, too; I lunch with him ever so often; he's frightfully gone on me; it makes me laugh!'

I realized then that all the conversation had been leading up to this. She wanted to be teased about the gentlemanly Mr. Saunders. Every girl who had a 'gentleman friend" was entitled to such chaff in the office, and she would have felt slighted if she had not had some to protest against, so I said the proper

162

things, while she giggled and begged me to stow it, assuring me that there wasn't anything in it – well, nothing much, anyway; and who was I to talk, she'd like to know, after lunching with three men all at once!

The Cameron Press was a revelation to me of the bitter struggles for gentility which go on in a big office where hundreds of employees meet daily, and of the fine grades which are recognized between them. The Cameronians were extraordinarily mixed. Before going there I had always thought, when the subject entered my mind at all, that there were only two sets of people; those who conformed to a certain standard, and those who did not. Whether they barely missed it or had no pretensions of attaining it made no difference, but I found in the Cameron Press innumerable nice distinctions, especially among the women, who discussed endlessly whether So-and-So was a lady, a real lady, quite a lady, not quite a lady or – final and incomprehensible damnation – 'No-class.'

To me, brought up rather snobbishly, these people seemed only pitiable and amusing during my first month at the Cameron Press, and then by degrees it was borne upon me that they did their work far more efficiently than I did mine; their brains were more alert, and they succeeded where I failed. It was a salutary discovery.

Encouraged by Miss Leslie, I tried to write a short story for the *Office Friend*: the payment was not good, but any extra money would have been welcome, however much trouble it took to earn. My plot contained all the usual features, and it was written in a style parodying that of Miss Leslie's pet writers, but she gave it back to me, saying that it was unconvincing, though she could not tell me why it failed to touch her heart. I re-wrote it, trying to take the idiotic tale seriously, because I knew that this is the only way to produce turgid fiction successfully, but it was beyond my powers of make-believe. I had three or four attempts, and then Miss Leslie, seeing that it was hopeless, gave the plot, which she liked, to the girl who lunched with the gentlemanly Mr. Saunders, and seeing nothing impossible in the situations, she made a good job of it. Ill-educated and a year younger than I was, she was the first person to make me realize the mental superiority of the rising lower middle class, over the falling upper middle class. She was one of the great majority of Cameronian typists who wore evening dress all day long, like waiters. Out of twenty-three people in Miss Leslie's departments, Miss Bullen and I were the only two who wore plain blouses and skirts, and we were rather looked down on for it.

Chapter 10: *Giving In*

I HAD a great deal of amusement out of the Cameron Press one way or another, but looking back on it, I think that my enjoyment of everything that happened lay chiefly, even at the moment, in anticipation of making a good story of it for Cullum at lunch at the Table, of which, at Ropes' invitation, I became a recognized member; or of telling him about it in the evening. After the novelty of the work wore off the days would have been dull and long if Cullum had not been always in the background, to magnify my pleasure. There was no point for me in anything into which he could not enter, but there seemed little that we did not share.

After the Cameron Press had disgorged its hundreds at half-past five, I used to meet him and we would spend a few of our joint shillings on dinner at some cheap restaurant where we could sit and talk afterwards. Sometimes, as it was young summer, the motorcycle took us both out to Kew or Richmond Park. Those were the happiest evenings I spent in London, because there were parts of Richmond where oaks and high-growing fern reminded me of the beloved Holmwood common, which I missed continually during the week. Very often we went to Janet's for dinner; she was considerate enough to invent household pre-occupations for herself at times, leaving us to talk alone. I think Cullum preferred these evenings to any others; he loved good talk, particularly when he was doing most of it himself, and Janet made a wonderful listener. Knowing the signs of inattention in her, I was sometimes aware that her thoughts were straying from Cullum's talk, to which she was apparently listening with shining eyes, but he, admiring her as much as I did, never noticed this, for Janet's eyes shone as spiritually when she was thinking of the excellent background made for her fair head by the dark wainscotting, as they did when she was following the conversation attentively.

I remember one delightful evening of which Cullum spent a large part in proving, with much elaboration, that the constitutionally lazy are the true benefactors of mankind, since it is to them that all progress is due. Janet started him on the subject by attacking the indolent way in which he always lounged in the evening, never stirring out of an armchair if he could help it. When Cullum did nothing, he did it whole-heartedly. He pointed out that in days gone by the energetic man whose dwelling lay a mile from the nearest stream uncomplainingly tramped that mile there and back carrying water whenever it was needed, and his successors might have done so for ever had not the lazy man to whom the exertion was unbearable, sat down and thought out a method of coaxing water along a pipe to the place where it was needed. The energetic man laboriously carried things on his back, with much sweating and panting, until the lazy man, desperately casting about in his mind for some way of easing the burden, hit on the idea of wheels.

'Those are only two examples. All through history it has been the same,' he said. 'We and we alone (I'm speaking for all physically lazy people) are responsible for the mental improvement of mankind.

Physical energy is content to expend itself unnecessarily, doing the same stupid things over and over again, but laziness cunningly thinks out labour-saving devices, primarily for its own advantage, of course, but mankind benefits incidentally, by saving time and strength which can then be devoted to worthier ends, to thought and art for instance. There should be a statue in every town, "To the Lazy Man Who Gave Us Time to Think." He deserves undying fame far more than the great and useless heroes of old, who were merely men at the mercy of their glands! Horatius at the bridge, Richard Coeur-de-Lion being magnanimous on his death-bed to the soldier who shot him and – er – oh – St. George tearing down the edict against the Church – they were only actuated by their super-stimulated glands, that's all,' said Cullum, relegating them to insignificance with a patronizing hand. 'All heroism is due to abnormally active glands, you know. It's a scientific fact. Horatius wasn't really any nobler than you and me, but his suprarenal glands, on which courage depends, secreted more freely, and Richard Coeur-de-Lion was a hot-tempered man as a rule, but just at the time of his death his system held an excess of parathyroid matter, which makes for generosity; and St. George's endocrine glands worked unusually hard whenever he was angry and excited together, making him especially foolhardy then – all a matter of glands.'

'Why don't you write an article about it?' suggested Janet, smiling.

'Oh, I have,' said Cullum. 'To-day. I looked up the stuff this afternoon. That's how I know.'

When Cullum was engaged elsewhere in the evenings I always went to Janet, liking her best when we were alone; we were closer then. It seemed to me that

167

when the three of us were together her decision always joined Cullum's in any friendly dispute, and once or twice, to my discomfiture, she drew out of the past and laughed at, with him, silly or intimate things that I had told her long ago – confidences that she had received seriously at the time. I never told her that this hurt, for as soon as we were alone together again we were back on the old footing, and I was sure that the change I seemed to have noticed in her was in my imagination only.

On Friday evening I went home for the week-end, and he came down on Saturday or Sunday. Even though I should see him in the course of the day there was always a letter for me on Saturday morning, because we had not been with each other the previous evening.

'My darling fellow,' started one,
'That's the only title I can find with which to pay homage to your male companionableness, which I love. Bless you, friend, the fact that you have a mouth which drives me nearly wild sometimes with the longing to kiss you, is really unimportant compared with the fact that you are the only woman I've ever known who will argue for twenty minutes on an abstract question without bringing it down to personal applications, generally first-and second-person-al applications. There must be precious few women who know men in general as they really are among themselves, because of the sex-pose that men adopt unconsciously before most women. One doesn't with you, I don't know why. Ropes and Raymond say what they really mean in front of you, sometimes in a slightly bowdlerized way, sometimes not even that, which is curious,

because when Ropes' fiancée was there we all talked in the way in which we wanted her to think we always talked, with restrained and painstaking intelligence! One explains the man's point of view to most women, but one takes it for granted that you have it.

'At the Table to-day, after you'd left, Ropes said, "I don't mind your lass coming, Hayes, because she isn't disturbing; you can easily forget she's a woman."

' "Bit uncomplimentary, isn't that?" Raymond said.

' "No. *She* wouldn't think so," said Ropes.

'There you are, fellow-my-lad, you're just "She," without a name to the whole Table when you're away!

'It's an intolerably long Friday evening – I suppose it's because I'm spoilt by seeing such a lot of you at other times that I find it hopeless to try, for a few hours, to go back to the things that kept me amused without you for twenty-two years. Dunno how they did! All I know is that they won't do it now.

'There must be literally hundreds of couples like ourselves, working in London in similar circumstances, and it is just possible that a few of them may be as sublimely happy, but they, poor fools, are going to mess it all up with marriage – get stale – get satiated – get over it, even the wonder and mystery of love, and settled down to mutual tolerance or contempt. Why will people try to cook porridge in a Greek vase?

'I am going out to post this now, and then to bed, with the same happy excitement I feel when I know I'm going to see you in a minute, because

I think I *am* going to see you; the indefinite dreams
that I've always had of you are becoming regular,
and very real, and I know that the part of me which
worships you, in spirit, finds you somehow in sleep.

'I kiss your eyes, beloved, wanting desperately
everything that I am not going to be fool enough to
take.

'CULLUM.'

In our minds, at that time, there was still no question
of marriage: the subject had been thrashed out and
closed, as far as we were concerned. Loving each
other as we did, both of us believed that we had
found an enduring treasure, for here was friendship
before physical attraction, but being cool-headed,
for young lovers, we remembered that the millions
of other lovers who had taken the vows we would not
take had believed it too, and the years had tarnished
their gold. Having constantly before me the example
of my parents' unhappy marriage, which had begun
in a blaze of passion, I insisted the more vehemently
of the two on the transience of love, once satisfied;
but in spite of this, I grew vaguely dissatisfied sometimes when we were most enthusiastically in accord.
Love, as Cullum idealized it for me, was desire that,
to gain eternity for its lovely discontent, renounced
even the hope of surcease from pain. This dream
of love unfulfilled satisfied my mind, pricking my
pride. Here was a man who, wanting me, still professed to wish for nothing more than the possession
of his own mind made richer by schooled desire.

My reason, disregarding my vanity, saw the splendour of the far-off ideal, while my hurt vanity and the
blind purpose of the whole world, to which my intentions were negligible, prompted me to use every

artifice that instinct taught me to stir the man in Cullum to the discomfort of the dreamer. I see now that there was no appeal of light touch withdrawn, of faint scent and unconsciously contrived effect, so banal that it did not serve Nature's turn in dealing with us, two people confident that they had harnessed her strength to their wishes. We were like engineers, pleased with the obedient power of a diverted river, and oblivious to the possibility of floods.

Sometimes I knew dimly that I was striving to break through Cullum's armour of ideals, but generally I obeyed the guiding force without realizing it, or actually against my will. I did not want to hurt the beloved boy, since even if I succeeded in waking in him half dormant desires, still I did not mean to marry him; and the stooping of love to hidden intrigues seemed such a desecration that it did not enter into my considerations at all. I did not know what I wanted.

'I suppose that young man is coming down this morning?' said Father at breakfast when I put Cullum's letter, unopened, into my pocket. He sighed deeply, though as we should be out all day, Cullum's visit would not disturb him. I nodded, hurrying through the meal, but at ten o'clock Cullum had not appeared, and by eleven I was in a fever of anxiety, knowing what his driving was like. Streaked with oil and dust he came in at twelve, with a good deal of skin off one side of his jaw. As he dismounted he smiled at me reassuringly, with a broad gleam of white teeth in a dirty face, and then pulled a grimace because the smile hurt. Some minor accident was always happening to Cullum on his motor bicycle, but according to him these mishaps were never his fault. I think he almost believed that the transport world was in league against him; and the police were especially unjust in endorsing his licence in unnecessarily large handwriting.

'Woman, come and wash your warrior's wounds,' he said. Road-grit had worked into the graze, and all his short after-life he carried a little scar from that accident. Vividly, I remember noticing it on a later and very different occasion. 'I'm lucky to have nothing worse,' he said when I had finished, 'the other fellow – a suicidal fool – was rather badly cut.' Whatever happened to Cullum, it was always the other person who suffered.

We drove out to Holmbush Tower, set on the edge of St. Leonard's Forest. In the farm-house near by, where we had tea, the boy leant forward to me and whispered: 'Don't turn round now, but in a few minutes, look at the eyes of the girl in white, sitting on your right alone. The envy in them is pathetic.'

Being with Cullum, I had not particularly noticed anyone else in the room. My skin was still glowing from his kisses, given lately in the wood; it must have been obvious to anyone who saw us talking, full of shared joy, that we were in love. But after that, each time that I looked away I met the eyes of the girl who was there by herself; they were fixed on one or the other of us with a look of resentment. She looked aside wearily when she saw that we had noticed her. She seemed several years older than Cullum, a colourless, plain girl, and her jealousy of our happiness touched me with easy pity.

'Let's go when you're ready. I can't stand that girl's misery,' I said. 'Poor thing, I wonder what she has lost? It must be agony to see people like us if you haven't got anyone belonging to you.'

Out in the great beechwood, under the high, silver-green ceiling of young leaves, the memory of her persisted. 'I wish that girl's expression wouldn't haunt me,' I said when we had long lost sight of the farm-house where we had left the bicycle. 'I keep trying to imagine what existence would be like for me if I lost you. I can't even picture it. I suppose I should live chiefly on recollections of the glorious days we've already had.'

'Probably. Women do live in the past, it seems. It's never finished for them. A man lives more in the future; that's why the majority of us can turn to entirely new adventures without much regret for what we leave behind. Women can't. If something took you away from me now it wouldn't be the thought of all I've had and lost that would hurt most, but the thought of the appalling amount that I should be missing in the future. That might drive me nearly mad. But you aren't going to get away, Esther mine!'

He pulled me to him, one arm holding me and the other hand under my chin. I did not know what urged me to resist as fiercely as I did, laughing at first, while one straightened arm held Cullum's face away from mine. The sudden determination in his eyes sent an unreasoning stab of fear through me. For both of us the game ceased to be a game, and as he roughly forced my head round, I sank my teeth into his hand, in obedience to a law older than the forest that held us. Over my outstretched arm, which he was bending, slowly and deliberately, with his, I saw and hardly recognized the straight line of his mouth and the blood-darkened face. Neither of us were playing as we fought; I was gripped by sheer, instinctive terror; the heritage, possibly, of some other woman's fear, long ago, among the trees from which these trees had sprung.

We were both young and strong, and desperately in earnest. I wrenched myself into a position in which my foot was locked round his ankle, and threw myself sideways. Unprepared, he was caught off his balance for a second, and then recovered. I was swung off my feet and forced down until Cullum was kneeling by me as I half lay on the ground, and I could not move at all; his arms held mine to my sides.

We did not speak at first.

'Now!' he said, when the silence had grown until I could hear the little noises of the wood above the beating of my heart. A jay chattered. 'You are not the only one, *darling*, who is occasionally possessed of the devil!' He kissed me angrily, hurting my mouth.

'Cullum, Cullum!' I begged.

'Oh, yes; I know your lip's bleeding!' he said, and wiped the blood off with his tongue. 'So is my hand.' His mouth pressed down, catching my cut upper lip between his teeth and mine. The stuff of my light summer dress had torn at the neck. Cullum's bitten hand crept down, closing over one of my breasts. With his head bowed over mine, he murmured something I did not hear, and drew me closer. Then the violence died out of him; he let me sink back on the earth, where I lay, beyond happiness or unhappiness or any feeling, with one arm over my closed eyes, trying to shut out Cullum and the whole world.

Presently I felt his lips gently touch my upturned palm.

'My God, Esther! I didn't mean – didn't mean – Sweetheart, look at me! Oh, Girl, what have I done!'

I tried twice to speak before I said: 'It's all right.

174

Oh, Cullum, I love you!' And he took me into his arms.

We sat so still, and for so long, leaning back against one of the trees, that wood creatures, birds and insects, and a field mouse, chirped and crawled and hunted close by us. Save for these, nothing disturbed the quietness of that green place, and when evening came, a great, strange stillness settled over it. We began to talk again, because the silence was oppressive.

'I can understand why the ancients worshipped trees,' Cullum said, 'they are everything that primitive gods should be, alive, beautiful, strong, and untouched by suffering. Early man liked his gods callous; it was their immunity from pain, and their indifference to it in others which made them seem greater than he was. Hold me, my dear! These trees were here long before we were born; extreme old age will make us horrible, but they will grow more and more venerable and lovely, and they'll be here, uncaring, long after we're gone. Kiss me, Esther! Our life's too short to love you in.'

'Trees are the saddest things on earth, I think,' I said when his arms had relaxed. 'Human misery doesn't impress itself on its surroundings as intensely as the agonizing sense of straining towards something which a wood has at night. That fills the air. If you've ever walked alone at night among trees – ? And yet, there's no joy to equal the exquisite unhappiness of coming close to the spirit behind inanimate life. I have that feeling sometimes. I think anyone does who has lived to a certain extent in contact with wild things for a long while. I suppose everyone in their life has one or two minutes when they seem to reach some underlying force. You get it from books,

I get it from being alone out of doors, chiefly at night. People like my mother find it in religion.'

Cullum said: 'I call it drunkenness, and mental drunkenness is the best thing in life; the pitiable people are those who can only get drunk with alcohol or women.'

'How amazingly lucky I am!' I said inconsequently. 'This part of England for my heritage of the land – you know –

> "God gave all men all earth to love,
>   But since our hearts are small,
>   Ordained for each one spot should prove
>   Beloved over all –"

and then you for my lover, and Janet for my friend!'

'I wonder if you've noticed,' he asked slowly, 'that Janet nearly always sides with me in any argument between us?'

'I have,' I said, 'at least, I've sometimes thought so, and sometimes I've thought I was fancying it, but she has gone back on a lot of things that she said before you appeared.'

'I'm sorry, I wish she wouldn't take my part automatically. Janet's opinions are formed by her inclination, not her reason. She's the completely feminine woman, just as my mother is. She would do the same. It's funny that both men and women should always find it infinitely easier to be loyal to a man than a woman.'

He was moody when we walked back, blinking as we emerged from the thick shade into the sun on our way to fetch Zoroaster. Going home, in record time for the run, he attempted to overtake every vehicle moving in our direction, in spite of my protests and the crush of traffic on the London-Brighton road. Through supper this irritable humour persisted; even my voluble sisters noticed it and subsided, and I gave up trying to change it.

As he was leaving I said, 'Cullum, you're not feeling rotten from the effect of that smash this morning, are you?'

'No, I'm not,' he said shortly. 'Women always ascribe everything to physical causes.'

He leant the bicycle against the holly hedge of the drive and put his arm round my shoulders, with his quick, sweet smile lighting up his sullen face. 'And they're generally right! Oh, bless you, dear, what a gentle way of showing that I've been dull, rude and snappy. I'm sorry!' He stared ahead, frowning at the distant lines of rooks flapping home towards us.

'We've been awfully young and far-seeing,' he said, with his long fingers pressing into my shoulder, 'and we've talked an awful lot of nonsense, but life's too strong for us to fight. We –'

While he paused, groping for words, I waited serene in the knowledge that what I had longed for had come, this man's surrender.

'I love you utterly, with my heart and brain; with my body too. I always shall –' I smiled triumphantly, and he pulled me to him – 'all my life, I know, and probably after, because I believe I've loved you before, and still dream of it; and so we may love again somewhere else. But it's *now* that matters. Let's chance it all, the taming of love. For me, that couldn't happen with you. We have everything on our side. Girl, I want you. Let's marry. I don't know why we were running away from the great adventure.'

'No, let things remain as they are!' I said, completely satisfied.

' "Haw, haw!" Oh, shut up, you brutes, this isn't funny!' said Cullum, to the rooks now overhead, and with one of his startling reversions to boyhood, he picked up a stone and hurled it at them.

As we were near the stable loft I whistled to the owls that lived there, and one of them hooted back.

'There! You hear? The wise bird is laughing at your capitulation!' I said.

Cullum stayed the night because it was too late for him to ride home when we came in from the drive, where we had spread a very little indecisive conversation over an hour and a half.

I became engaged to him three weeks later. This was not what I had intended, but Cullum bent on getting his own way was irresistible. He had a slogan, 'I love you, I want you, and I am going to have you,' which he gabbled off each time we met, or wrote on odd pieces of paper and sent to me in official envelopes, by his firm's messenger-boys, while I was in the Cameron Press. These notes, which arrived for me constantly, attracted a great deal of attention in the office, and I could give no satisfactory explanation of them.

The actual engagement happened absurdly and rather unexpectedly, as the important events of life generally do. We took a picnic lunch one Saturday into the Redlands, and while we were eating, Cullum discussed with me an idea for a short story; he used to talk over his work, not because he wanted criticism or suggestions, but because he found it helped him to get his own thoughts clear to try and explain them to someone else. After the meal, he lay back on the dry ground, smoking, and evidently far away in thought; I was sitting cross-legged in my favourite position, propped up against a tree-trunk, a yard or so from him. The sun was drawing the strong, resinous scent out of the trees; the smell of the pines in the warm, sleepy stillness seemed to go to my head suddenly. My eyes travelled over him slowly, over the warm red-brown hair and the strong hands that were playing absently with pine needles, and the sturdy, lean young body; they came back to his face, which was half averted and curiously sad, as usual when he was absorbed in his own thoughts.

An impulse of intense hunger for him moved me.

'Cullum, I will marry you!' I said in a low voice.

For a moment he did not seem to have heard at all, and then he came back from afar with a jerk, aware that I had spoken.

'All finished,' he said. 'I had the last; I'm so sorry.'

'Finished? But – what?'

'Sandwiches.' He saw the blankness of my face. 'Didn't you say – ?'

'I said I'd marry you!' I told him with a choky little laugh.

'Oh, my dear – ' Once Cullum had realized the situation he was most adequate.

'You beast!' I said contentedly some time later. 'You ruined the dramatic value of what is quite possibly the only occasion on which I shall get engaged! I could spank you!'

'If you think it would be any consolation to you, try!' said Cullum and obligingly rolled over on to his face.

I did try, but it stung my hand and he only laughed.

'That's rotten, sweetheart! Now I'll show you how it ought to be done – ' He sat up, pulled me across his knees and smacked me uncomfortably hard.

My family and Janet had been expecting the news. We were able to astonish no one, since even the Table showed no animation over what we considered the wonderful and incredible announcement. Raymond Cole, with his easy man-of-the-world air, told us that he had known we should come to it in time, and Ropes said, 'But I thought you were engaged, all along? Baby snatchers, both of you.' However, they stood us a lunch.

Gerald Hemingway was gloomily resigned, and kept out of my way, but young McDonald refused to consider the engagement at all. 'Perrhaps!' he would say to any mention I made of the future. By importunate energy he succeeded about this time in getting on to the administrative side of a big political organization in the Midlands. It was a Labour organization, and he held Conservative views, but he wanted the experience and left Holmwood. He wrote to me regularly once a fortnight, whether I answered or not, and it was interesting to see how rapidly his letters improved.

Cullum asked me to tea at his house to meet his family.

'Don't spring the great fact on them at once,' he said. 'When they know you a little we'll let 'em down easy, especially Mother. She knew that I was more or less engaged to Paula McMillan, and so she was prejudiced against her from the start; it would be the same with you, and that wouldn't be fair to either of you. She's mother-blind enough to think that nothing could be really good enough for her son.'

'You never told me you were engaged to the McMillan girl?'

'Well, it was nothing very definite, and honestly, when you turned up I clean forgot all about her. That's how it ended.'

'But what did you do about it? How did you break it off?'

'I didn't do anything. Now I come to think of it, I suppose I behaved awfully badly. I didn't go to see her and when she wrote I kept putting off answering, till at last I thought she must have gathered that I wasn't engaged to her any more, so I didn't write at all. Yes, I was a cur!' he said, but the realization did not seem to weigh heavily on him.

'Anyway, I gave her a jolly nice ring, and she's stuck to it, so she did get something out of it. I wish I'd got it back to give to you, now – not as an engagement ring, of course, but I'd like you to have it.'

'Robbing Peter to please Paul!' I said, not knowing that this was a habit of his.

His mother and I took a mutual dislike to each other when we met. I disliked the way in which she doted openly on Cullum, extolling his cleverness in his presence. Apparently Cullum was so accustomed to it that it did not make him feel uncomfortable: brought up by such a mother, he could be forgiven his occa- sionally naïve conceit. I wondered that he was not more spoilt. Plump and placid-looking, she had an abundance of untidy hair of a beautiful colour, a little lighter than Cullum's. She was one of those hypo- critical women who find an idea that reflects to their credit in every subject and constantly begin a sentence, extolling what they consider their virtues with 'I am afraid –' 'I am afraid I am terribly soft-hearted over animals; I can't bear to see them hurt,' she said, and in answer to a conventional remark of mine about the weather, 'I am afraid I do enjoy this very hot weather, though I keep thinking of the poor wretches in the East End who can't get away into open spaces. We ought to think of them more often, don't you think?' 'I am afraid I'm devoted to children,' and so on.

Cullum's father listened with the non-committal

half-smile which he kept for his wife's remarks. Arthur Hayes was a nice little man, but I had been told that he had been called one of the wittiest men in the House of Commons and I hardly dared speak to him. He was very dark, and his skin was dry and pale as parchment, and covered with minute lines, as though the flesh under it had shrunk greatly. Cullum's personality seemed boisterous beside his, and yet the two were alike in some ways. The elder Hayes had the same charming voice as his son, and he used it effectively. I never met anyone with a more impressive way of making commonplace remarks; they did not sound commonplace when he made them.

He was discussing with the other guest, an American woman social worker, who had been studying industrial conditions in Teneriffe, the life of the Canary Island peasant, who drags sustenance out of the barren mountain sides, by building, with enormous expenditure of labour, a small terrace on which to grow a dozen banana trees.

'Those poor, ignorant people are just wonderfully industrious,' she was saying earnestly, 'but their morals! Well, they don't seem to know the meaning of that word. Do you know, they have illegitimate children, like rabbits!'

We appeared to gratify her by our expressions of surprise.

'Like rabbits!' she repeated, nodding her head sadly. She seemed much concerned by this singular fact.

'But why particularly like rabbits?' asked Mr. Hayes. 'Like all other animals, surely? After all, the marriage service –'

'Oh, I wasn't meaning that. I meant they have them so often – like rabbits do. Breed so quickly you know. Seeing how Nature's up against them in everything, on the mountain sides, poor soil and lack of rain and all, you'd think they wouldn't want so many children, but once they've got them, if you forget what those children are, I will say it's fine to see how the parents work to bring them up. They're stupid and sinful, but they show great parental feelings.'

Mr. Hayes mused for a moment, presiding over a pregnant silence, and then he pulled his pipe from between his teeth and cleared his throat.

'Their minds,' he said in his impressive manner 'are like manure heaps on which beautiful flowers flourish.'

His remark electrified us. We tingled mentally. On the face of the American I saw the same joyous light which no doubt was shining on mine. We had been privileged to hear Arthur Hayes, one of our wittiest M.P.'s, at his highest conversation level! (Undoubtedly we had.)

'That's so!' breathed the American. 'When I saw them dragging those great stones all the way up the mountain side for the sake of a few miserable bunches of bananas, well, I said to myself, "Those people jest can't have *heard* of Texas!" '

(I stored in my memory this example of Mr. Hayes' noted wit, but when I came to think of it later, the words had lost the magnitude that he had lent them, and were not even appropriate to the subject. They reminded me of some of Raymond Coles' painstaking and usually irrelevant epigrams. It was the same with the majority of the elder Hayes' remarks: his sonorous delivery made them sound as weighty as the pronouncements of an oracle, but in the six months in which I was often at the Hayes' house, I never heard him say anything profound, though I often thought I had until I came to examine it. I suspected, at last, that this applied to his wittiness in the lobby.)

183

For the rest of the afternoon I listened eagerly, but we were such a small herd that he cast no more of his remarkable artificial pearls before us. The American woman took the lead, and she talked to us about motor cars all through a protracted tea. She had already owned an incredible number of cars; she was an expert on their ailments, and there was no checking her in her determination to teach us all she knew. Nothing is duller to listen to than the technicalities of a subject on which one is not an enthusiast. We were all fidgeting. Cullum rolled imploring eyes at me.

'Aren't you glad, Mrs. Hannon,' he said, stemming the tide for a moment, 'that a car is so much cleaner in its illnesses than a horse. What was that disease you were telling me of the other day, Esther? The oozy one?'

'Glanders?' I said wonderingly.

'Yes, that's it. Have you ever seen a horse with glanders, Mrs. Hannon?'

'No, I shouldn't care to. Now, where the American car scores over the English car is that –'

'Well, you should take the first opportunity, for it's very interesting,' said Cullum firmly. 'The horse's neck swells up, and the gatherings break open; or if they don't you squeeze them until they do –'

I remembered Kipling's *The Story of the Gadsbys*, and enjoyed the way in which the boy, firmly but with a courteous air, paid her back in her own coin for boring us. Someone should have treated us like that when we talked theology at the Coles'.

' – and there's always a lot of matter inside. Pus, you know, which spurts out when you press it. Then you wash out –'

'Oh, don't!' said Mrs. Hayes, and Mrs. Hannon set down her cup deliberately and did not finish the biscuit with which she had been emphasizing her points, between mouthfuls.

'How just disgusting!' she said. 'With cars – '

But the boy's imagination was not to be curbed. 'What colour is the stuff that comes out, Esther? Green?'

'Grey-green,' I said, backing him up.

'Almost yellow at times?' he suggested with gusto.

'Yes, but not as runny as you'd think from the way it comes out.'

'Ah, sticky, isn't it, and you have to keep washing it to prevent scabs from forming?'

'Oh, do stop these horrid details, Cullum! You're turning my stomach!' came from Mrs. Hannon.

'Just as you like,' he said. 'Of course, it may sound beastly to you, but to us, who are frightfully keen on horses, it's every bit as enthralling as the insides of a car: one simply can't imagine that other people don't find it interesting too.'

We talked of other things, avoiding mechanics.

Arthur Hayes' eyes twinkled at his son, who had never had anything to do with horses in his life, and then he smiled at me.

He seemed quite pleased, about a month later, when we told him that we were engaged. Mrs. Hayes often kissed me, but I never felt that she liked me.

Chapter 11: *Possession*

LIFE had not shone for me, until then, as gloriously as it did in those days. The whole world sang.

'Green days in forests' we had in plenty in the week-ends, and in them we planned the 'blue days at sea' that were to come after the publication of Cullum's next book, when we should marry and buy a yacht with the proceeds. His first book was not selling very well, though he never admitted it, but according to his reports, his publishers seemed abnormally enthusiastic about the chances of his second.

Hearing that I was in a boarding-house, Mrs. Hayes often asked me to stay at her house, keeping ready for me, whether I came or not, the bed in the little room that had been Cullum's dressing-room and den, and opened out of his bedroom. I could not understand, feeling her resentment for me, her evident desire that I should marry him. I think she wanted grandchildren.

It was unfair to throw us together as much as she did. She had no right to sacrifice me to her son, but motherhood was a blind passion with her; nothing mattered to her except Cullum's good, and of that she had a short-sighted view. I think she would have sacrificed herself or anyone else with equal eagerness if by so doing she could gratify some whim of Cullum's. Maternity in such women is a fierce flame which entirely consumes their judgment, as well as their sense of right and wrong.

Stimulated all day long by the knowledge that we were not far away from each other, made hungrier for one another by the restraint of meeting in public at lunch, we came back in the evening to what was practically a self-contained flat – no one else slept on that landing – wanting each other with the exaggerated intensity of strained nerves. As an older, married woman she should have seen that this state of affairs was very bad for two young people as passionately in love as we were.

The next two months were a gradually increasing strain to both of us because we were living in an irritating semi-intimacy, with no barriers between us but our weakening resolutions. All through the day I used to long feverishly for the coming of night; we were gloriously happy in the torment of unceasing desire, grateful to Mrs. Hayes for leaving us so much alone together, and we talked a great deal in those days about the sexlessness of beauty, meaning, unspecifically, the beauty of our own slim young bodies, and we were willingly drugged by these excellent theoretical narcotics. I sometimes suspected that we were reassuring ourselves. Was anyone, we asked, as invincible as we were, having recognized the strength of the physical forces arrayed against us – nothing blind or unprepared about us. We were armed! – and passed on to a higher plane of companionship, leaving them conquered? In our financial situation there was no hope of marriage for some time, and we were strong enough, we said, to wait.

When Mr. and Mrs. Hayes went out in the evening, we used to buy food outside and cook it, very badly, over the gas-fire in Cullum's room. I could boil an egg as hard as anyone, but there my domestic ability ended, and he was no better. I remember that it was

187

at this old, instinctive playing at owning our own establishment or cave, that we discovered that the water in a saucepan which is not enough to cover three potatoes may be enough to cover four, and more than enough for five. For quite half an hour we argued with great solemnity over the immense moral principal which both of us felt must be involved in this tremendously significant fact, but we could not decide what it was. We took ourselves very seriously at times.

Till all hours of the night we used to talk with the door open between us, cutting short the sleep that we badly needed, to restore the lost balance between rest and the energy that we expended, in those circumstances, faster than we stored it. Sometimes, to finish a discussion, Cullum in marvellously patterned pyjamas came and sat on the side of my bed, and then, unconsciously, our talk would become punctiliously impersonal. We were vividly aware of our nearness.

At no time in that period was there a perceptible violation of the natural reticence which had always been between us; the first edge of shyness was gradually worn away by constant companionship; we drifted into an exquisite, tantalizing physical familiarity which accentuated in some way the reserve that still remained between us.

I do not know what Mrs. Hayes thought of our relationship; I think she believed me his mistress; certainly she must have intended it, and yet, having done so much, she was horrified by the really innocent flippancy with which Cullum and I sometimes spoke of other people's affairs. Words seemed much more blatant to her than actions; they do to many people.

The effect of our unnaturally exciting, thwarted existence was more apparent in me than in Cullum. I grew rather thin and listless, but he became correspondingly restless, and we tramped all day long in the week-ends which he spent at Holmwood, striding along happily, mostly in silence, through woods, and streams, and climbing over or through hedges. We used to draw a straight line on the map before we set out, and the game was to see how closely we could follow it across country. It was great fun, but it used up what little recuperative force the country air gave me. Ropes' wise eyes at the Table noticed the marks of tension in both of us, but he said nothing at the time.

I had long got over my first aversion from him, and as time went on I liked him more and more. He was the quietest, wittiest man I had met; he never gave advice, but his rare suggestions carried weight, even with Cullum, who, as far as everyone else was concerned, went his own way uncaringly. As it had been about the high collar of which Ropes disapproved, so it was with the terrible beard with which Cullum came back from his three weeks' holiday in August. Ropes' sarcasm got rid of it when his mother's entreaties, and mine, had failed.

Having only been with the firm a few months, I had no right to a holiday that year, and Cullum's departure on a yachting trip with friends left me unduly desolate. Childishly, I saw the present as eternity, and could not feel very much comforted by the thought that, like all three weeks, these must drag through to an end one day. Ticked off in days on my office blotter, they seemed interminable: frayed nerves were largely responsible for the state of depression into which I sank, but it made me realize as I had not done before how completely I had delivered myself into Cullum's nice hands: I, who had boasted valiantly to him six months previously, and to myself long ago, that no living thing should ever touch my heart!

His letters were the one consolation.

'After this, holidays together!' he wrote. 'I'm in
good company, but all day long things happen which
only you could fully appreciate. A boat would be
your ideal setting, my brown girl. Heartless object,
you didn't trouble to write to your Lord and Master
yesterday! All right, my dear, if there's nothing
when we go ashore this afternoon, I shall stick a pin
into the snapshot I have of you, on Jenny, and if I
still don't get a letter by to-morrow morning's post
I shall jab it into Jenny, which I know you would
resent more.'

Then he came back, having laboriously grown a short
beard, one of the tufty, aesthetic sort that will not meet
in the middle. It was the best he could do, and of a
reddish colour, but he was inordinately proud of it.
Convinced that he was the embryo of a great novelist,
he was resolved to begin looking the part now.

Defiantly he swaggered to the Table with it the day
after his return, having basked all the morning in the
criticism and attention it had drawn from the people
in his firm.

Ropes' fiancée, Alison Mann, was there, a charmingly pretty girl, who pleased him immensely by saying
that she would now be terrified if she met him in a
dark lane.

Raymond recoiled before the strange growth with
exaggerated symptoms of sickness, but Ropes, to our
immense astonishment, took no notice of it at all.
Half way through the meal Cullum, stroking the two
little tufts, was conquered by his curiosity.

'Well, Ropes, what do you think of my beard?'

Ropes rested serious eyes on it.

'Just for one moment, when I first saw you,' he said in his deep voice, 'I thought my Redeemer had come for me!'

The rising young author, helped by my scissors, got rid of it the same evening.

At lunch, forgetting the other girl, we started up one of our favourite kind of intellectual hares, the kinship of pity and love, and ran it merrily through complicated doublings and twistings, glad to be together again.

Ropes, talking of the pity innate in maternal love, began magnificently, 'That pampered fable, the woman's mind – '

'But Rob, you know you don't really *mean* that!' said his fiancée when he had finished, and to our horror, after floundering into explanations at which she smiled indulgently, the strongest-minded member of the Table took back nearly all that he had said.

Raymond scowled, loathing, quite comprehensibly, the intrusion of the deadly practical female mind into men's discussion of theories.

'No passion can be considered great unless it is socially impossible,' he said. This was one of his two favourite aphorisms at the moment; the other was 'For women, marriage is a matter of opportunity; love, of importunity;' and though neither had any bearing on the course of the conversation, he managed to introduce them both, blushing each time.

'Possibly pity and love are compatible in the case of the majority of women,' I said, answering Ropes, 'but you must remember that there are a large number of women, like myself, whose interest in anything declines as soon as it becomes weak enough to pity. Illness, helplessness, any kind of pitiable weakness doesn't appeal to us at all, rather the opposite. Where we pity we despise.'

'The attitude of the healthy savage!' commented Ropes. 'And a very good thing, too. Mankind is getting softened by too much ready sympathy. It's the fashion to excuse anything and everything. We bear with too much, good and bad, in these days. We're too indiscriminately kind.'

'Neither of you will ever be accused of that!' Cullum broke out. 'God keep me from falling into your hands, Ropes, if I am ever in need of a friend; you'd be as merciless as Esther! Can't you make allowances for weakness? – "Too much gentleness in the world!" – Everyone is still far too harsh towards anything that they don't understand, and they understand so little! There are extenuating circumstances in every case; of course there are! Why can't you see that?' He spoke with so much feeling that we were taken aback. He flushed, and Alison Mann kindly covered the slight awkwardness of the moment, caused by a man having said, in English and in public, something that he really meant.

'I confess to feeling drawn to anything that I can look after and boss a little,' she said. 'Rob says it's because it flatters my vanity to be needed; I tell him it's the reason why I'm going to marry him!'

Cullum smiled at her. 'Thank goodness everyone isn't as hard as these self-assured, righteous people! All the same, they and their kind are in the majority everywhere, unfortunately.'

The incident closed. I pick it out of a number of such recollections of Cullum pleading for tolerance. If they were appeals to us for understanding, they were pathetic, for they failed; we condemned easily and ruthlessly.

A few weeks after this, Ropes told us jubilantly that an uncle had offered to pay half the expenses of six

192

months' study in Berlin. He was to take his final
medicals at the end of that time. He went abroad
almost immediately, and before he went we gave him
a lunch, at the end of which he asked Cullum and
Raymond to keep a friendly eye on Alison, who lived
rather a lonely life in Putney with a married sister.
Both of them promised; I should have done so too, had
I been there when the matter was mentioned, but I
had returned to the Cameron Press punctually at
two o'clock for once. There had been trouble that
morning. Miss Bullen had asked me for a certain
address, and I had given it to her from memory.

'Don't guess. Look it up in the book!' she snapped.

'It isn't in the book.'

'And why not?'

'Well, I never put down the addresses I know.'

'Miss Sieveking, give me the address book!' she said
in an ominous tone. She looked through it and found
that there was hardly an entry in my writing, though
I had been on the *Office Friend* three months.

'This,' she said, with an awful look, 'is very, very
serious!'

She went into Miss Leslie's room, and after a few
minutes they came back together, Miss Leslie looking
very worried, Miss Bullen very fierce.

' – Never heard anything so unbusinesslike! She says
she remembers them all. Nearly all of them!'

'Well, does she?' asked Miss Leslie.

'So it seems, but that's not the point. It's the
unbusinesslike principle. . . .'

This was the burden of Miss Bullen's complaint
during the long discussion of my fate which followed.

Miss Bullen was for sacking me on the spot. Miss
Leslie, who wanted to keep me, pointed out patiently,
over and over again, that if they did, they would not

know any of the host of important addresses which I kept in my head: other delinquencies of the same sort were discovered; telephone numbers, advance payments and appointments were not written down as they should have been; I trusted my memory implicitly and rarely made any entries; it was actually the extent of my lack of business method which saved me; even Miss Bullen was at last brought to see that if I left suddenly there would be a terrible muddle; they would have no records at all of so many important things.

After this, though fairly secure in my position of living references, I thought it wise to be punctilious about trifles for a few days.

At first, after Ropes' departure, Cullum went over to see Alison Mann, or took her out to dinner, once a week, and Raymond followed suit at the beginning, but his other social engagements interfered, and after a time he gave up the habit. Cullum soon complained that he found it a tax. I gathered that Alison's sister, preoccupied with her husband and children, found the girl rather in the way in her ménage, and did not care who came to see her, or where she went.

Once when he proposed a duty visit, I suggested coming too, because he grumbled at the dull journey there and back by himself. Like Olive, he hated being alone. I was prepared to do it for his sake, or for Ropes': Alison, though she was very sweet, I did not find particularly interesting: but Cullum told me that she had said she did not like the society of other women; she was even more feminine than Janet. I was relieved to escape the little extra trouble; I was beginning to feel really worn out. London life did not suit me, and the unnatural conditions in which I was living made it more trying.

When Cullum had taken Alison to a dance one

evening because I had a raging headache and could not go with him, he sat on my bed after he got back. protesting humorously that it was not fair on the morals of a bachelor if he had to dance with other men's fiancées who clung langorously and very noticeably did not wear corsets. (Alison was inclined to plumpness.) Still feeling nautical from his holiday he described her neatly and technically as a 'beamy little craft that missed stays.'

Then the week between his visits slipped into a fortnight, and after a time I heard no more of Alison. I was too absorbed in my happiness to give another thought to her.

It was a glorious summer for me, in spite of a growing feeling of malaise. The days fled too fast. Being run down in health I caught influenza badly when it swept through the office. I was in bed with it for ten days at the Hayes' house, too ill to move to my boarding-house, or to go home. Cullum did most of the nursing before he left for the office in the morning and when he came back in the evening. When he was engaged in the evening, as he was once or twice, I missed him badly. When I came back to work Miss Leslie was so shocked by my appearance that she sent me away for ten days' convalescence, as I had had no holiday. I crawled thankfully back to bed. I was no longer feeling ill, but simply tired out. Cullum came in, after work, full of a great plan, and kissed me, as he insisted on doing throughout the illness, disregarding my protests that he would probably catch it.

'I shall, officially!' he said on that occasion, 'we're going away together!'

He told me of the little fishing village, West Mersea, in Essex, where he and his party had put in for a night

195

during the holiday. None of the local people knew his name or whether he was married or not; few of them would even remember having seen him. It was then late September, and he knew that a fishing smack could be hired for five pounds a week, including the services of the owner, who would act as cook and skipper.

'You want sea air. Well, I'll take you to Mersea, and we'll hire a smack. Think! A week in a boat together in this weather! It would be ideal. It would mean sharing the cabin at night, of course, but we should be little closer to each other than we are now. What do letter-of-the-law restrictions matter to us now? You know I love you well enough not to do anything that you don't wish, beloved. Oh, can you imagine anything finer?'

'Don't! It is so tempting,' I said, 'but I'm not going to have you pretending to have 'flu if you haven't, and I'm not going to pretend to be Mrs. Something-or-Other when I'm not!'

'Oh, damn that prejudice of yours! Coming up against it in your mind is like seeing a woman in a gorgeous evening dress with a bit of thick woolly underclothes showing at the neck! You needn't do the fibbing; I'm not so squeamish!' He knelt down by the bed and slipped his arm under my shoulders. 'Don't you want to come, sweetheart?' he said persuasively.

I rested my hot cheek against his cool one, smelling the nice blended fragrance of tobacco, shaving-soap and youth that Cullum brought with him.

'Yes, I do! You know that. Oh, it would be glorious! Promise that it will be all right?'

'I promise, my dear!'

Everything went smoothly. London was full of

influenza at the time; no one questioned Cullum's illness; probably several other people in both our firms took a little holiday on the same excuse.

Twenty-four hours before we left Town – with his mother's expressed approval – some change took place in Cullum; I could not make out what it was. He lost all enthusiasm for the trip, and at the last minute would not have gone, if the boat had not already been engaged by telegram. I was afraid that Nemesis was upon him, in the shape of influenza, but once we reached the little village in the great salt marshes he regained his spirits. We had a week of those fine, crisply warm autumn days which open mistily and close in a hushed calm. The fishing-smack and all connected with it delighted me. Save the lines of a fine horse in full gallop I know of nothing lovelier than the lines of a well-built boat, and those East Coast fishing-smacks with their low sterns and flush decks are wonderfully seaworthy boats, and a joy to see under their wide spread of brown canvas.

Cullum decided we were to be Mr. and Mrs. Chaldicott-Hume – 'Chaldicott with two t's,' he insisted on explaining each time he had a chance, at the local pub and to the wife of the man who owned the smack. I kicked his ankle unobtrusively. It was an excellent *nom de péché* he considered, because it sounded convincing; no one would be likely to adopt such a mouthful of their own free will.

I enjoyed being called 'Mum' by Charlie, the sturdy little fisherman with a face like a wrinkled apple. He had the distinguished manners common among East Coast folk, which did not preclude his using the most appalling language before me, in a cheery conversational way. He took a fancy to me.

'If all women were like you, Mum,' he said to me

one evening, to Cullum's delight, 'there'd never be any trouble with the men!'

I am sure he meant it kindly, though it was one of the most uncomplimentary remarks ever made to me.

Under Charlie's direction, Cullum was bringing the smack down the Blackwater to her berth in Mersea Quarters one evening.

'There's the Nass beacon; you'd better let me take her now, sir,' he said unnecessarily. Cullum had been yachting every summer since he was fourteen, but like every other fisherman, Charlie had not the slightest respect for an amateur's seamanship.

As usual, the Nass End cormorant, outlined black against the vivid evening sky, was sitting in solitary state on the basket-shaped Nass End beacon, which marks a submerged mud-spit running out into the estuary. Charlie told us that the bird was always on this perch; no one had ever seen him fishing, and no one had ever seen more than one there. He did not think there was another cormorant in the immediate neighbourhood at that time; they are not exactly rare birds in Essex, but uncommon enough for the presence of two or three together to be remarked on.

The bird stayed on the beacon as we drifted slowly towards him on the tide. The customary evening calm had set in with the ebb; the sun was going down in glory, crimson and gold, behind the flat expanse of the marshes, and as it was an evening of exquisite peace, the young male mind turned automatically to thoughts of slaughter.

'He'd make a fine shot perched up there, wouldn't he?' said Cullum, taking an imaginary sight with the boat-hook.

'She'd not stay there for you to get close enough to

hit, sir,' said Charlie in his sing-song Essex voice. 'She'll move, soon enough now. See?'

The cormorant slowly stretched out his wings, looking like a Chinese decoration for a few seconds as he stood silhouetted against the red sky. Then he launched himself from the beacon, the weight of his body bearing him down almost to the water before he lifted and flapped leisurely away, sweeping round in a wide circle until we had passed, and then returning to his vantage point, from which, until the night hid him completely, we saw him surveying the waste of mud-bank and darkening water.

'Wonder if anyone has ever had a shot at him?'

'Well, I couldn't rightly tell, but Hunky – maybe you've heard tell of my cousin Samuel George, Hunky that is, who saved they five Burnham smacksmen off the Buxey Sand last season?'

'No. Did he?'

'Yes, Mum. Had a drop too much that night. Got a Humane medal for it. Well, Hunky, he says he's been out and shot that little owld bird. He does say he killed her, but I say, "Well, boy, but there is the owld bird, right enough!" And he says, "Yes, mate, but she's another one!" And I say, "Well, she doesn't look it!" So I can't rightly say. I never see the cormorant gone, but he does say he killed her. Still, you can't believe they Georges! If you was thinking of a bit of gunning, sir, we'll lay up for duck to-night down Sal'c't Crick. You fetch me off from the Hard at two to-night and we'll pick up my owld gun-punt and go down to the pans in the Crick.' I found out afterwards that these saltpans in Saltcott Creek are wide, shallow openings in the sea-wall, where the wild-fowl come down at night to feed.

Cullum looked at me doubtfully.

'I don't suppose Mrs. Chaldicott-Hume – ' he began to Charlie.

But he had bemoaned to me some time before that since the Hayes family moved to London, he missed the shooting that he used to enjoy as a boy in Warwickshire; so I insisted that he should go.

'All right, then,' said Cullum, not very keen, because he said that punt-gunning, which he had never tried, did not strike him as offering much sport. Scattering half a pound of duck-shot among a number of sitting birds at one shot seemed too wholesale a method of killing: the odds were too much in favour of the sportsman.

Charlie looked at him strangely. 'You've not been gunning down these parts!' he said cryptically.

We turned in early, half dressed, because it was cold that evening and the night promised to be colder still.

It was as Cullum had said: sleeping actually in the same cabin, within a few feet of each other, had made little difference to our relationship, save that it had, if anything, increased both the sense of intimacy and the sense of reserve that went with it. Flung almost into each other's arms, by inclination and Mrs. Hayes, we were accustomed, if not physically reconciled, to this state of constant stimulation and control.

'This is very hard for me, but it's worth it,' Cullum said, kissing me good-night before he turned in himself.

The wind was rising, and it was blowing against the set of the tide. Contrary wind and tide mean misery in a small boat at night. The dinghy, made fast astern, bumps against the side, held alongside by the wind. She did so then, at maddening, irregular intervals, for what seemed an eternity. Shivering with cold, Cullum let go her painter from one side, and, standing in the dewy cockpit with bare feet, cursing hard, worked her round the rudder with the boat-hook and with much difficulty made her fast on the other side. She bumped impartially wherever he tied her, and however long the rope he gave her, which was the only remedy he knew for bumping, except tying a bucket over her stern so that the tide would hold her against the wind. He hunted frantically for the canvas bucket that we knew was on board somewhere, but could not find it. Sleep was impossible until one o'clock, when the tide changed. Then we slept soundly until four a.m., when it was too late to do anything.

When we met Charlie later in the day on the Hard, the little stone jetty, he accepted our shame-faced explanations without a word. His was the invariable courtesy of the East Coast man, but he looked at Cullum with the glance that fishermen keep for amateur sailors. With perfect tact he said that conditions, the moon and so on, would be even better that night. He also brought us an alarm clock.

There was wind against tide again, and we anticipated another disturbed night, having forgotten to ask him what he had done with the canvas bucket; but the dinghy did not bump. She seemed almost reluctant to come alongside when we drew her up at half-past one, jumped in, and cast off. The tide should not have been running very hard, but we seemed to be getting swept down rather fast in proportion to the headway we were making.

'Pull!' I said.

'I – am – pulling!' said Cullum, obviously rowing hard; 'but she's extraordinarily heavy. Is there a lot of water in her?'

I peered down in the darkness.

'No, I can't feel much.'

He had to put his back into it to get her to the Hard, where a dark figure was waiting.

Charlie stepped in, and without a word leant over the side, untied a line, invisible in that light, from the ring below the scull-hole, and hauled in and emptied the canvas bucket which he had fixed there, unseen by us, before he left us in his own dinghy, the previous evening. In the semi-darkness I could feel him looking at Cullum.

'I'll lay that stopped her bumping!'

'Oh, yes,' said Cullum in a subdued tone, 'it was most effective!'

I should have liked to give Charlie a shilling and our permission to tell us what he really thought of Cullum as a yachtsman at that moment: conjecture is so much worse than knowledge. Silently and easily we rowed off down Saltcott Creek.

For a long while I sat in the dinghy alone, anchored in mid-stream, watching the serene moonlight on the shining ripples of the dark water, listening to the calling of unseen sea-birds and wondering where the two men had got to. Lying flat on their faces in the tippy little gun-punt with the old duck-gun mounted in her bows, they were paddling themselves as quietly as possible down the 'crick,' using hand-pads, which slip on like gloves, and get the paddler's hands chilled to the bone in the water. A biting wind was blowing over the marshes, but I had made such good recovery in the last few days that, well wrapped up, I did not feel the cold at all.

I heard one shot, and a few minutes afterwards their voices as they rowed back. Once the birds are scared it is useless to hope for a second chance. Charlie, encouraged by Cullum, was carrying on a one-sided argument on the relative values of mother's milk and

202

beer. To the fact that he was reared almost exclusively on the latter, Charlie attributed his present freedom from all ailments. A bottle of beer had been left in my charge in the dinghy, to which Charlie was now returning like a swiftly homing bird, and no doubt this had suggested the subject.

They came back empty-handed. A punt-gun can only reach its quarry on the water, or just as they are rising, and the birds had been flying a good deal that night, added to which the water was lumpy, and the gun is aimed by the boat. They had only had one good chance, at a group of widgeon feeding among some reeds. Patiently they had stalked up to leeward, as widgeon have scent as keen as a dog's as well as eyes like a lynx's; and then a curlew, rising for no apparent reason at all, had startled the shy creatures and put them up. They had fired on the off-chance, and missed.

Having changed his mind about the odds being too much against the birds, in East Coast wild-fowling, Cullum was bitten with this duck business.

'We'll go out flighting this evening in the dinghy with an ordinary gun, if Charlie has got one. I know the places now. Lots of singles and pairs came over low while we were trying for those widgeon. We won't trouble Charlie to come.'

We borrowed an old twelve-bore from him: an incredibly disreputable gun, actually with string round the stock and barrel, and corroded with rust from long association with salt air and long dissociation from oil. He gave us some special cartridges of his, at which Cullum looked dubiously.

Hidden in the reeds at sunset, I waited in suspense for the moment when that appalling weapon would have to be fired, but only two birds came near the place where they had passed almost continuously the night before, and these two came together. One was a diver, swimming, and the other a flapper duck. Cullum fired both barrels.

There was a blinding flash and a roar. The dinghy rocked as if a squall had struck her. A pall of smoke blotted out everything, and the water in all directions, it seemed, was pounded into little columns of spray by duck-shot. Cullum said the gun kicked like an elephant gun, though I do not suppose he had ever handled an elephant gun, and he swore he heard the loose pieces rattle as he fired.

Through the thinning smoke we saw the startled diver dive, and the flapper flapping away.

Our luck was out, but doggedly determined now, we got up for the morning flight. It would be too galling to have nothing to show when Charlie came off to us later on.

We had five shots: the same terrific performance each time, and the same result. Either the remarkable gun was hopelessly out of the true, or Cullum had lost his straight eye. We differed about it; I clung to the second explanation, because in the one try I had, I knocked out a few tail feathers from an otherwise unhurt redshank, and so the first alternative seemed too unflattering. But there was really little doubt about it.

Mortified, despairing and with our blood up, we rowed back up the 'crick' towards Mersea Quarters in the cruel light of a bitter dawn. Feeling too ruffled for any more sleep, Cullum got the smack under weigh with terrific exertion, shouting to me to do things simultaneously at different ends of the boat. We tacked out towards the Nass End, that famous trap for unwary yachtsmen.

On the beacon sat the cormorant. His placidity was somehow more than either of us could bear.

'We can't shoot the brute; let's scare him off,' said Cullum, 'I like the way he dips when he launches himself.'

We stood on, stood right in, far closer than we had done when the bird flew off before, and still he appeared perfectly unconcerned. The tide was rising, so that even if we touched we should not be aground for long.

'Look out, it's getting shallow,' I said.

'Right. Lee-ho!'

And as we came about we stuck by the stern.

Cullum, jabbing with the sweep into soft mud, said and did what is usual in the circumstances, but the cormorant, who must have heard and seen it all many times before, treated us as though we were not there. We settled down to a few minutes' wait.

'I'll make that blasé bird move!' said Cullum, and picked up the gun. With anything less antiquated it would have been a ridiculously easy shot and Cullum took long and careful aim. It seemed safer for the cormorant if he did, so I made no protest. There came again the spurt of flame and the tremendous crash. The smack, lifting on the tide, rocked a little, and everything was obscured for a second by blue smoke. Shot splashed the sea all about us. To our astonishment and horror the cormorant fell dead into the water.

We did not retrieve the body, and when the tide freed us we cruised about for a while, not feeling inclined to face West Mersea having removed one of its most distinctive landmarks. To have shot the cormorant seemed futile and inexcusable. Both of us realized in the next two hours all that the Ancient Mariner felt about the albatross. Then we returned to pick up

Charlie, sailing back with half-averted eyes past the incomplete-looking Nass End beacon.

We told him about it when we were well out into the Blackwater again, away from the beacon on whose unusual bareness he had not remarked as we sailed out.

Without comment Charlie picked up the binoculars Cullum had brought and focussed on the Nass, now far astern. Then he handed the glasses to me. Sitting contemplatively on the beacon was a cormorant.

'But we killed it!' I said.

'Yes, of course we did,' said Cullum, who had not yet seen, surprised at my tone. 'Why?'

Charlie merely looked at the amateur sailor in the way that fishermen do. He smiled politely and incredulously.

'She's been the only cormorant I see about Mersea for a long time,' was all he said.

For nothing on earth would we have shot that bird again, but we could never decide in our own minds what it was that sat imperturbably on the Nass End beacon for the rest of our stay, and probably long after. Was it the identical bird that Cullum, and possibly Hunky George too, shot at and hit once at any rate, or was it his successor, from some hidden reserve of cormorants which supplies vacancies at short notice, or do cormorants have ghosts?

There was what they call in West Mersea an 'easterly loom' that day, a mirage effect in which trees on distant land that is normally out of sight are visible, apparently growing straight out of the water. It was the time of the equinoctial gales, and we had a hard day's sailing in a stiffening easterly wind. After four days in that extremely bracing air I was feeling really fit again and immensely in love with Cullum. He was in his element. Standing with the tiller between his knees, bare-headed, bare-armed, and with the sun lighting his happy, freckled face, he made an unforgettable figure. This is my second outstanding memory of Cullum. When I recall him one or other of these two scenes spring first into my mind. There swept over me then, with a singing of blood in my ears, the realization of how much I wanted him.

When we were back on the moorings in the evening, Charlie lit the lamp for us in the comfortable, dusk-filled cabin, and pulled the hatch over, shutting out the fading red of the sky.

'Well, then, I'll be "something" off now, Mum, if there's nothing more you want,' he said, and left us.

We lounged on our bunks for some time, one on each side of the cabin, saying nothing, but enjoying the close companionship that follows shared physical exertion. 'Come up on deck,' said the boy at last, and his voice startled me. From the deck we saw the twinkling lights of the village, half a mile away, making tiny broken paths of gold over the water towards us. He made room for me on the hatch, and sat close to me, not touching me. There were frostily bright stars, and a glow over that part of the marshes where the moon would rise soon; sea-birds were calling like lost souls. We seemed to be surrounded by feathered spirits. Occasionally, close over head, sounded the dry whirring of their wings, but we could not see them in the semi-darkness. We sat there, I believe, for hours, in this dim, most glorious night, and quite suddenly the moon rose, flooding the water with light and silvering the black shapes of the deserted smacks near by. We were utterly alone. It felt as if nature's eternal sense of waiting had come to a breaking-point of strain. Cullum's hand, burning hot, closed over mine. Trembling, I drew mine away, and went below, feeling unreasoningly that I must get away from him. For a long while I sat with my head in my hands, hearing him walking to and fro just above, before I started preparing to turn in. He swung himself down through the hatch before I was ready, and stood looking at me.

Desire in the eyes of the beloved man is the most wonderful sight earth holds for a woman.

'Esther, how beautiful you are!'

We both laughed shakily at nothing. He undressed, as I had seen him do often enough before, but there was new glamour over everything that night. Cullum, stripped, was an unusually fine human creature. His body was one of those entirely beautiful things whose loveliness hurts. He was lithe, and the moulding of the long arms, lean and muscle-grooved, was splendid. Wide shoulders tapered down to narrow hips, set over narrow, deep thighs, and his fair skin held an almost transparent sheen.

He came over to me and instinctively I drew back, full of the happy fear of women. He caught hold of me and kissed my mouth, and throat, slipping the thin silk from my shoulders.

He let me go, and hesitated. 'No, my dear, I –'
And I held out my arms to him.

He took me then, and kissed me until my senses merged in a throbbing ecstasy of pain. All through the soft, warm darkness of that night we lay in each other's arms, and slept a little, and woke to kiss and whisper, glorying in the wild, new, blinding wonder of love.

Chapter 12: *Breaking*

IN the morning light we were shy with each other.
'I say, Cullum,' I said, realizing the high-sounding
fact with amusement, 'are you aware that you are
technically a seducer of innocent maidens? One
maiden, anyway. How wonderfully sinister that
sounds!'

'Doesn't it! And you're my victim!'

The idea struck us as supremely funny. It was
impossible to think of Cullum in such a light, or of
me, either.

'It's your own fault,' he said. 'You trusted a good
young man – I am that, really, on the whole – which
anyone experienced in such matters would tell you is
fatal. To the bad man, satiated with conquest, one
woman more or less is nothing. He's quite willing to
do without her. His attitude is, never run after a
woman or a 'bus, because there's sure to be another
coming round the corner in a minute. Women are all
alike to him. But the good young man like me wants
one special woman, and it isn't fair – in fact – oh,
come here! I can't talk consecutively when you watch
me with such eyes, Esther!'

With his lips touching mine he murmured something
at which I felt my face turn scarlet, and he laughed.

Cullum, as the possessive lover, was more exacting,
more autocratic than he had been; gentler too. He
made the darkness of the nights bright for me with

words. Love, separating us from the rest of the world, as all lovers are isolated in spirit, changed the flesh of this man into flame, for me.

We made love humorously, which was as it should be.

'I believe the whole idea of sex was evolved by the old gods, wearied by centuries of life and appalled by the prospect of eternal boredom,' said Cullum when we were lazing on deck in the sun the next morning, while Charlie was below, preparing lunch. 'A terrible conception, everlasting, goal-less existence! I can't think why people are so keen on having it. Lack of imagination, I should think – At any rate, the old gods looked round desperately for some unfailing source of amusement to lighten the tedium of immortality, and invented the whole gorgeous, ridiculous business of love. They knew that watching it from on high would keep them entertained for ever. Looked at dispassionately, through the eyes of a god, it must be funny, you know, to see man strutting about the earth, striving to be dignified, and constantly getting tripped up by sex and forced to make himself grotesquely undignified and absurd. Because, of course, the practical side of love, viewed impersonally, is the most comical thing that any ingenuity could conceive. Luckily, we can't view it impersonally, for long.'

On the last day of our brief, stolen honeymoon, Charlie looked up at me with a smile while I was steering.

'You've not been married long, Mum, if I might say?'

'What makes you think that?'

'The bloom on your face.' He added in a fatherly manner, 'Bless you, it's good for the eyes to see young people like you and the gentleman!'

About a week after we had both officially recovered from the effects of 'flu, Cullum took me to a dance at a new cabaret place which had sent an invitation for two to his paper, hoping for a little publicity. As we walked in, Cullum stopped dead by the door.

'Oh, heavens!' he exclaimed, 'there's Paula!'

She was standing with a group of people on the other side of the room, not facing us; but as if she felt his presence she turned and her eyes travelled round the room. She saw him, and for one instant her lovely, impassive face was charged with joy. She took a step forward, saw me, and stopped, and remained staring wide-eyed at Cullum.

'This is awkward!' he mumbled. 'Wait here a minute – d'you mind? – I'd better – she thought I was abroad, you see.'

He went over to her, and at his coming her eyes lit up pathetically. He drew her aside and they had a few minutes earnest, rather excited conversation. He kept glancing round at me. Her expression changed as he spoke; surprise and disappointment came first, and quiet anger, it seemed to me, and surprise again. When he left her, her face looked as though he had struck her. She took no notice of us for the rest of the evening. Cullum was too irritable to be questioned.

'The girl's a fool,' was all he vouchsafed as explanation when he came back to me, and as I had a hearty dislike of people who showed curiosity, we did not talk of her any more. The incident entirely spoiled the evening, but in the enchantment of the night we forgot it.

A week later the Coles asked us to dinner. Now that I was engaged to Cullum, Mrs. Cole felt bound to invite me with him. Save that Paula McMillan was not there, the whole dinner was reminiscent of the one at which I had met Cullum: the conversation was almost the same. I wondered if he spared a thought to that easily forgotten girl to whom he had been engaged. He did not appear to. Having an admiring, uncritical audience in Mr. and Mrs. Cole, he was at his best as a conversationalist. The possibility of being sent abroad by his paper had put him in unusually good spirits.

After dinner we played, for very small stakes, a family card game, on the lines of Coon Can, which was always played at the Coles.'

'We don't really *gamble*, you know,' Mrs. Cole explained. 'We only play for money to make the game more interesting.'

This was the kind of subtle distinction which my mother would have understood more easily than Cullum or I.

Cullum won continually. According to the Coles, he always did. He must have made about three shillings, after repeated winnings, when Mr. Cole, beating him for once, said, 'Done you this time, my boy. Pay up and smile!'

It was a friendly game in which we each kept our own score, paying in pennies as we went for the sum of whatever cards were left in our hands when someone 'went out.'

The prosperous City man, rubbing his hands in anticipation, showed more satisfaction at the prospect of making about sevenpence, chiefly out of his family, than he probably evinced over his most successful business deals.

'You only get tuppence-ha'penny out of me, anyway,' said Cullum.

'It's positively unfair,' I said jokingly, 'the way in which luck looks after you! I think I shall have to audit your accounts!' Saying this, I whipped out of his hand the four cards he had not been able to get rid of, just as he picked up the pack to shuffle. I only saw the cards for a second before I mixed them in with mine and returned them to the pack, making some silly remark about the devil and his own, but they blazed into my brain. Cullum was cheating.

No one was paying any attention to us at the moment. The Coles were settling up with coppers. My eyes met Cullum's: he was caught off his guard, with no time to dissimulate. His face had grown white and his eyes were appealing. There was no question of whether he was cheating deliberately or not. His face admitted it before he could control his expression.

We went on with this futile game, avoiding looking towards each other. I do not know what I said, throughout the rest of the long evening, except that I talked a great deal, sitting there, half-stunned with sudden misery, knowing, but incapable of fully be-lieving as yet, that Cullum cheated at cards – cheated at cards for a few pence – cheated! –

Cullum ceased to win all the time; I suppose he was playing fair.

'Aha, I've broken your luck, Cullum!' said Mr. Cole.

Cullum cheated! Over my brain floated the black cloud of this knowledge, like a fog threatening to descend, to settle down on my mind and make me realize what had happened, and then I should not be able to pretend any more to this excited gaiety that was making the Coles laugh now. But I knew that I must go on pretending, go on being garrulous among these garrulous fools, who did not know that my world was crumbling under their eyes. Cullum cheated at cards! I knew that there were people who did that, just as I knew that there were people who committed murder; both acts seemed equally incredible and remote from my life.

We left at last. I was staying with his people at the time, and we went home by Underground, in dreadful silence among a noisy crowd of late travellers. In my bedroom once more I said:

'We might as well talk about this and get it over.' I had reached a stage of nervous, unnatural calmness. 'So you cheat at cards, Cullum! While playing with friends – with me – for paltry sums. Not that this makes it any worse, only somehow – '

He caught me in his arms, kissing me, denying nothing, because he knew that it was too late, begging for the pity and understanding that I did not possess. I waited impassively until he let me go.

'I'd rather you did not touch me!' I said, young and hard and wounded.

He went into his room, and I crept into bed, crying weakly for hours in the darkness, desperately conscious that in the next room was Cullum, for whom my whole being was clamouring. Unable to fight against the overwhelming shock of disillusion, I remained awake, hearing the slow quarters and hours chiming from the church near by until, worn out with emotion, I lay there without thinking, longing with an agony of intensity for Cullum's comforting arms. I went to him at last, driven by desire stronger than any I had known.

He was asleep. I kissed him and he stirred, seized my arm, and drew me to him. Defiantly I blotted out for a few moments the raw, intolerable new ache which I carried with me, like a mental shadow, in the days that followed the unhappy waking from this night of fitful, exhausted sleep.

I left the Hayes' house and went back to my lodgings, wanting to see things in their fresh perspective, apart from the intoxication of Cullum's presence. I had worshipped Cullum, believing him to be the embodiment of my impossible ideals. He was always good at realizing quickly what anyone would like him to be, and adopting the role, unconsciously. He had played up to my dreams very well.

For three days I did my work at the office much as usual, and at lunch time went to the Table keyed up with the expectation of meeting him. He was not there, however. The longing to see him, if nothing more, became so acute that I wrote to him. We had not parted with any idea of finality; actually we had parted in a very matter-of-fact, hurried manner, being both very late in starting for our different offices, and the understanding had been that we should see each other at the Table, I having left the Hayes' house for the time being. I do not know how he explained my sudden departure to his mother; excellently I have no doubt.

He answered with a remarkable letter, vaguely worded, but evidently intended as a final good-bye. Mercifully, a shock supplies its own anæsthetic; I could not take in this second one all at once.

'I know it is useless to make excuses to you, with your cool, strict straightness, which I loved, as you know, – because I haven't got it myself, I suppose,' he wrote. 'In your code there is no excuse for cheating at cards, nor for lying, and I have lied to you in all sorts of ways, trying to seem what I knew you hoped I was. Sooner or later I knew you would find me out; it is almost a relief now that the time has come. I am a weak cad, but I wonder if you can understand how terrible it is for a man to live with the shadow of his real self always lying ghost-wise between him and the infinitely desired dream which is close enough to be touched, and to know that if he reaches out to his dream, assuredly the shadow will reach out too and destroy it? You made too high a pedestal for me out of your ideals, is it altogether my fault that I have fallen from it?

'You are a temptation to deceive, because you never suspect falseness. You remember the story I told you of having saved a boy from drowning near Liphook last summer? That was all an invention. I tell you that as an instance; there are so many others. Now that I know it will make no difference one way or the other, since you've found me out in something else, confession is a relief.

'And yet of all the things I've told you about myself, most of which are untrue, none of them was consciously invented. My damned imagination works too well; I say what it or the wish of the listener prompts, and at the time I believe what I am saying myself. It's the auto-intoxication of words, and afterwards I realize what a contemptible thing I've done, but then it's too late to explain; no one would have the courage to do it then. Can you understand? – Oh, no, I know you can't! Perhaps, somewhere, I shall find someone who will.'

There was a good deal more of it. The writing of that letter would have been an emotional indulgence to any author; Cullum must have particularly enjoyed it, I thought. (I had grown bitter in a few days.) It ended:

'Not the least part of the hell I'm going through is the knowledge that you are suffering damnably too. Writing this, I'm crying, as a man – the decent

216

sort of man that you should have loved – does not
do! I've got the job abroad, and shall keep out of
your way until I go. That will be better for us
both.

'With all my will I hope you will forget me, as I
shall try to forget you; only with my heart I pray
weakly that you'll think of me sometimes, because
I know that I shall always remember. Good-bye,
Esther, sweetheart.'

His letter left me dazed for several days. I could not
believe that Cullum had gone out of my life for ever,
nor that he was the contemptible romancer and cheat
that life had suddenly proved him. I only knew that
I wanted him. My mind recognized that he was
worthless, my body was crying out for him; reason has
no more power to recall love than to bestow it.

The days were desolation: there was no meaning in
anything, but happily there was work that had to be
done, and necessity is the mother not only of invention,
but of that strange unreckonable force, human endurance, which makes it possible for a man or a woman
to get through the day's trivial jobs when their world
has smashed under their feet.

But the nights were intolerable, for in them there
was no escaping from desire.

Night after night I used to lie, with every muscle
tense in the torment of physical longing, my arms
round the pillow for the comfort of gripping something,
wishing that tears came easily to me: they would have
helped. Until sleep came. And then sometimes I used
to dream of him at Holmwood or, once or twice, in
the boat. In the dreams we would be happy, till a
vague sense that something was terribly wrong crept
into it, and though I could not recall what it was,

I would cling to him, afraid. I grew to dread those
dreams, recalling vividly, as they did, the departed
glory that had transfigured my world. Waking from
them, I sounded the depths of the wide range of emotional experience, trying to alleviate, if only for a
moment, the endless, hopeless strain of wanting
Cullum, whom I despised.

I went often to see Janet, to escape the unaccustomed
loneliness of the evenings. My free hours, which I
had counted like a miser, had become heavy burdens
that must be borne somehow; they were easier if shared.

She had seen Cullum, and I asked for news of him,
ashamed of my eagerness to hear of him. To my
astonishment, he had told her of his own accord
exactly what had led up to the breaking of the engagement. She told me that he had impressed her as being
very much distressed.

'The role expected of him!' I said. 'I'm sure he even
felt it – while he was here!'

'That may be clever,' she said, 'but it's not worthy
of you. It is the sort of thing that Cullum would not
stoop to say. He was very sweet in speaking of you.
It was you he was thinking of, more than himself.'

'Cullum is naturally kind,' I said. 'It's one of the
nice things about him. But I'm not. I remember we
agreed one day that kindness and weakness generally
go together, and he said it was a pity that I hadn't a
little more of both, and of course he was right. When
I'm hurt I can't think first of anyone else's trouble;
nothing exists but my own pain. And the thought that
I allowed myself to be loved by Cullum, by a man who
can stoop to what is, to me, the meanest form of
trickery – ' (Janet had known of the relationship).
I caught hold of her hands and buried my head in
her lap, feeling the need of human contact. 'I can't

tell you what that means to me, I can't bear to think of it!'

'But my dear, cheating at cards, after all – !' she said. 'Of course, it's wrong, but if I had been in your place –'

'Oh, I know,' I said wearily. 'If it had been any nice woman she would have gone on loving him just the same! But I have none of that maternal kind of love which sweeps pride aside. For me, love is based on respect, on pride in the other person, and once that is gone, I can't love them any more – with my mind,' I added. 'Cullum cheats at cards. Admits it because for once he had no chance of lying successfully. He is not even particularly ashamed of it, as long as he is not found out. Well, to me cheating is incomprehensible, and therefore unforgivable.'

'But if it was for a few pence only, why is it so dreadful? I am not excusing Cullum, but I think you two ought to come together again; you are making yourselves wretched for too small a cause.'

'It's the littleness of the sum he can cheat for that makes it so despicable; can't you see that?'

We argued for a long time, and I said bitter things.

'I can see one thing,' she said at last, not unkindly. 'There is only one thing that you love, and that is your own pride. It's wounded, and there lies the whole extent of your trouble. Don't think me unsympathetic; I am very sorry for you both, for it all seems unnecessary.'

She was kind to me, but Cullum had touched the maternal side, which was as dominant a factor in her as pride in me. He appealed not only to that part of her nature, but to the woman's natural preference for the man's side of any cause. Before these two primitive instincts the artificial tie of friendship broke down.

She said prettily that I was welcome at all times, but she made me feel that I was not wanted. And yet I did go back, though it made me unhappier each time, but I was urged by a longing to hear news of Cullum. Janet and I grew apart as I should not have believed possible in so short a time. Cullum wrote to her, too, very touchingly; as he could so easily once he had made himself believe the appropriate sentiments. Janet was completely won by the obvious sincerity with which that letter was written, and was annoyed by my heartlessness when I laughed scornfully at it.

Gradually the dull resentment against Cullum that smouldered in me, because he had broken my dreams and made me ashamed, flamed up into a slow, growing hatred. It was a quiet passionless hatred; after that one outburst the first time I saw Janet after the breaking of the engagement, I did not speak bitterly of Cullum to her again. I never mentioned him at all unless she did, and yet I was always hoping that she would talk of him: for I still cared for him.

She must have read by my face that I was becoming more and more unhappy. She put her hand gently on my harm just as I was leaving her house one day. 'Esther, you need comfort that I can't give you. I wish I could. Why don't you pray?

'No!' I said fiercely, jerking my arm from her hand. 'I didn't pray in the height of my happiness. I am not going to whine now!'

'That is nothing but arrogance, which doesn't help anyone to bear sorrow.'

'There you're wrong, St. Janet! Arrogance may be an abomination in the sight of the Lord, but it's sometimes one's salvation in a time of trouble! I believe that stubborn pride which is deeply rooted in anyone's character is the one thing that will carry them through a trial in which the rest of their world has forsaken them. It is the last defender of the stronghold when goodness, courage and hope – usually in that order – have given way! I'm rather an authority on pride, according to you, so you can take my word for it.'

'My dear, I'm not joking now. Be serious for a moment. Why harden yourself when this may be God's way of helping you to find Him? You wouldn't listen to Him when you had Cullum, and perhaps that's why you have lost him. Now things are changed; why not give Him a chance?'

'Very flattering of Him to consider my soul worth the price of another person's honesty!' I said. 'But He'll have to try again!'

'You hurt yourself as well as me when you talk in that way. To turn to God now wouldn't be "whining," even if you didn't share your happiness with him. When my kiddie was playing about happily, he didn't need me all the time, and I understood that, but as soon as he was hurt he came to me and I didn't consider that whining. A mother – or a father – may respect the child who prefers to stand on its own feet at all times, but will not love it as much as the child who turns for help in its troubles. Cullum at least recognizes his own weakness. You saw what he wrote to me about wanting my prayers.'

'I did,' I said, 'and I thought it quite one of the best-written passages! But if there is a God I'd rather He respected me than loved me. I have had just about enough loving lately! There, don't look so concerned. There are plenty of other things besides religion left in the world for me. Horses, and trees and books. After all, since you are sure I've no heart, it follows that it can't even be chipped, doesn't it? Only my sense of proportion has gone for the time being, and already my one-sided sense of humour – which Cullum, by the way, never really liked – has recovered enough now to let me see that it's funny that he, of all people, should have chosen me, of all people, and that I should have made an idol of him!'

With an effort of will I made myself stop these frequent visits to Janet after this. It was too disturbing to the peace of mind for which I strove to be with her, in her house, when I knew that Cullum had lately been there, and the rooms seemed full of him still. If it was only my pride that was wounded, as she said, then pride is more vulnerable than I had thought, for the scar did not heal with the passing of the days, as I told myself vehemently that it would.

'Soon it won't hurt so much! It won't! Soon it'll be better. Oh, surely it must!' I used to say to myself at night, with my face buried in the pillow and my fingers gripping the iron of the bedstead side, for the queer comfort that the pain of the sharp edge pressing into my hand gave me after a while. But it was not so; the dragging weeks brought no alleviation.

I was thrown very much on my own society. Cullum and Janet I had lost; I could not go to the Table for lunch any longer, for Raymond was Cullum's friend, and knowing nothing of the story, believed that I had broken the engagement and had treated him rather badly: unfortunately, Ropes, for whose company I would have given a great deal, was out of reach. My own people at Holmwood heard only that the engagement had ended, and took it for granted that it was by mutual consent.

'We weren't really suitable, Father. He didn't

care for horses, you know,' I said carelessly, and that seemed to him an adequate explanation. Olive, the romantic-minded, was loud in her lamentations and pestered me for details. Gerald Hemingway's open rejoicing jarred on me, and one of my most satisfactory friends in all that time was, unexpectedly, young McDonald, who had come back from the North, greatly improved, with only the trace of his stammer left, and had secured a post nearer home. We met in the week-ends and I found him a relief because, after saying non-committally, 'I never thocht ye would marry him, somehow,' he did not refer to the subject again, not from tact – he had none – but because it held no interest for him, having nothing to do with his career. Jenny my mare, was my greatest friend, but she was in foal: I worked father's other horses hard. About six hours a day in the saddle on Saturdays and Sundays ensured heavy dreamless sleep for those two nights, and this was the sweetest thing that life held for me just then.

During the week I wrote a good deal, finding it an outlet for the feverish creative energy that possessed me. I had begun, at last, to get myself a small market for short articles in some of the cheap Cameron Press publications. I was working in this way in my boarding-house bedroom one evening when I was told that some young gentleman wanted to speak to me immediately.

Surprised, I went down and found Raymond Cole, disturbed for once out of his assumed blasé air.

'Look here, Esther, I know I dropped you pretty abruptly,' he said, too much in earnest to waste time on conversational preliminaries, 'but frankly I thought at the time that it was a damned shame the way you chucked Cullum. Now I believe that it

223

was probably his fault, but it doesn't matter about that now. This business with Alison is urgent. You know Cullum is being sent by his paper to Madrid, as a correspondent. He's going to-morrow.'

I nodded. Janet had written to me.

'He's persuaded Alison to go too! It seems that they have been very thick for some time. Cullum is getting her to chuck Ropes – come away with him first and tell Ropes afterwards, when Alison and he are married. He's told her he'll marry her later, in Madrid. Cullum, without a penny! So likely, when he's made excuses not to do it in England. But she believes him, of course. It's damnable, with Ropes away.'

'But this is absurd,' I said. 'It's absurd!'

That is how it struck me for the moment. The full significance of the facts was too much for me to understand all at once. They seemed merely ridiculous.

'You see, I feel I'm a bit to blame about it, too. I've been slack about looking her up, though I promised Ropes I would. But you know how it is – other things crop up; but I did drop in this afternoon, and she told me this jubilantly! Cullum wasn't there. Apparently this rotten affair has been going on for some months!'

'It can't have been,' I cried. 'Oh, surely not!'

I realised, then, what this meant.

'It has. Since a little while after Ropes went to Germany, she says. She's wild about Cullum, and was terribly cut up when I told her about – you, you see. Lately, I mean. He's given her to understand all along that there's been nothing much between you and him since he got to know her, when he says he broke off his engagement. About three months ago. I told her that was a lie, but she won't believe it, naturally. She doesn't know what to believe, poor girl. This has come as an awful blow. But she must be made to see the truth. In a way, I'm responsible to Ropes; I know what it would mean to him if she went off like that without any warning. Cullum has been lying to her right and left, and he always was plausible. But he evidently doesn't mean to marry her if he's made ingenious excuses to get out of doing it in England before they go. We must make her realize that, for her own sake, as well as Ropes'. You'll forgive me, Esther, but there isn't time to mince matters – they're off by the first boat-train to-morrow – and frankly, you were Cullum's mistress quite lately, weren't you? He gave me to understand it when he came back from West Mersea.'

'Yes,' I answered mechanically, sick at heart.

'Can you prove it?'

'I could, yes, with one of his letters. But Raymond I can't show it to you, or anyone: you don't understand.'

'Oh, I know this must be pretty awful for you, but don't you see this isn't the moment to consider that? I'm sorry. But she's the sort that must be looked after.'

'I suppose so,' I said. 'What do you want me to do?'

'The only thing is for you to come round with me now. Together me can make her believe the truth.'

'Oh, no!' I said, shrinking back, 'I couldn't do that. Raymond, please! You don't know what you're asking – '

'You simply must. Poor little thing, she was crying her heart out in indecision when I left. Her wretched sister is away, and she's alone with the servants.'

He insisted. I was too dazed to resist. While he secured a taxi I got ready, doing things in the detached, unreasoning way in which one behaves in dreams; and as we drove out to Putney I was physically aware of nothing except the extreme coldness of my hands and feet, a sensation that always came to me when I was afraid.

He sent up his name, and when Alison, red-eyed and pale, came into the drawing-room, Cullum followed her.

I caught my breath.

With lips that felt curiously stiff, I smiled slightly at both of them, trying to keep myself from trembling. Seeing him again now was an ordeal that I had not expected. Here was Cullum unchanged, save that for the first time there was no answering light in the beloved face when his eyes met mine, only apprehension.

'What have you come here for?' he asked, and instinctively his hand reached out to Alison. He touched her arm reassuringly and she glanced up at him with troubled, trusting eyes. Those two stood together, as if facing an enemy, throughout the interview in which I broke down, slowly and mercilessly, the pathetically heroic image of himself that he had built in her eyes, and broke, too, those fragile, irreplaceable things, her first visions of love incarnate (for Ropes, who was worthy of love, had never reached her heart, which Cullum had taken so easily).

'I want – I've got to explain certain things to Alison,' I said, hearing my voice sounding very dry and expressionless, and as if it were someone else's. All the time that I was speaking I had the illusions of standing by, listening to someone else.

That made it just possible to go on, to show her
Cullum as I knew him to be, as rather a pitiful cad.
And she was so gallant in her disbelief that I had to
pity her: I could not even hate Cullum now that we
were face to face again, and it had become an effort
to remember that the changes of the last two months
were real. I had a senseless impulse, all the time, to
go to him and forget this useless misery in his arms.
But he was thinking only of Alison, the one thing
that at the moment he wanted with all his heart.
And I was trying to take her from him. I had become
the enemy.

Oblivious to everything but that, he cried to her
passionately, 'It isn't true, my dear. I didn't really
love her – not after I knew you.'

('Cullum! Oh, dear heart – don't!' I said under
my breath.)

'The engagement was only broken off three weeks
ago,' said someone with my voice, 'and he was my
lover then, Alison.'

'Oh, it's not true!' she said, with a motion of her
hand as if to ward off what I had said.

'Cullum, isn't that the truth?' I appealed to him.
'Tell her!'

He had the look of a hunted animal in his eyes.

'The engagement, yes. 'Lis, darling, I couldn't get
out of it, things had gone so far. The other thing is
not true, I swear!'

'I believe Cullum,' she said.

I smiled a little. 'So did I. I expect various other
poor fools will, too, at different times. You must
believe Raymond and me, Alison. Why should
I tell you this? Do you think I'm proud of it? It's
agony to me to know it's true, can't you see that?
But if you want proof, it's here, in this letter from

him, written long after he swore to you that I was nothing more to him: – but can't you believe me without that?' I said, speaking hardly above a whisper because it was such an effort to speak at all. 'I would so much rather not show you this.'

'I don't want to see it,' said Alison.

'You must read it,' Raymond urged.

'Perhaps you'd better.'

I held out to her the exquisitely tender, intimate letter Cullum had written to me a fortnight after we came back from the boat. I knew every word of it by heart: many times it had sent the hot blood racing into my face. It was very explicit.

She began to read, but her self-control gave way, and she sank into a chair, crying terribly, with her hands over her face.

Cullum, on his knees beside her, put his arm round her.

'Alison, sweetheart, can't you understand? God knows I didn't want to do that. She wanted it – how could I help it? All the time it was you I wanted, you whom I loved in my thoughts, even when I took her. It was because she wanted me –'

'Oh, not that, Cullum!' I cried aloud, stabbed by the knowledge that now he was speaking the truth; but he did not hear, he had forgotten me, and everything but Alison, to whom he was pleading to give him what he believed then to be his one chance. 'In some ways I've been rotten all my life. You could help me to find my soul if you came out with me and married me. No one else can, Alison; I need you. If you give me up now –'

'Oh, why are you all torturing me!' Alison sobbed, 'what have I done that I should go through this?'

'You'll suffer less now by hearing the truth,' said Raymond, 'than you would suffer later if you trusted Cullum blindly.'

'You don't understand; I love him,' Alison said. 'What does it matter what he has done?' With her tear-stained face and disordered hair she looked childish.

He turned on me savagely. 'Damn you, why should you rob me of my one hope, through sheer spite? 'Lis trusted me, and I would have played fair with her.'

'Ropes trusted you, and you have not played fair with him,' I said, 'and I trusted you too.'

'Why should you, who are as hard and cold as iron, now, sit in judgment on me. If I've hurt you, aren't you taking a hundred-fold revenge?'

I did not answer. I could not force myself to speak to him directly again.

'Cullum has failed in loyalty to Ropes, who was his friend,' I said to Alison. 'And to me, whom he loved a little while ago – though I can't expect you to believe this – as much as he loves you now, – as much as, soon, I suppose, he will love someone else. Do you think he would be loyal to you, whom he has already deceived about his engagement?'

Brain and heart and body, I felt bruised. It seemed to me that we talked on and on for hours, forcing Alison to recognize the facts.

'You know now that he has lied to you all the time. Do you still mean to go with him to-morrow?' I said at last. I felt that if we had not won now, I could not do any more. I had ceased to care what the issue might be, longing only to get away; not to see Cullum's unhappiness, and hers, any more, not to torture myself any longer.

'No. Oh, no! Please go all of you. I can't bear any more.'

With a despairing little gesture of good-bye, Cullum went out, and the servant and I put pretty, broken-hearted Alison to bed; she was in a state bordering on nervous collapse. She was made for the sheltered places, and life, with which she had played like a child, had hurt her more suddenly and brutally than she was built to bear. On her wrist I recognized a bangle of mine which Cullum had taken to be mended while I was ill. I had forgotten it. It was one which we had once pawned in order to be able to go out to dinner together. I remembered that he had wished to get back the ring he had given Paula McMillan, in order that I might have it, in the time of his love for me. The one who held his heart, at any period, held all his heart.

Chapter 13: *The Ditch-and-Rail Jump*

'THANK God that's over!' said Raymond with fervent distaste as he drove me back. 'But we owed it to Ropes. What a contemptible cur our Cullum is!'

'I suppose we owed it to Ropes,' I said dully, 'I think that it was the right thing, the only thing to do. But I am not sure that I did it entirely for Ropes' sake, nor for Alison's,' I added, having few illusions left about myself. 'Perhaps Cullum was right when he called it revenge! I don't know. Most of us are curs sometimes, and he's a pitiable sort of cur, who means well in a weak way. It's always himself he deceives first. Just for the time being he honestly cares for Alison, as much as he can love anyone.'

Too exhausted to relax, I did not sleep until well on in the next morning, and I woke feeling feverish and thoroughly unwell, aching all over as one does with a temperature. I got up shakily because the servant told me that the same young gentleman wanted to see me, at that early hour. I had had nothing to eat but a biscuit in the office since lunch the previous day, and the room kept turning black all round me.

I learnt from Raymond that Alison and Cullum had gone by the seven o'clock boat train after all.

Raymond had telephoned early to hear how she was, and had been told that Mr. Hayes returned after we left, and insisted on seeing her. 'And no one can touch Cullum at talking,' Raymond said with grudging admiration. 'Poor little Alison. I suppose it will be left to us to break this to Ropes. There's nothing else we can do, is there? Will you tell him?'

'No!' I broke out angrily. 'Why should it always be me? Do you think, like Cullum, that I'm not human now. Because sometimes I can manage not to cringe when I'm hurt, do you think I never feel? Don't you realize what it will mean for me to-night, oh, my God, knowing – ' I pulled myself together. 'Sorry, Raymond, I've got a rotten head this morning, a real splitter. That's what is the matter. Perhaps I had better write. Breaking things to people isn't your strong point, is it?'

After he left, I wrote a telegram to Miss Leslie telling her that I was unwell and could not come that day, Friday, but was sure to be back on Monday. I could not face the drudgery of the Cameron Press that day. A great longing for Holmwood came over me. Into my brain, which was too tired and sick to think clearly of anything, crept pictures of the common; the common when it was very wet and green, as it would be now, in November, with dew-jewelled autumn cobwebs lying thickly on the gorse. I wanted, as desperately as I could still want anything, the oaks and high holly trees of the country where I belonged.

I reached Victoria before nine o'clock, not having waited for breakfast because I was feeling too ill to eat, and I was consumed with impatience to get back to my own country, the one loved thing that would not fail me. I did not think at all on the journey, but with the beat of the train there kept hammering through my head the knowledge that soon, very soon, when I could feel again, something was going to hurt me damnably. But not yet. In this blessed respite from the misery of feeling I was so completely numbed in spirit that the detached part of my brain was playing abstractedly the riding game that I always played in trains. I rode in imagination parallel with the track, about a hundred yards away, and as the train rushed past hedges and ditches I had to choose my jumps quickly, look back to see what my landing would have been like, and gallop on mightily to meet the next fence as we drew level with it. I could actually feel myself taking the jumps; it was the only thing that I could feel, but soon, soon now, I must meet the realization that was waiting for me. Cullum had got Alison and they had gone away together; but it did not matter to me; not very much; not yet. Later I should mind, when something had stopped going round in my head.

From the station I walked home over the common, feeling a little less giddy and sick. A keen wind was blowing, and it cleared my head. Gerald, on Gracious Lady, cantered up and reined in by me.

'What are you doing here on a Friday? Coming to the meet?'

'Where?' I said stupidly.

Gracious Lady, impatient at being checked, was sidling away.

'Ripley's field,' he called. 'Sorry, I can't make her stand. Eleven o'clock. You might do it if you raced.'

'Yes!' I shouted back. 'I'll come!' And I began to run.

Hunting! That was what I wanted. Physical exertion that would keep at bay a little while longer the understanding which was going to hurt unbearably.

Gasping for breath I reached home and met Moon in the yard.

'Is the Major hunting to-day, Moon?'

'No, Miss, he's out shooting. We didn't think you – '

'Saddle the Lepper while I change. I'll be down in less than five minutes.'

233

'Miss Esther, whatever are you thinking of? Why, I hold the Lepper isn't fit for the master, let alone –'

'Damn you, Moon! Will you do as you're told?'

The little jockey who had carried me about as a baby was deeply pained by my tone. I smiled at the look on his face. It was good to do all the hurting myself, for a change!

'I'll get you fired if you don't!' I said. 'You understand?'

I stopped in my hasty dressing to change my blunt spurs for a prize pair that I had never used: they were beastly things, meant for show. The feeling of nausea came over me again as I ran, sideways to keep from tripping, down the stairs: and to steady myself I took a drink of neat whisky. Acting on an empty stomach, the spirit, to which I was unaccustomed, pulled me together for the moment and I went out to the Lepper permeated by a glow of exultation. He laid back his ears, showing white in his eye, as I tried the girths.

'Pull them in a bit,' I said. I knew the Lepper hated that. He reared. Moon obeyed with an air of injured dignity, and the Lepper made a grab for his arm. My crop caught the animal hard across the muzzle. I liked the dry sound it made.

'Now, you devil!' I said through shut teeth, 'Moon, give me a leg-up and then get out of the way at once.'

The Lepper reared wildly as soon as he felt the unaccustomed light weight on his back. I brought the handle of my riding-crop smashing down between his ears. He dropped back on his fore-legs and began to kick, and the keen-rowelled spurs, striking downwards and backwards to reach the softest part of the barrel, ripped the skin along his sides. I used my heels again and again, choosing the same place. It was the first time in my life that I had deliberately inflicted pain on an animal, and I enjoyed it with every faculty in me that could still feel joy or suffering. He made an attempt to crush my leg against the yard wall, and I used the spur on that side mercilessly, and my crop too, to force him away from it. Squealing with fury, he leapt through the yard gate and bolted up the drive. I was still horse-sane enough in my madness to get him on to the grass at the side to save his feet from the hard road: I did not want him lamed; I wanted to ride out the agony in my mind, for the thing from which I was running away was overtaking me. The whisky had freed me from the confused, sinking weakness of the early morning. I could think now; I could not help but think.

The Lepper, stretched out at full gallop, swung out of the drive on to the Mill Road, where we slithered dangerously on the wet, tarred surface. By luck no traffic was passing, for the beast was almost beyond my control, though he still responded a little to my hands. He took the bank by the side of the road with a bound, and we were on the common, thundering over the uneven, mole-humped ground. He flung up his big head and neighed shrilly, and then the thick-muscled neck bored down, dragging the reins through my hands. I did not care when he got the bit full between his teeth. Riding very long, I could reach with my heels the tender part of the barrel, and jabbed my spurs savagely into the lacerated skin. Memory broke like a wave over my consciousness, flooding it with disconnected images. Cullum's face as he knelt by Alison, begging her to stand by him when I had turned against him – Cullum's dim-lit, hungry face in the cabin of the fishing smack; Cullum's mouth; and little things that he had said, came back to me; endearments, and then the vague, last-minute excuses that

235

I had argued against before we went to Mersea. I had made him come! That, too, was true, among other things which he had said yesterday.

Due to the cutting wind, or perhaps because I was crying without knowing it, my eyes watered; blinding tears fell and dried on my cheeks.

('It isn't true, Alison. I didn't love her – not that way – not after I knew you' – 'Damn you, why should you rob me, you who are as hard and cold as iron?')

Wild pace goaded an over-stimulated mind. I realized everything with unbearable clarity. Cullum was with Alison now; they were going to their new life together, and I had no part in it. I should not have a part in anything of Cullum's; never any more. But I could still feel the touch of his hands on my body, those beautiful hands that had loved me, and would love Alison. For her, now, the nights would mean whispering and soft laughter, and sobbing, ecstatically caught breath; and Cullum. I remembered the little hollow between his lip and chin, and the delicious softness of the skin of his throat, where I used to kiss it. All hers. But she could not love these things as I loved them; for surely, no one could!

There was a wide ditch before us. The Lepper took it with hardly a pause in his tremendous, rocking stride, and swept on again faster, pulling savagely. My arms were growing cramped with the strain. The continual drag and jerk on the heavy curb must have hurt his mouth severely, but he seemed insensible of it. He was an enormous, powerful beast, nearly seventeen hands, and the burden of my weight was nothing to him: he moved superbly. I relaxed my grip and sat back in the saddle, thrilling with the joy of danger.

(Cullum's long arms, lean and strong – 'I have loved you in dreams all my life, and I believe that after death

236

I shall love you again.' 'Esther, I want you, come
here!')

The thud of the Lepper's hoofs and the creak of
leather worked out an accompaniment to my racing
thoughts. Exultantly I knew that nothing I did could
stop him now, and I used my crop constantly on the
sweating flanks.

Bushes and trees rushed past. I heard the hounds in
the distance; we were too late for the meet, then. The
brute threw his ears forward and plunged through a
piece of swampy ground with his head up, listening.
Sliding and stumbling, we were through the boggy
patch, and his feet resounded on the road that bounded
the common; in my ears echoed Cullum's voice saying
unforgettable things. 'I can foresee dreadful trouble
after we are married because I shall want you to give
up hunting. I've become a coward for you because
I love you. Your body is so beautiful that I can't
bear the thought of it running any risk of being
broken. It's mine, and you're not to spoil it, beloved.'
This was from the letter I had given, uselessly, to
Alison.

The road divided just ahead, one side being the
Ripley track. Leaning right over the Lepper's neck
I caught the rein low down by his mouth, and put all
my strength on it, slashing the other side of his wet-
streaked neck. He took the right track, and wrenched
his head free, hearing the hounds again, much nearer.
The gate before us was open and we shot through, into
the Ripley field. The swell of the ground hid the hunt
from us, but by the cry of the hounds they were not
questing, but running free already.

'They've drawn the hazel-nut spinney,' I thought
irrelevantly.

Cullum always laughed at the same things as I did:

and to have exactly the same sense of humour is a great and uncommon bond. I saw Cullum standing at the tiller, wrinkling up the corners of his blue eyes in the sun that turned his hair to a copper glow. He wasn't mine now! He had never been really mine; nothing was mine except the shame of having loved him; liar, and poor contemptible cheat, who could cheat himself with his own lies.

A fleck of dazzling foam flew up and caught on my sleeve. The exhilaration of speed had got into my blood; I was not crying now. Between us and the hunt was a fence and water jump which could not be taken from this side. There was a three-foot wide stream, and then a steep bank with iron railings above it. For a bet, several of the more reckless of the younger hunting people had tried it, from the other side, and it was particularly difficult even then, because the landing after the drop was on sloping, wet clay. Coming from this side it was absurd to think of taking it; but there was a gate lower down.

From the brow of the rise I saw the hounds strung out in a mottled, broken line, streaming away from us, and their clamour surged back to us on the wind. The Lepper had not once slackened his breakneck gallop; I could feel the lathered, reeking body straining forward now. It was the moment, if I meant to take the gate, to try to turn him, but a spell of crazed excitement held us both. I heard someone shouting from the other field, and, as distinctly, Cullum's words, sincerely spoken:

"Lis sweetheart, can't you understand? God knows I didn't want to do it. She wanted it so much – how could I help it? All the time it was you I wanted, you whom I loved in my thoughts even when I took her. It was because she wanted me. . . .' And in his letter to me, 'Your body is so beautiful, I cannot bear the thought of it being broken. It's mine – '

All my cunning of hand and heel and voice I used to madden the big beast under me, half mad as he was already with the smell and sound of the hunt, carried to him by the wind. Standing in the stirrups I shouted back inarticulately to the gesticulating figure in the further field, and then, laughing and drunk, crouched down and rode for the jump.

The Lepper never refused a jump. As we galloped down the last stretch to the stream I felt him quicken and shorten his stride, gathering himself for the tremendous effort; and, cool-headed now, I chose the ground for him, and touched him lightly with crop and heels as we both braced for the leap.

He rose splendidly. It is strange how long a big jump seems to take. I saw the ground drop away quite gradually. We were over the stream, and the fence was sinking before us, and then below us. It was right under us. I thought for a second that we had cleared it, and then I knew that we had touched and were falling. I wondered, as the ground came up to meet us, slowly at first, and then faster, whether I was going to break my neck.

I broke my left hip and thigh instead; the horse rolled on me. I suffered one second of intense shooting agony, and heard shrill screaming, my own, I suppose, before I sank into thick, deep blackness from which I was drawn, unwilling, back to the light and to such pain as I had not conceived to be possible. They were lifting me on to a make-shift stretcher of rails.

Dimly I saw a man's face as he bent over me.

'Cullum? I muttered, dully.

'Esther, dear, bear up if you can; we'll get you home as quickly as possible,' said Gerald's voice, and I realized that of course it would not be Cullum. I should never again wake to see him.

Pain sent me unconscious once more when they began to carry me, and through the nightmare transit home I drifted between dim, pain-stabbed darkness, and the full consciousness of agony.

The London specialist who set the two crushed, splintered bones with a splint and weight came into my room to see me again before he left, when the effects of the anæsthetic had worn off.

'Fairly comfortable, my dear?'

'Well, I thought it would be worse.'

'Oh, you'll soon get used to your nice little weight. You'll get quite fond of it.'

I gave the feeble smile required by professional jocularity.

'Shall I ever be able to ride again?' I asked, not that I minded one way or the other at the moment, but one day I hoped to care again. Pain is a great aid to sanity.

'Oh, there's time enough to see about that later! All that you have to think of at present is mending yourself, you reckless little girl – what a long little girl you are by the way; I thought we shouldn't have enough bandages to go round!'

'Tell me now, please, whether I shall be able to ride. I think – Oh, I think, it saves one so much to know the truth at the beginning, instead of finding it out later!'

'Well, yes, I expect you'll probably be able to ride again – if you want to, and to walk too. But there will be a certain amount of disability.' He took my hand and patted it, peering down at me keenly. 'Most people, you know, don't want the truth, but I think you are of the sort that can stand it?'

'It's an ability that grows with practice!' I said.

240

'One or two facts won't upset me now. What is likely to be the permanent result of this accident?'

'Well, I consider that you ought to be thankful to get off, after a smash like that, with merely stiffness and a limp.'

I said nothing for a moment, and he began to talk soothingly.

'We hope that it may not be very noticeable. The joint is badly damaged, but you have youth and good health on your side, and of course – '

'Oh, I'm content!' I interrupted, and turned my head away; glad for the moment, with a feeling of sullen pride, that I had spoiled irreparably the fine strong body which Cullum had loved.

Our local doctor gave me a morphine injection and I slept fitfully, dreaming with an undercurrent of uneasy sensation, throughout the night that I had dreaded, when Cullum would be with Alison.

Chapter 14: *Strain*

DAY after day through the succeeding three months I lay immovable, with little to do but think, and in my worst hours my imagination, free from control through weakness of body and spirit, endlessly showed me pictures that I desperately wanted to shut out of my mind. Crying out in the darkness against the misery of flesh and spirit, I believed sometimes that nothing human could endure such a strain for a long period of this terrible forced inaction, by which I was imprisoned with memories. Surely, I thought, something must give way, either flesh or spirit, and bring relief. 'I can't bear this. I can't!' I whispered to the tedious night, which meant to me now only a horror of unoccupied sleepless hours, and to others, Cullum and Alison, meant everything that I had lost. In the day I could pretend, before others, to a stoicism which I did not possess, but the night disarmed me and brought me low. Sweating and taut-muscled, in the paroxysms of intense feeling, I waited almost expectantly for the ghastly minutes to pass and give me ease that did not come, but the limits of human endurance are set wide when one is nineteen. There is a pitch of unhappiness, differing with individuals, beyond which age cannot feel any added sorrow very keenly; young nerves hold unimpaired their full capacity for recording pain. And as youth suffers more easily, though its griefs may be transient, so it suffers more deeply, too; a fact which older people forget once the small, niggling troubles of every day and every year have blunted the sensitive surfaces of the soul. They see that youth has compensations for its sorrows which age lacks, but then youth cannot perceive its consolations, and age sometimes can. There seems to be no alleviation for the devastating sorrows of youth. Fortunately we forget this, or we should not dare to bring children into the world.

My over-zealous memory brought back to me, in those months, trifles connected with Cullum which had long passed out of my mind. A host of vivid forgotten details attended unbidden on my thoughts of him, and I re-lived scenes in which he had played a part, – not once, but daily. Pride, so Janet had said, was the dominant element in me, 'the chink' of Cullum's old theory, through which I was most vulnerable, and she was right: it was largely pride through which I suffered, but it was pride that could not stop my caring for Cullum, knowing how unworthy he was, and knowing that he did not want me. It could only punish me terribly for loving him.

Seeing them now in their pitiless new perspective, I recalled the happenings of the last weeks in which Cullum and I had been together, searching them for warnings that I should have noticed. There were plenty. Little occurrences took on a fresh significance now that I knew that it was Alison whom he had wanted when he first possessed me – when he possessed me because, as he said, I had made it impossible for him to refuse! The searing flame of that knowledge burned always in my consciousness.

I was blessed in those days by the constant companionship of the greatest of all antidotes to mental torment, acute physical pain. It is even more efficacious than work as an anæsthetic for the soul; for while it lasts it leaves no room in the brain for remembrance. As the strong, torn hip muscles began to knit up, frequent muscular spasms set in round the smashed joint, and I became too worn out by pain to be able to bear it quietly when it came. These fits of keen agony, which left me shaken and gasping, drove out of me all desire save that of bodily peace, and when this came it seemed the goal of all possible human longing. I wished for nothing else – for a little while.

People were very kind in visiting me during the first month, while I was still a novelty as an invalid. The interest wore off, naturally. Boredom succeeded pain for me: but two friends never slackened in the task of entertaining me. Gerald Hemingway devoted to me many hours which his out-of-door spirit might have grudged, and regularly in the week-ends came Carlisle Jamieson McDonald, the heavily cultured youth who was succeeding beyond anyone's expectations, save his own, in a private secretaryship to an under-secretary. Gerald brought me the books that he thought I should like to read, and the other, those which he wanted me to read.

Coming fresh from the world of affairs, these two imbued me, temporarily, with a desire to return to it. Personality is a mental scent, and Gerald brought the smell of wet pine woods and saddle leather into my sickroom. Carlisle, pregnant with portfolios, fairly reeked of state intrigue, or so his newly-developed ministerial manner suggested. The reaction from their cheerfulness made itself felt, after they had gone, in spells of despondency in which I did not want to read, and unfortunately I could not write while I was ill. No ideas would come. Instead, I used to count the maddening lines of flowers on the wallpaper, feeling unreasonably irritated if the pictures were not straight with them. Blindfolded I could have made a map of the little cracks in the ceiling.

In spite of the indifference of my will, my body healed comparatively quickly.

The Sunday before I was to be free of the weight on the foot was my birthday, and early in the morning a great commotion sounded in the passage outside my room. For convenience at meals, a sitting-room on the ground-floor had been made my bedroom. I heard the pictures banging on the walls, Mrs. Barrie's shrill protests, and Olive's deep voice saying, 'She *shall* have the wretched beast with her for a treat!' There was an unaccountable amount of trampling, and then came my lovely mare's nervous, high-pitched whinney-ing.

'Jenny!' I called excitedly, and whistled on my fingers, as I used to do, to bring her in from the common when she was turned out to grass in the summer. She had been led past my window several times, but I had not been able to touch her for months. It was brave of Olive to lead the startled mare, who sidled and jibbed, through the front door and along the narrow passage, for the child was terrified of horses. She turned the handle of my door, but it was Jenny who pushed it open, and found the way round the table to me by herself, prick-eared and frightened in such unaccustomed surroundings, and unhappy at leaving her foal.

She muzzled my face and hands, and reaching up, I pulled her neck down to me and buried my face in it, feeling very close to tears. Jenny's corner was one of the few soft places still left in my heart.

Gerald was particularly good to me when I began to get about again on crutches. Sometimes his devotion was a solace, and at other moments only an added irritation, because, leaving me unstirred by anything but slight sympathy, he said frequently the things that would have transformed earth for me had they come, even now, from Cullum. The usual lover's sayings, they were idiotic, and they sounded it because Gerald said them, and not Cullum.

His new, uncharacteristic gentleness and patience touched me. He was always there when I needed someone; I grew to rely on him, and when he made love to me humbly it soothed my sore vanity, and I was too weary to resist.

The little-satisfied desire which Cullum had woken in me was eating into me. Gerald was young and clean-run and eager. The surge of tingling new life in the air, when spring rode laughing over the earth again, infected both of us one golden day in March when I limped out on to the common with him for the first time. The rough tufts of grass were bending in long ripples before the gay wind, as though the common were being stroked by the invisible hands of spring. I was just learning to walk with a stick, and was resting for a moment, thinking of what life had been like at this time the year previous, when Gerald's long forbearance broke. He made love to me passionately, surprised at my sudden responsiveness. His touch fired my blood and I lavished on him some of the pent-up emotion of six months' longing for another man. In my thoughts it was not Gerald that I kissed. (Cullum had once said that, knowing my powers of make-believe, he would be more afraid of my being unfaithful with him, in thought, than to him, in reality, if I ever cared for anyone else.)

'Esther, you do love me, then?' he said when the moment of emotion had passed. Vehemently I assented, trying to convince myself, and later I made no protest

246

when he took it for granted that we should be married one day, though the engagement was never definite. For a month I forced myself to believe that it was Gerald I wanted now, even though I knew at the back of my mind that the shadow of Cullum lay with me still, but I thought that in this dear friend's arms I could close my eyes and dream. It was as pitiful a self-deception as most of Cullum's.

I longed so much to find some means of shutting out loneliness and reality that for a while it seemed possible. Of Gerald's side of the question I never thought at all. He was happy, and I intended to give him all that I could, but by the time that I was well enough to go back to London and take another job – my old post had been filled long ago – I knew that I could not go on with this pretence. I could not bear Gerald's touch after a time, and he noticed it at last and asked for the explanation which, coward now all through, I had put off giving him from day to day.

His reception of the wretched, wounding truth almost made me regret that I had told him. His kindness was the most cutting reproach that he could have offered.

'All right, my dear,' he said, after a long pause, when my halting, shamefaced attempts to make him understand had trailed off into silence. It was he who tried to comfort me, gripping both my hands very tightly as if striving to express by the contact the things his inarticulate, matter-of-fact nature made it hard for him to say.

'These few weeks have been wonderful for me, but I've always been afraid of something like this. I sort of felt at times that there must be something wrong, or you wouldn't have turned to me. Why should you? But if I could have been the man you wanted –' He broke off hurriedly. 'Well, don't worry about me;

I shall get over this unhappiness – as much as you have got over yours!'

It was essential that I should get a job as soon as possible. My accident had been expensive for Father, and apart from financial considerations, I was eager to have something to do, to take my mind off myself. The limp proved to be more pronounced than the doctor had expected, and I was unduly self-conscious when walking in public. The galling contrast between my old, active self and the maimed, clumsily moving creature I had become made it an ordeal for me to cross an open space if I thought – as I always did, often wrongly, no doubt – that people were remarking on my ungainly gait. I resented the alacrity with which older women gave up their seats to me in public vehicles, though physically I was glad of it. The pity of strangers is horrible when one is young: it nearly broke my spirit during the first months in which, by degrees, I began to go about again. Knowing that the leg would never be any better, I had a morbid fear lest people should think that the infirmity was congenital; I do not know why this should make it any worse, but I hated the idea; and I imagined, being over-sensitive about it, compassion in eyes that held only curiosity, or not even that.

The interest of my new occupation, when at last I became a sub-editor on a small farming paper, cured me of brooding over my disability, though I never grew reconciled to the unsightliness of my misshapen left hip and thigh; having once gloried in my body I now avoided seeing it as much as possible.

Ropes was back in London, qualified, and a house-surgeon at one of the big hospitals by the time that I found work. It was good to see him back sometimes, on his free days, in his old place at the Table, though the life had gone out of the lunch-time meetings, which we tried to revive. Raymond, ostensibly careworn when he remembered his new junior partnership, still attempted to lure the conversation towards an opening for his latest *bon mot*, and Ropes, supercilious, abrupt and quietly witty, was outwardly the same as before, but the lack of the hilarious nonsense which Cullum had contributed was like the loss of effervescence in a wine that is meant to sparkle. We no longer gave tongue on the trail of any of those unwieldy ethical quarries (the durability of friendship, the education of women, or divorce law reform), which human puppy-packs love to harry, nor did we now discuss ingenious, untenable theories with enthusiastic gravity. No reference was made to the past, save accidentally, till Ropes said suddenly one day:

'It was good of you two, you know. I mean, about Alison. I didn't answer your letter, Esther, because there seemed nothing worth saying about the whole business. But I know you both did all you could.'

'There seemed nothing worth saying about the whole business,' was characteristic of Ropes.

'Oh, that's all right,' I answered awkwardly.

'Sorry, old man, that we couldn't – ' said Raymond.

Both of us felt curiously relieved and yet embarrassed now that he had broken the silence in which that topic had been shrouded.

'Have some of my tobacco, Ropes. West Indian stuff. Smuggled through out of bond by one of our clients.' Raymond proffered his pouch to ease the uncomfortable pause, in which Ropes was fingering his pipe absent-mindedly, staring down at the table-cloth with inattentive eyes. He looked dubiously at the unpleasant-looking black stuff which Raymond affected, and declined.

'Try it. It's not half as strong as it looks.'

'Neither am I!' said Ropes.

Raymond had to hurry away earlier than usual to lend his support to the tottering finances of the world's fuel market, in a conference with several men whose heads, he knew by experience, were stronger than his own. On Ropes' sound advice he swallowed, one after the other with much fuss, three pats of butter, in preparation for discussing oil, over many troubled waters, and then left us.

This was the first time that Ropes and I had seen each other alone since Cullum and Alison had gone. I did not like to intrude, by any expression of sympathy, on the privacy of his feelings. I knew enough of Ropes to guess that here was pain even more poignant than mine, for his nature was slower to trust, and more tenacious than mine.

(I could remember Cullum holding forth, with the perfect self-assurance of his age: 'The mind of a normal woman is not as receptive to extremes of feeling as a man's: the emotional range is smaller, if more frequently travelled –')

On Ropes, of all people, this blow should not have fallen; his hard, unprepossessing manner was a shield that protected one of the most sensitive natures with which I had come in contact. Like all people who care for few things in life, he was more defenceless against hurt from the things he loved than the general run of men. The first rawness of my wound had passed; I felt instinctively that it was not so with Ropes.

'How does it feel being a full-blown medico?' I asked, for something to say.

'Very wearing. Like Raymond, I am weighed down by new responsibilities. As a student when I was asked to diagnose a case I hurried off a prayer to my patron,

St. Alexius' (Ropes was a Roman Catholic) – 'but now that I'm a doctor I daren't call in unqualified assistance. I guess, uninspired.' He asked me with professional interest about my damaged hip, which was still terribly painful at times. Though it grew better it never ceased to hurt when I was tired.

'Rotten for a girl to have a handicap like that,' he said. 'Looks matter so much more to a woman than to a man.'

'Good for my character!' I said. 'As Raymond would have enjoyed observing – several times – women are like those sale notices, "All the goods marked in plain figures," for us it's "All the good marked by plain figures," and henceforth that will apply to me.' I could not yet bear to refer to the deformity without joking about it.

'So you haven't entirely lost your sense of humour?' Ropes said, righting his pince-nez just as they seemed to be sliding off. 'Come to that, nor have I. Worse luck. Wonder why people say that preserving a sense of humour helps you in times like this. It doesn't. To see that your own tragedies are really rather ludicrous doesn't lessen the tragedy. Only robs you of the mean comfort of self-pity. Take the satisfactory position of a man like Henley, who either had no sense of humour or could mislay it long enough to write gorgeously about the unconquerableness of his soul under the bludgeonings of chance. Not surprising that the menace of years finds and shall find him unafraid. He's got a belief in the importance of his own personal drama to keep him going. A sense of humour knocks that to bits – leaves you writhing under the injustice of things, plus the knowledge that you're only a figure of fun in the eyes of whatever gods there be.'

'There's no need to explain that to me!' I said. 'I

know that most cruel things in life have their damnably funny side if looked at from the right angle.'

'We're all acting to an audience of ourselves, all our lives,' Ropes said, 'and it's much easier to act nobly, isn't it, if you believe you're the hero of the play than when you know, having a sense of humour, that you're the clown as well?'

'I was sorry for you when I first met you, knowing you were more or less engaged to Cullum,' he went on, mentioning his name for the first time. 'I should have been sorry for any girl who intended to marry him, and you struck me as particularly unsuitable. I knew Cullum was a liar through and through. You seemed incapable of seeing it. But I was fond of the boy. People are. I thought that in his own curious way he was an idealist.'

'He is,' I said. 'He's always convinced of the justice of whatever course he wants to take.'

There was a long silence here.

'Anyway, I never dreamed that he could stoop to anything innately petty or mean. Alison is mentally so much younger than you are that, apart from every other consideration, it was not fair.' The deliberate calmness of Ropes' tone was a strange contrast to the expression of his eyes.

'Have you heard anything about – them?' I asked diffidently. I knew nothing except that he had not married her, which I had learned from her sister.

'I had one letter from her, not saying the commonplace things which one would expect in the circumstances. For her it was rather a remarkable letter. She doesn't write easily. She seems to be growing up quickly, with Cullum. Probably it means she's unhappy – Oh, why wasn't I here! If only I had been here!' he said with the first note of feeling that I had

heard in his quiet voice. The look on his face shocked
me by the depth of its emotion. With the exception of
one other occasion, this was the only time in which
I saw him moved, for a second, from his habitual
attitude of indifference to all things except his work;
but it was easy to see how sour his soul had turned.
Ropes, whose comments had been sarcastic but kindly,
was often scathing in his criticisms now.

I saw a great deal of him. He formed a habit of
dropping in two or three evenings a week at my
boarding-house. Sometimes we talked, or if I had
brought back some work to finish from the office, he
read or smoked in the arm-chair in my bedsitting-
room, to the thrilled horror of several elderly boarders
of both sexes, who were convinced that he was my
lover, since he had been allowed into a room which
undeniably held my bed, even though it might be
disguised as a sofa during the day. That was con-
clusive. The old ladies believed the worst because they
secretly hoped it was true; the dear old gentleman
because, in the virile period of his youth, it would
have been so.

Besides an increasing amount of work on my paper,
for which I ran the section devoted to horses, I was
doing a good deal of freelance journalism now. Ropes
was one of those companionable people whose presence
in no way hinders concentration on something else.
After association with Cullum, of whom one was
vividly aware at all times, I found this quality of
self-effacement most endearing.

I learned by degrees the outlines of Ropes' history.
The son of a Dorset gamekeeper, he had won a scholar-
ship from the local school to a better one, and from
there to the University. Without boasting of it, Ropes
never tried to disguise his humble origin. His charm

253

was that he did not pose at all, as Cullum's was that he posed so well. Ropes' parents had died when he was ten, and since then he had fought his own way up to his present position. From the little he told me of the struggle, I gathered that it had been very hard: he was still financially straitened. There had only been one softening influence in his life, his protective love for Alison, who was the only woman who had mattered to him at all.

'You are actually my first woman friend,' he said 'for she, of course, was not a friend.'

He kissed me once, unexpectedly, and because he was pleasantly masculine I took his fine, ugly face between my hands and kissed him again: afterwards, I think, both of us felt embarrassed.

'Don't let's do that again,' I said, 'neither of us really meant it!'

'Certainly I didn't!' he said with a disarming smile, 'but as I come here so often I thought it was about time I did something like that, just out of politeness.'

'Wretch!' I said, throwing a shoe at him, and then a Thesaurus. He ducked, and as they crashed against the door and fell on the floor, the old people below must have thought, with tremors of delight, that he was knocking me about.

'Stop! I didn't mean it,' he said as I picked up another book. 'Sit down, there's a good girl, and put your hair straight; ruffled up like that it looks almost attractive, and if you appealed to me at all, which you don't, I should kiss you again, for my own benefit this time, not yours.'

'It's a pity, from my point of view, that we can't care for each other,' he said later, when I had picked up the missiles and we had settled down, one on each side of the gas fire. 'Mentally you mean more to me than she could, and you are the tall, dark, thin kind of woman I admire and prefer, theoretically, to Alison's type. But the unreasonable attraction which can't be classified as either mental or physical is missing, and it's that unknown quantity which makes all the difference between a companionable woman and an adorable mystery. To me you're one of those women – lots of young, charming nurses at the hospital are the same – whom I consider eminently to be desired but not desirable. While Alison – Oh, well, just the sight of Alison set my blood racing. The memory of her still moves me like that. It's all incomprehensible. And darn' silly.' He sucked away at his pipe.

I introduced Ropes to Carlisle McDonald, and they appreciated each other's sterling qualities. I often went out with McDonald; life was becoming full again, and moderately happy, except at times, when the old longing would sweep over me again; I had not outgrown hating Cullum, because he still mattered to me more than anything else in life.

Ropes' wit scored against the Scottish lad's slow, sound arguments, but McDonald seldom realized that he had been scored off, and taking the doctor's gravely spoken absurdities quite seriously, he disposed of them with unnecessary elaboration, as a steam-roller might crush a flower.

McDonald was much annoyed when a Scottish-American friend of ours took out English naturalization papers.

'Leaving out the v-vexed question of the supeeriority of races,' (his stutter was almost conquered now,) 'which we will not discuss before Miss Sieveking, still I hold that the man has l-lost by changing his nationality.'

'So he has,' said Ropes, without a moment's hesitation, 'he has lost the battles of Bannockburn and Saratoga!'

'Now how could that be,' said McDonald, with his invariably patient condescension to the impracticability of the Sassenach mind, 'when the last of these was focht in 1777?' He always knew dates, 'And he was not even born then?'

Triumphantly he proceeded with the congenial task of reducing an elusive absurdity to a self-evident one. Afterwards he talked to us informatively about land-policy, of which he knew a great deal.

'That lad will be a very eminent man one day,' Ropes said when he had gone. 'Nothing will be able to keep him from getting anything he really wants. My poor girl, I fear he intends incidentally to marry you!'

'Yes, I know,' I said, 'when I first realized it, I thought the idea colossal cheek on his part: now I feel rather honoured. But I don't mean to marry him.'

'I'm glad. You wouldn't suit as partners. He's a fine fellow, but not a gentleman by birth,' said the astounding Ropes.

'But surely that consideration –' I began, intensely surprised. Snobbishness was the last thing I expected from Ropes.

'Oh, I know I'm not one either, but then you'd be equally unwise to marry me, though if I wanted you I should get you to do it.'

I laughed at his insulting self-assurance, and reached for 'Thesaurus.'

Chapter 15: *Surface Healing*

ABOUT a year after Cullum went away, the immaculate Raymond, looking very self-conscious, came late to the Table one day, with one cheek showing a short tear in the skin; the flesh all round was slightly discoloured. Any bruise showed very distinctly against his dazzling complexion.

Ropes, who had been distrait in manner, looked hard at the damage and wagged his head reproachfully.

'At last!' he said meaningly. Despite his stock of cynical epigrams, Raymond was an impeccable young man, whose aggressive superiority to the common failings of mankind riled both Ropes and me at times. Now his face certainly looked as though it had been scratched by someone.

'Don't be a fool!' he said irritably. Raymond was seldom ruffled: he blushed his wonderful, all-embracing blush. 'I don't know what rot you're thinking, but anyway, this graze is nothing.'

' "Nothing!" ' Ropes turned sadly to me. 'The blasé lamb, fresh from the slaughter of his dewy innocence, describes his first adventure as – "nothing!" What is the decadent youth of England coming to!'

'We aren't decadent,' put in Raymond quickly, seeing the chance of introducing a new epigram. 'Nowadays a v –'

But he was not to be let off.

' "Nothing!" Thank goodness, in my young days,'

257

interrupted Ropes, who was twenty-eight, 'we had at least the courage of our indiscretions.'

He chaffed Raymond unmercifully.

'If you want to know,' Raymond told him sulkily at last, 'it was a pigeon that did it! I've given up explaining to people, because no one believes me: I know it sounds fatuous. I was fearfully late for an appointment yesterday evening and, cutting across the Royal Exchange when it was getting dark, I dashed round one of those whacking great pillars just as a beastly pigeon, flying at a tremendous pace – they can, you know – came swinging round the other side. We both swerved too late, and collisioned. It may sound silly, but it's no joke having a big pigeon hurtling into your face. It took me by surprise, too, and there was an awful second just before we met when I saw its eyes looking horrified, right close to mine. They seemed the size of sixpences.'

'And though there are eyes into which even you could gaze happily for some while,' Ropes suggested, 'we are to take it that this was emphatically not that kind of bird?' He turned to me and indicated Raymond as if he were some strange specimen. 'First "nothing"! he says, and now he calls it – "a pigeon"!'

The scorn that he threw into the words made the unfortunate Raymond blush again. 'Do shut up about it!' he said 'I've been disbelieved at home, the people I dined with last night screamed with laughter when I told them what had happened, and everyone at the office has been funny about it all the morning, till when I had to interview two men just now about a deal I had to tell them in self-defence that I was tight last night! They were respectful and sympathetic about that!'

'How are the mighty fallen!' said Ropes. 'The old

spirit of the race is decaying: our young men are assaulted by pigeons in public places! And we used to be a nation of sportsmen! In my day a young man prided himself that there wasn't a virgin or a pheasant safe within two miles of him. But where is the typical young Englishman now?'

'Talking of virgins,' Raymond tried again, 'don't you think that nowadays a v – '

But I was already answering Ropes' last remark. 'There never was a typical Englishman, of the type in which foreigners firmly believe because we have put him across them in fiction. You know the familiar figure I mean, inarticulate, dogged, undemonstrative, big and efficient. He usually wears on his ruggedly handsome face a scowl of that ruthless determination which, like the roast beef of old England, might have done so much to make us what we aren't, if we had as much of it as the inventors of the English tradition have given Continental people to understand. He is always pure English, without even a trace of Irish, Scottish or Welsh blood, and yet I've only known one person who could claim with any certainty that his family had been pure English for as much as six generations back, and he was a voluble, dark little fellow with a pointed beard, who might have passed anywhere for a Frenchman. Nearly all Englishmen say they're partly Irish, or French, or Welsh, if they aren't Scottish – but most of them are, I don't know why. Scottish blood seems to be everywhere.'

'I don't think it's that Scots blood is really so prevalent,' said Ropes, 'it's because everyone who has had a great-grandfather from north of the Tweed, remembers it, long after they have forgotten what their great-grandmother was.'

'Who knows for certain what his female relatives are

in these days of emancipation?' put in Raymond, seizing the loophole for the saying that was burning a hole in his brain, and running it off at great speed so that he should not be disappointed again. ' "Now adays a virgin of twenty is an anachronism; of twenty-five, an improbability; of thirty, a tragedy. No woman can be said to be her own mistress until she has tried the obvious alternative." The man in my room in the office said that this morning. I think it's rather neat, don't you?'

'I'm sure we shall,' Ropes told him kindly, 'towards the end of the week, when we're more used to it.'

'Going back to what we were talking about,' I said, now in full cry after this Cullum-like subject, 'Silence is another attribute of the complete Englishman of fiction which you don't often find among the people of England – particularly not among the writers who started the idea! We're a talkative lot – aren't our historical men remembered far more easily for what they've said than for what they've done? Think of Nelson, and "England expects every man to do his duty" jumps to the mind before any details about Trafalgar: probably the clearest thing you remember about the Armada is Drake's "We have time to finish our game, and beat the Spaniard too." Bloody Mary, who was a figure of action if you like, is memorable for saying that Calais would be found engraved upon her heart when she died. What do you know about Latimer the martyr, except that he said before he was burnt something about having this day lighted a candle in England which should never be put out? I don't even remember which side he was burnt for, but I remember his words, and all I can recall of any of the Georges except the last is that one of them said he wondered how the apple got inside the dumpling.'

'No, we aren't a silent people,' Ropes said, 'in spite of the famous inarticulateness of the traditional Englishman. Curious that the only man who complies with the description of that admirable person, – doggedness, quietness, efficiency, undemonstrativeness and all, is the man who would most fiercely repudiate the idea – a rather typical Scot! McDonald, for instance.'

It was the most successful reunion we had had at the Table for very many months: we seemed to have recaptured some of the old spirit. Then, just as he was leaving, Ropes said abruptly.

'By the way, you two might as well know. Alison came back two days ago.'

We sat silent, staring at him. He went on expressionlessly after a moment, as if he were announcing some trivial arrangement. 'We're going to be married pretty soon. Probably some time next week. I'm not asking you two to the wedding because we aren't having anybody.'

The Table society finally disintegrated after Ropes' marriage. Raymond's time was increasingly taken up with business lunches, and now, on his free days, Ropes went home to the little flat that he took for his wife close to the hospital. There Alison's child was born five months later. I heard of it, without surprise, from Raymond, who had been expecting the news too, though neither of us had seen Ropes since the day when he announced his immediate marriage; but we knew the covert goodness of Ropes.

I did not see Ropes again for a long time. I think that Alison felt disinclined to meet me, and he was wrapped up in her to the exclusion of everything but his work.

Relieved, in a way, to be rid of the associations of the Table, I went elsewhere at midday: it was a stupid, half-unconscious longing for some tangible tie with the past that had drawn me back there after my accident: the memories it evoked often hurt. One by one the links between my present life, and that period which belonged to Cullum, were wearing thin, and breaking. I never saw Janet now, the Cameron Press had been left behind, Ropes and Raymond had gone out of my life. I was busy, making a fair success of my unimportant work, and in a negative way I was tolerably content. It is one of life's kinder traits that, after a while, the consolations to which one turns as an escape from a crushing grief loom larger on one's horizon than the grief itself. I did not feel the one-time misery keenly now; nor, on the other hand, did I feel anything else very much. I seemed to have lost, to a great extent, the power of feeling keenly; and that, I thought, was more gain than loss. To go 'secretly armed against all fate's endeavour' at twenty years old is a great freedom, to be obtained only at a great price.

Life was no longer empty, but it seemed rather pointless. Besides my actual pleasure in writing, the satisfaction of making money, rather than the want of the money, kept me working exceedingly hard. In days gone by, the lack of the few extra pounds a month which I earned now had curtailed so much of our enjoyment, when money meant the possibility of meals or excursions with Cullum, that their coming was almost an irritation now that they could buy me so little that I really wanted. I was able to buy the clothes that I had coveted while in the Cameron Press, because Cullum would have liked me to be well-dressed: for clothes for their own sake I cared very little.

It was pleasant to run across Ropes one day, by accident, about six months after Alison bore Cullum's child, when we met in the City restaurant that I

262

frequented. Evidently he, too, now avoided the Marlborough Restaurant, where the Table had been. He came over to me and we talked as though there had been no interruption of our friendship. Telling him of any small strokes of luck that had recently come my way, I put them in their best light and made much of them, determined that he should think the world went very well with me. Ropes remained unimpressed by the catalogue of my good fortunes. It was hard to deceive Ropes or to deceive oneself in his presence.

'Glad your job is turning up trumps. That's the main thing after all,' he said, after the meal. 'I, too, see existence as an amusing spectacle at times, as you seem to. But I'm twenty-nine: you have discovered unduly early the art of standing aloof the better to appreciate its humour. Unfortunately, I think the attitude is genuine in your case. Pity, you know.' He smoked for a while in silence. 'You used to be avid to taste everything; are you really content to have become an onlooker? Sound philosophy, perhaps, but not natural.'

'It isn't a matter of choice,' I told him. 'If one has a gammy leg at twenty, when every normal person's life should be ninety per cent. physical, one has to be a mental giant to make up for it if one is going to participate much in life. And by degrees during the last eighteen months it has been borne on me that I was not predestined to be a blazing star shining over Darkest Literature, as I secretly believed when I was about ten, and hoped long after that! So I must be an onlooker. I can't dance, you see, as I used to, and that cuts me out of a good deal automatically, and then I still dislike meeting strangers for fear they'll be sympathetic – curse them. If they don't say they are, they look it, or I think they do, which comes to the

263

same thing. I do hunt sometimes; I feel it's a kind of duty to my self-respect to do it, just because I'm afraid. I do it to prove to myself that I can, but I go through an awful attack of nerves beforehand, and am clammy with fright all the time; I am afraid of having to admit to myself that my nerves have more control over me than my will. You are the first person I've told that I dread hunting. The first jump feels simply ghastly and twice I've lost my head altogether for a moment when we were right up to a fence and I felt Jenny getting ready to take it. I "pulled" her, making it look as if she had refused the jump herself. It'll ruin her temper and what is left of my nerve if I do that often. Isn't this a humiliating confession?'

Bitterness possessed me again: 'Hunting is the last of the old interests to which I still cling. Ropes, it was not quite fair of you, who have got Alison, to ask if I am content – I! Content!'

I was envious of him, and I could not help showing it at that moment. There were times, and this was one of them, when it seemed to me that physical fitness, and the actual possession of the beloved, was the best that life had to bestow. Starved of these things, I hungered for them.

Ropes looked at me wonderingly, and I noticed, behind the ever-slipping pince-nez, fresh little lines round the kind eyes. He, also, had been working much harder than was officially required of him.

'Yes, I've got Alison!' he said, 'Alison who is so grateful for what she calls my kindness that she tries to respond to my caresses, hating them! Oh, I've been through hell, too!' The suppressed vehemence of his tone was an unexpected revelation, coming from Ropes, of a soul in torment. A strain severe enough to have broken down this man's self-control meant suffering

264

which appalled one's imagination. It is not good even to contemplate some degrees of human misery. He turned his head away, striving for composure, and I felt as if I were intruding. When he looked back his eyes still held the same terrible unhappiness.

'Oh, God, Esther!' he said, speaking as if involuntarily, 'you can't know what it means to me to see Alison, day after day, a changed, quiet, sweet woman, utterly absorbed in that child, not just because it's hers, but because it's Cullum's, and she loves him! Her eyes stray to the baby continually when it's not in her arms. And then they come back to me guiltily, and she tries to pretend the love that she would like to give me, and can't. And she thinks I don't see the effort it costs her! It's that pretence which breaks my heart. She smiles at me, trying not to shrink when I make love to her! I can't help it sometimes, wanting her as I do. She gives me everything I ask. I think it wouldn't be so bad if she wouldn't let me touch her at all, but to hold her, submissive because she thinks she owes me that, and to know – Oh, well, lately I've tried not to bother her in that way. It's the greatest service I can do for her. Think of it, just to refrain from troubling her! Seems such a rotten little thing to be the best you can do when you care for anyone as I love her. And yet it's just about the hardest of all. But I'm only a man after all, and because we're together sometimes it's more than I can do. – She can't loathe my caresses at the time as much as I loathe myself afterwards for having given way. You remember what an irresponsible child she used to be, always bubbling over with chatter about something? She sits for hours now, silently, holding the child tightly as if she were afraid of it being taken from her, and staring at nothing with a dead, far-away, hopeless

265

look on her face. The kid is a boy, you know, with hair like Cullum's. If she had loved me, even a little, I should have been fond of the child.' He passed his hand over his face, trying to brush away something. 'Shouldn't have thought it possible to be so jealous of a child.'

Now that the dam of silence was broken, words poured forth, tumultuous, ungoverned; and dreadful in the insight they gave into a man's writhing, naked soul, which is only fit for a god to see.

'Once, when we went to a dance, she did get back some of her vivacity just for a time – Oh, yes, under the stimulus of champagne! We had a good deal. I needed it; I feel desperate sometimes because things are so hopeless, and I gave her a lot on purpose. Can you see the humour of a man making his adored wife slightly tipsy in order that for once she should not feel repelled, against her will, by his affection? I did! I still do. Very funny indeed.'

'Ropes, don't!' I said. It was horrible to hear this even though I knew it eased him.

He went on as if he had not heard.

'She was kinder than usual that evening; she is always kind. I think Alison would rather die than consciously hurt me, because she is grateful to me – for the child's sake. But I was surprised to find she had any passion in her, though I don't know why I should have been. I knew that a woman can be ice with one man and fire with another – that's maddening when you know the one you want loves someone else – but I had given up hoping for that sort of thing from Alison, for me. This isn't a thing one ever mentions, if one has any decency. But one gets past caring for the pretty little decencies of life, sometimes! She was a bit tipsy, which was my fault, and that, of course, accounts for her response to my love for once. And at last, love-drunk in my arms, she called me "Cullum!" Laugh! Why don't you? I did!'

I shall never forget his face; I should like to.

He told me, afterwards, something of Alison's life with Cullum. It was an ordinary, pitiful story. The first few months in Madrid had been gloriously happy, but the radiance of the early days had dimmed very soon. Neither trusted the other whole-heartedly. Alison knew now how unstable Cullum was, and because he was aware of it, he thought that she was always watching him, and accused her of it one day.

Cullum's ingenuity parried the question of marriage whenever it arose. It was always going to be as soon as his paper sent him the cheque he was waiting for, so that they could afford a car and enjoy a little honeymoon, touring the country, or take a short sea-trip. He complained of the delay, due to the notorious irregularity with which, he said, foreign correspondents were often paid, though he pretended that he himself was treated with more consideration than the others. Cullum always let it be understood that he received preferential treatment everywhere: being the exception to every rule was a necessity to his queer vanity. By chance, Alison discovered that the money had arrived many days before, but he explained that away, suggesting that it would be better if they waited to marry until his present job finished and they knew definitely whether he was to stay in Madrid or move to Rome. Finally they agreed to put it off until they were settled in Rome.

Alison was with child by this time, but Cullum was so jubilant over the prospects of the job in Italy that she still felt secure. The arrangements for this wonderful new post were as good as made, he told her: it was only the usual red-tape formalities that were holding up the appointment, and these would be finished within a fortnight, or at most by the end of the month. Though by now she was beginning to know something of the extent of Cullum's imagination, Alison believed him, as many people did, all his life, because he believed himself implicitly at the time. He is well armed who is armed with sincerity; sometimes it is like a sword laying waste; a dangerous weapon, for it is almost irresistible.

Cullum was travelling between Madrid and Rome fairly often at that period, staying in Italy for about a week at a time, ostensibly trying to hurry on the arrangements for his transfer. From one of these visits he did not return, but he wrote to her, a very remarkable letter. Ropes told me the gist of it in his own words.

'That's not the phrasing Cullum used,' I said, 'I think I can give you that! He said something like "If I could only make you understand what it is costing me to go . . . every fibre of me aching for you, the soft, dear whiteness of you . . . unworthy to touch you, my beloved . . . the double hell for me of knowing that you are suffering too . . ." and probably something about "God's will." Isn't that right?'

'Yes,' said Ropes, astonished, 'it was more or less like that.'

I laughed, and my own laughter wrung something in me. Would there never come a time when Cullum's actions should have no more power to move me?

'I've had that letter, you see. Alison's edition was bound to be strongly reminiscent of mine. A man may make love to many different women, but I think in his heart it's always to Woman, not an individual but an idea, the epitome of all his women, and he must

268

make love in very much the same manner to every individual, because they are all one to him.'

'So you know that letter of Cullum's by heart!' said Ropes. 'You still care for him, then?'

'I don't think I do,' I said. 'It is hard to be sure. The dream I was in love with, the ideal he impersonated, has pretty well faded out of my mind, but nothing else has taken its place. Only I've realized by now that love, for a worker, plays a very insignificant part in life; it isn't very important except at odd minutes. Some time ago I exhausted my store of emotional energy, and since then I've found that there are other things of more lasting interest for me than sex affords. I don't know how much I still care about Cullum. What I miss most isn't Cullum, but what he stood for in my imagination. I've discovered, as many people do, that a man or a woman can afford to live without their ideal, their supreme satisfaction, whatever it is, as long as they believe that, somewhere, it exists. Even if they have no hope of attaining it, still the belief that it is there, if out of reach, is enough to keep alive faith in mankind, and the ultimate goodness of the universe, and all that sort of thing. And that matters enormously. But to realize that the shrine at which they worshipped is not only empty, save for a little dust, but has always been empty – Oh, that comes hard. It's better to cry for the moon than for a mirage. Tell me, how did Alison get back to England. Had she any money?'

'Very little. He left her practically none. She stayed on in Madrid for a fortnight, simply unable to believe what had happened. She kept to the house most of the time because the tradesmen were insulting whenever they saw her. They were dunning her for long-overdue bills all the time; but she seems to have got

269

used to dealing with that sort of thing by then. It had gone on continually the last part of the time with Cullum, who paid up nothing, if he could help it, after he started his trips to Rome. It isn't surprising that Alison has altered, and become unexpectedly capable: it was an extraordinary experience for her. She stuck it, pawning things one by one, always hoping that Cullum would come back, till she was absolutely penniless and the landlady threatened to turn her out for non-payment of rent. Then she somehow managed to borrow enough from the woman to cable to me, and I cabled back the money for her fare home. You would hardly know her for the same person if you met her now. And that cur, Cullum, is safely out of the whole affair, in Rome! It's not on himself that his actions recoil.' Ropes was calmer now.

With a wry smile, because of the little sting of remembrance, I quoted something that Ropes had helped to write:

'The wonder groweth with the days,
How Fate looks after Cullum Hayes!
When, as the Bible says he "oughter,"
He casts his bread upon the water,
Lo, it returns upon the tide,
Well buttered on the upper side.
No wonder war is with us yet,
And, baulked, the Balkans fume and fret,
And trade is in an awful plight –
Fate has not time to put things right:
It's much too busy all the days,
In doing jobs for Cullum Hayes.

– Do you remember all four of us supplying lines of that in turn, one day at the Table, because Cullum used to say so often "The other fellow always pays; it's in my horoscope"? But I didn't realize at the time just how true that is!'

'So far, the toll of Cullum's habit of carrying conviction when he's lying has been your partial disablement for life' (Ropes alone knew why the accident had happened; the rest of my world thought it the kind of thing that was bound to come to me eventually.) 'the wreck of Alison's happiness, and through her, of mine.'

'We pay for the butter on the upper side!' I told him. 'Before me, there was a girl to whom he was engaged, whom he threw over. We met her one day, and the whole incident was queer. I don't know what happened to her. I wonder if his luck will always hold!'

'My God, if I could get hold of Cullum and make him pay! Anyhow. I shouldn't care what happened to me afterwards as long as he suffered, first, as much as Alison, and you, and I have suffered, and probably that other girl too. I'd cheerfully hang afterwards, and so would you, I believe, in spite of your hard-garnered philosophy of looking on! You aren't the type that soon forgets, or forgives. And I don't believe that you've done either. Wouldn't you die happy if you had got even with him, even or nearly, for the waste of these months of pain. Wouldn't you!'

I struggled with my pride, and told the truth. 'Yes, Ropes, I would.'

Ropes sent me some Continental newspapers a month or two later, marked in pencil at the long account of the unsavoury divorce proceedings in Rome, in which a young English author was cited as co-respondent. One paper reproduced a photograph of Cullum and the smiling portrait of the young wife of some minor Italian notable.

'An interesting example,' Ropes wrote, 'of the tire-some monotony with which a man loves one woman under different forms, on which you remarked. You and Alison have nothing in common in looks, but here – do you notice? – are her eyes, and your mouth as it used to be.'

(Something vaguely suggested Paula McMillan, too, in the shape of the face and shining, sleek blackness of the hair.)

'I don't want these papers back,' his letter ran, 'you can have them to keep or destroy as you like; (but, fool, I expect you'll keep them!) To me, this seems to throw a good deal of light on the last stage of the Madrid affair!'

Two of Cullum's letters, which had been read out in court, as part of the evidence, were printed below the pictures. They were beautiful. His style had gained in the two years since I had known him. Reading them, one felt almost ashamed at having stumbled on something delicate and lovely, that should not have been given to the world to paw and soil. My accursed memory, recalling unprompted passages from his letters to me, made me catch my breath in distress: some of the printed phrases stung, so close were they in shape or meaning to others in letters which I still kept. Ropes knew me well? I had never been able to bring myself to burn these sole proofs that I had once been happier than the gods allow.

Ah, but there was subtle humour in the second letter, for anyone who could appreciate it! He described to this girl, charmingly and convincingly, having met her all his life in dreams! Had there been any one with me to share the joke, I should have found it ludicrous enough, but no one was present when I read that letter; I was under no obligation to myself to seem amused, and laughter costs so much. Iron entered into my soul again. I remembered how cleverly Cullum had played on my credulity that evening at Holmwood when he told me of this enchanting bond of dreams. – 'I've always seen you among trees. Here sometimes, because I remember that big tree with no branches for some way, and then one that bends down nearly to the ground and up again. You sit in the crook very often and read there!'

Of course I did. Anyone would, if that garden belonged to them and they loved books. It was a safe guess; it seemed to me miraculous, at the time. – 'I used to see you in another place; I shall know it when I see it.' That, too, was quite safe.

In the letters came a passage of which Ropes had specially marked the end.

'– your glorious eyes, that hold in them, when you are grave, all the sorrows of all the lovers in the world. I, loving you, wonder sometimes what lies behind those eyes, or if, indeed, there is anything at all. For even when you are in my arms, our love, the greatest reality I have known, is still nothing more than a dream. We know only the pleasant outer shells in which our natures hide from each other – but what does that matter, when you are so beautiful that I hardly care at all whether your thoughts are as profound as your eyes suggest, when you smile at me enigmatically in the silence that wraps you like a cloud sometimes; or whether, as I occasionally suspect, *mia cara*, your mind is all taken up with trivialities, such as what the world would say if it knew, if hat-brims will be wider this year, or the price of butter.'

'The price of butter!' Certainly, Ropes must have seen the twisted humour of that phrase. I wondered if, kinder where he loved, he had kept those letters from Alison. They must have been very like some of hers, but more intense, for I believe that Cullum loved this Italian girl better than he had loved anyone until then.

He married her as soon as the divorce was made absolute: there were no children from the marriage, but the three years that followed seem to have been the happiest of his life. In them he wrote his one magnificent book, *The Tale No Woman Will Understand*, fine-wrought, polished work which was unlike anything that he had written previously and yet was unmistakably Cullum's, and stamped with the charm of his personality. Had he published it under an assumed name I should have known the author; it was full of Cullum's fantastic ideas, which had pleased me of old, but now in the strangely woven web of his imagination lay jewels of thought. He had become a fine craftsman in words; they were selected fastidiously and lovingly used. Under the characteristic quaint gaiety of his work ran a current of inexpressible sadness. Reading his book, I could hear the ring of Cullum's voice clearly in the peculiar turn of many sentences; but it did not stir me any longer. Emotionally I seemed to have become completely apathetic at last, and I was glad, and a little surprised that nothing but my mind responded to this ardent, lovely expression of his love for another woman. He dedicated it 'To Fione Hayes, because unfortunately I have nothing more worthy to offer her.'

The book failed financially, although the majority of good critics praised it. Incomparably finer than *The Chink*, it did not even win the limited popularity, much exaggerated by the author at the time, of that first

274

book. Through his books, which deserved a better fate, Cullum suffered his only reverses of luck.

After the publication of *The Tale No Woman Will Understand*, Cullum and his Fione settled in London, and he joined a small, ambitious publishing venture which promised to flourish. He did a good deal of abnormally mature work at that time, and I heard of him once or twice through acquaintances though I never ran across him. I did not anticipate being disturbed by a chance meeting, if it ever came about. Time had dulled even my memory of that unhappy period of intense emotional distress. Thinking of it, I seemed to see all the figures of that queer business as puppets dancing in an atmosphere of unreality, myself among them. Those distant happenings did not feel as if they had occurred to me; and once one has begun to see oneself objectively in retrospect, all personal memory of participation has already died. Unmoved, I read his last book several times, because it was an enchanting net of romance woven by an eager lover to catch other lover's hearts – they must have been very little hearts that slipped through – but besides joy in its good workmanship it brought me nothing except a passing, pleasant regret, no deeper than that which the first signs of autumn usually brought me. I caught myself trying to conjure up a little of the old, poignant longing, and wondered if it had ever been as keen as I imagined. As an emotion, it was far less perceptible to me now than the annoyance of having a manuscript rejected by an editor, or the anticipation of one of Carlisle McDonald's visits.

He and Gerald Hemingway were the only two old friends whom I had kept. Gerald was shortly to marry Olive, and when we met, which was not often now that I was working on a French paper, and living in Paris with my mother, he was unnecessarily demonstrative in his gratitude to me for having refrained from marrying him. As he explained to Olive, the similarity between us on unimportant points had been responsible for his long infatuation with the larger shadow while the little substance was growing up.

That grave, presentable young man, McDonald, had become the dominant factor of my existence. Our acquaintanceship had ripened into a close, satisfactory friendship which made little demand on my emotional side and a great deal on my mentality; the unsought role of chief friend and confidante to the able young politician was exacting to live up to at times. He had not asked me to marry him as Ropes had predicted; instead he had intimated to me that this was what he expected of me eventually, and without waiting for my comment, had gone on to discuss more debatable subjects. He was as quietly certain of my ultimate compliance with his plans as he was of his own success. Scottish self-confidence is no less irritating for being usually well-founded. I was prepared to accept the inevitable. It would be in many ways an excellent arrangement. The years had worked great improvement in the ambitious Scot; he was by far the most interesting man I knew, even in Paris where I moved continually among interesting people. I admitted to myself that I wanted a lover, but my pride forbade any hidden liaison. I liked power, consideration, and the excitement of scheming for success; all these were assured to the wife of that fore-ordained statesman, and on his side he considered that I had a good deal to give him. Our marriage would be a fair, reasonable deal, and I had set up reason as my guiding star, following it as directly as I could, now that emotional exhaustion had turned to satiety.

I did not like being made to feel anything in those days. The books and plays and music that I preferred all appealed to the head; and for the people who did their thinking with their hearts, I felt even less sympathy than I had felt formerly. For those who cried out under suffering that I knew I could stand in silence I had none at all; suffering may sometimes strengthen the weak, but those who are naturally independent it makes hard. Still, the years had taught me that I could be swayed in certain circumstances by nearly every impulse that I had ever condemned as incomprehensible in other people, and that in any crisis I always behaved fifty per cent. worse than I should have expected!

Chapter 16: *Again*

LATE one evening, a day before I was expecting McDonald for a visit, Ropes, like a messenger from the past, arrived unexpectedly at my mother's flat and asked to see me.

We had not met for over two years, but I knew that they had not dealt very kindly with him. He and Alison had been living apart for some time; the position was indefinite and prejudicial to both, but on account of his profession and his religion he could not let her divorce him. The separation had been by mutual agreement. He looked much older, I thought, as I greeted him.

He told me enough of his domestic history for me to imagine the rest. 'It was because of the child. My fault, of course. I couldn't stand him about the place after a time.' He laughed shortly. ' "What a darling little boy; he's not a bit like his Daddy, is he?" dear old ladies used to say to me. That was their mistake! He is going to be very like Cullum. Clever and cunning too. I couldn't bear the sight of him, and Alison cared for nothing else. If we'd had a child of our own it would have been different, I suppose. I think she's happier away from me. She is willing to come back to me if I want it, but I know that she only married me for the sake of the baby, and there are some things a man can't do.'

Through everything he said showed the underlying fact that he still loved her, and wanted her.

He began pacing up and down the room. 'Cullum is in Paris!' he shot at me suddenly, speaking with deep, controlled excitement. 'Did you hear about the wind-up of his firm?'

'No,' I said, 'I am very much cut off from news of my old world. What has happened?'

'Bankrupt some months ago. Two of the partners lost every penny they had. Not so Cullum, of course: nor the other partner. Cullum cleared out, with this other man – taking just a little more of the money than was found quite justifiable when the books were examined! It is only lately that it has been brought to light how much fat he saved from the fire. It might not have been discovered at all; rather cleverly done, the whole thing. The other man was traced to the States and then lost sight of; Cullum disappeared and it was thought he had joined him. But they've found him here, under an assumed name? They believe so, at least.'

'Oh, Ropes, this can't be true!' I said. 'It's too terrible.'

'Still able to be surprised at Cullum's doings? Alison disbelieved it at first, too. I envy you both that curious, unquenchable faith which women have in men like Cullum, and from my heart I envy him his knack of inspiring loyalty! I was not so surprised! But, my God I was glad, glad!'

All this time he was pacing the room, speaking jerkily. 'The police believe that there's no mistake. I made enquiries and found out about this from a great friend, a big man in the Service. There's an extradition order of arrest out for him, but in the case of an alias someone must identify the person. I jumped at the chance, got this chap I know to use his influence.' Ropes' smile was ugly. 'It'll be good to help in bringing Cullum down at last!'

I sat still and silent, considering. The coming of Ropes, with his intense preoccupation with things that I had put aside, was like a stone hurled into the surface-quiet stream of my life; stirring the depths, it brought to the surface again forgotten feelings and desires.

'To help in bringing Cullum down after all this time, now that he has over-reached himself at last. Yes,' I said, drawing my breath sharply, 'that would be good.' Temporarily one can bury hatred or love, under the accumulation of every-day interests, but a very little thing will serve to resurrect either. I remembered Cullum's happy saying, 'With me, the other fellow always pays.' We had paid, Ropes and I! Alison had paid most of all perhaps, but she had kept something, she had the child; we had nothing.

'I can believe what you tell me easily enough now,' I told Ropes. 'Just at first, in spite of repeated proof, it is difficult to credit such things of anyone who has ever been – a friend.'

Tired from the journey, he walked up and down the room restlessly for an hour or more, refusing anything to eat or drink, too excited to feel bodily fatigue.

'You can't think what this means to me – or rather, yes, I think perhaps you can; you, alone, of all people; that's why I came to you. I am so afraid that this man may not prove to be Cullum. Suppose he gets away scot-free again!'

'Where is his wife?'

'In London. She doesn't know his whereabouts. At any rate she says she doesn't; and has heard nothing of him for a month or two. Women are magnificently loyal to Cullum.' He sneered. 'He has left her without a penny.' He took two or three turns in silence, and then went on again. 'They're smart, these French police! Do you know how they found him, if it is

Cullum? Through Mlle. Heloise Passonom.' He named the great French comedienne whom I had seen several times in London and Paris. 'It was noticed that a young man of whom nothing was known, of no discoverable income, had been sending her expensive presents, and they made inquiries in England, and found out what I told you. He has been here two months, too infatuated with this woman twice his age to get away while he can. There's irony in that, isn't there, that the woman who lets him down at last is old enough to be his mother? She is the first woman he has really wanted, I imagine, that he can't get, and that's why.'

He had now a nervous trick of hitting the palm of one hand with the other fist. Up and down the room he paced, doing this, with a strained, gloating expression on his face which I should have found repellent if I had not been too moved myself at the unexpected prospect of revenge to care for anything but that Cullum was within reach of justice at last.

'At six o'clock to-morrow morning the police are going to his hotel.' Ropes stopped before me, and his weary face lit up. 'The identification before extradition is a purely formal matter. One of the English police, and someone to identify the man, has to be sent from England: I got this man I know, who can do pretty well as he likes in his own sphere, to arrange for me to come, and I've got the written order. But there could be two, instead of one, to recognize him! If you wanted to come! The policeman with me – stolid chap – knows I'm in with authority and is most deferential. If I introduce you to the police as someone who knew him also, coming so there should be no mistake? Ah, Esther, after all these years to get even with Cullum! No, not to get even, but to pay in part what I owe him!'

'If I care to come!' I said, one hand at my throat where something seemed to be tightening. 'Yes, I want to come! Thank you, Ropes! Do you know, for two or three years I have been believing that I did not hate Cullum any longer?'

Ropes smiled unpleasantly. 'I thought your character was almost as vindictive as mine. When it comes to the test, there's precious little difference in behaviour between hearty agnostics like you and professed Christians like me! I have taken these two days off as a holiday. A holiday! It's the first I've had for a long while; it will be the best I've ever had. If only it is Cullum!'

2

It was still dark when I went to the gendarmerie with Ropes the next morning, and he explained that I had known the suspect well in the past and would confirm his recognition. In my favour was the fact that I was of the press, an English-French reporter on a paper that was on good terms with the police, and they were about to carry out a smart coup in conjunction with the English force, and neither Ropes nor the English policeman spoke French fluently. There are means of arranging these things; they made no objection to my accompanying Ropes to identify this 'James Cartwright,' in fact the two *agents de police* were effusive and gallant; they talked to me incessantly as we drove to the shabby little pension where the man who called himself James Cartwright was living. I hardly knew what I answered them; all at once I was sick with apprehension at the thought of seeing Cullum again, if indeed this proved to be Cullum, in such straits; and yet I was desperately anxious that we should find him. As we left the taxi in the mean back street that was just waking up, I glanced at Ropes' set, worn face, and he grasped my arm steadyingly as we toiled after the flustered, protesting, half-dressed proprietor and the police, up many flights of winding stairs.

The hotel was a miserable place, with stained paper peeling off the walls. The air was oppressive with the mingled smell of staleness, garlic and whitewash which clings to poor French houses.

I had grown unaccustomed to climbing many stairs since my accident; the shooting pain in my injured hip was sickening for the moment as I leant against the wall of the landing, holding tightly to Ropes' arm while the proprietor knocked at the door. There was no answer.

I heard Ropes mutter: 'God, if he's gone!'

They seemed to knock endlessly. A black haze gathered and danced in the corners of my eyes. I had to fight it off with all my will. The proprietor's master-key could not be used because the door was locked from the other side, with the key left in the key-hole. Surely they rattled at that door for many minutes, for hours!

'Pull yourself together!' Ropes said to me sharply and shook my arm.

'I'm all right, really,' I told him.

The two burly French policemen were breaking open the door.

The lock gave way and they went into the room. I shut my eyes for a moment, stupidly overcome. And then one of them, the big one with the thick white face, came back into the passage, and began to speak, spreading out his hands in Henri's particular gesture. How queer and unreal it all seemed.

He was saying: '*Il nous a bien échappé, le coquin!*'

'Escaped us?'

His voice receded to an immense distance. It was as though it came to me muffled by the darkness that was gathering again.

'*Il est mort.*'

So Cullum had escaped for ever, and was dead – in that room, where the senior policeman was standing on the threshold, giving instructions in a disappointed, business-like manner to the proprietor. A doctor must be fetched at once, he said, and there were other offices to be performed – '*mais il est bien mort,*' he added, with a lift of the shoulders, as he turned to us. 'Enter then, Monsieur! Madame would prefer to stay outside? This is the man!'

But I longed to see him again. I limped into the ugly little room behind Ropes, who had not let them know that he was a doctor.

'Yes, that is Cullum Hayes,' he said.

Crowned with the appalling dignity of death, Cullum was lying there, in the bed, with one hand under his head on the pillow. I knew it for the position in which he usually slept. Dignity sat queerly on Cullum, even then. His head was turned towards the door, so that he seemed to be looking at us, though the eyes were almost closed. Death must have made him look a little younger, for he did not appear to have altered at all in the three years since I had seen him. The little white scar on his chin, acquired the day he came to me at Holmwood, showed up clearly even against the waxen whiteness of his face. The lips were drawn back into a slight smile, in the contraction of death, for he had been dead some hours, and the eyelids had begun to lift a little, so that he seemed to be watching us slyly from under them. It was as if he were laughing at us.

There was an empty glass on the table by his side, and books and a fountain pen. On the floor by the bed lay an unfinished letter, crumpled as if his last intention had been to destroy it, but his will or his strength had failed. The agent in charge picked it up, and seeing that it was in English, asked me for a rough translation while we waited for the other policeman to return. He had gone for a doctor, and the unhappy proprietor had disappeared, bemoaning the unfortunate publicity which this *sacré affaire* would bring on his respectable establishment. Already his laments had attracted a small group of people into the passage, where they questioned, and whispered information, and peered. No doubt he was now informing his neighbours of his misfortune, in which the whole street would revel. The *agent*, the English policeman, Ropes and I were alone in the room, with Cullum.

'I think this can be left unread,' I said. 'It is only a love letter.'

'*Ça se peut bien!*' commented the Frenchman, 'but I would ask Madame to translate it a little. It is possible that there may be something of importance.'

It was to Heloise Passonom.

'Here, beloved, is a little flower of triumph to add to your glorious bouquet – to-night, by your acting, you have made a man laugh who knew that he was going to die within a few hours. Even you, to whom my praise means nothing, will be pleased, if only for a moment, by this last gesture of homage from a lover who turns from you to the only other possible mistress. You have never been mine, would never be mine even if I prolonged this agony which living has come to be; I can make sure of death, at least.

'I wonder what I shall have found before to-

285

morrow? Wise men have said that death is the opening of a door into the place where there is no more forgetting, so that waiting for me are all my past actions, and all things that I have known in this life, clearer and more intense in their existence than they were on earth. Then your image will be there, clothed in your amazing beauty, and my unbearable need of you will be there too. That is so terrible that I don't think it's true. The only memory I want to meet again is that once I held you in my arms for a few seconds, and that you kissed me – you! – that for one moment you did not laugh at me for being little more than a boy, as you always do.

I would take into eternity, if I might, the memory of that kiss, without the knowledge that you gave it on an impulse of kindness, no more: and I would keep with me, too, the ghost of the scent of your hair, and the delighful echo of your voice, and the recollection of the light in your eyes when you smile. And all but this, if God is merciful, I shall forget.

'Heloise, I can't endure this any longer,' (the writing here grew very bad, as though the words were scribbled hastily) 'I love you. There, it's done. Heloise, I applaud you, you played well to-night. My darling. . . .'

'*Je vous remercie, madame,*' said the *agent de police.* '*Quel type original, hein? Permettez, je prends la lettre pour l'enquête.*' He asked a few questions of Ropes, and made a note of the answers.

I stood for a moment looking down at the rigid figure in the bed, and there surged over me like a flood the old consuming passion for this man. It swept aside the years that the locust, hatred, had eaten, years in which

I believed that I had lost the power to feel. The old sorrow and desire tore at me again as fiercely as they had ever done. I remembered nothing of the past, knowing only that here lay my youth and my dreams, dead with Cullum; for this man's body had been my heaven, and I loved him. How was it possible that he had died, when he was so great a part of me, and I still lived? Many things had dimmed Cullum's picture in my mind. Somehow, once more, I had not been prepared to find him so terribly the same to look at. This was Cullum the boy who had laughed with me, and said 'I have loved you in some life that is past, and I believe that I shall love you again'; who had said, 'you belong to me for ever'; it was not the man through whom I had grown bitter and hard in these sad, useless years.

Ropes said 'We'll go now,' and came to my side.

In that second I would have given anything – oh, all that I still possessed, to have stooped and touched with my lips Cullum's thin, smiling mouth, but I did not kiss him because I knew that at the end he had been utterly sincere, as he had always been in his own strange way, and that when he died his last thoughts were of this woman, Heloise, whom he loved. I had no right to kiss him.

'Good-bye, my dear,' I whispered, and could not keep my hand from touching, once more, his wiry, dark red hair, playing for a second with the funny tuft above the ear where he could never get it to lie flat.

As we left the hotel, Ropes shouldering a way for me through the chattering cluster of errand boys and housewives round the door, the first reporter arrived, a man who lived in this district and was on the staff of the same paper as I was. News travels even faster in Paris than in London, and the distraught proprietor

287

and his wife had soon confided their misfortunes to the whole neighbourhood. The other journalist's face fell when he saw me.

'But you have always the best luck!' he said, 'I thought that I was without question the first kite dropping on the carcase this time. Well, fortune of war! I'll tell Parmentier' (the news-editor) 'that you are on the story. How much space shall I ask him to hold?'

It struck me as curious that at this moment I must ply the profession in which Cullum started me.

'About a quarter-column,' I said, with laughter that made Ropes glance at me anxiously. 'The story is worth just about that. But you take it. You can always make more of sensation-stuff than I can.'

'On no account, *mon vieux!* It is of course your story.

'Oh, I don't want to work to-day,' I said, 'A friend, my fiancé in fact, is arriving from England.'

'Ah, in that case!' he said, grinning, and hurried in.

THE END